THOUGHTS OF LOVE

"What are you thinking, Adam Cassidy?"

"Actually, I was thinking that for a woman I really don't like very much, I rather like you, Miss Mariette Donovan."

She smiled then, turning to her side and dropping her head against her palm. "Indeed. And what makes you think that I want you to like me . . . or even that I care whether you do or not?"

"I think it matters." Before he could prevent it, Adam's fingers spanned the space between them and lightly touched her hair. "You've the most magnificent hair, Mariette . . . the color of pale flames . . ."

She smiled prettily as his hand circled her neck and coaxed her to him, his fingers lacing through her hair. When his mouth sought the intimacy of her own, she scooted out from beneath his hand and quickly disengaged his fingers from her tresses.

"I don't know what you think you're doing, Adam Cassidy," Mariette shouted hotly. "But I'm not one of the wanton women you have met in your travels. I'm a lady—"

Adam gave her a wry smile. "Ladies need to be kissed, too, Miss Donovan."

CAROLINE BOURNE

EDGE OF HEAVEN

ZEBRA BOOKS
KENSINGTON PUBLISHING CORP.

For Dawn Willoughby, who first suggested that I continue the story of the Donovans of Philadelphia begun in Allegheny Ecstasy *and* Allegheny Captive.

ZEBRA BOOKS are published by

Kensington Publishing Corp.
850 Third Avenue
New York, NY 10022

First Printing: October, 1994

Printed in the United States of America

Prologue

Rourke House, Philadelphia, 1856

"That's right, children. Old Cousin Webster Mayne's hand continued to live after it was lopped off in the fire of 1788. And to this day, we of Rourke House, continue to watch the mouseholes and the niches and crannies, because it lies in wait there . . . just as surely as Webster's hideously deformed ghost strolls the corridors, watching us when we sleep, and trying mightily to find his lost hand—"

Ten-year-old Cassandra's immediate reaction was to argue that Webster wasn't hideous and deformed—because she had seen him many times in the past few months—but she kept quiet, for fear that her mother might become angry and end the session.

Hannah Gilbert did not really enjoy their family history, but she did so enjoy entertaining her children with tales of ghosts and goblins. She watched the faces of her children, twelve-year-old Miles and the pretty Cassandra, aware that only Miles's eyes were as wide as china saucers suddenly darting around the large, semi-dark attic chamber in search of the terrible phantom. They loved the stories, and when too long a time passed without them, they enticed their mother to the haunting shadows of the attic to tell them what they'd heard no less than a thousand times before.

"Do tell us again, mother," entreated Miles, "about the day he kidnapped you and took you off to the Alleghenies, where he gave you to the young man and woman. Tell us about how he fell from the balcony and splattered himself on the cobbles below."

Hannah smiled, her reminiscences those of her mother, Carrie, who had told her the story many times during her own youth. She had been just a baby when Webster Mayne had snatched her from the loving arms of her family on Christmas morning, thirty-four years ago, and might have killed her if he hadn't had a change of heart.

Then, her thoughts moved forward, to skim the past few years. Her son had grown away from her, his adoration of his rebellious "Uncle" Roby a cause of it, Hannah was sure. Though Miles generally got along with his family, he frequently rebelled against her authority, and the authority of the men in the house, with the exception of Roby, and the only times he truly acted like a child was when she agreed to come to the attic to tell ghost stories. Then he was her precious boy again, and ofttimes she would extend the sessions of storytelling, just so that she could watch the childlike animation in her son's face that she might not see again in days, or even weeks. Sometimes she had the feeling her son hated her, though for the life of her she couldn't understand why.

In the moment of hesitation before her mother could collect her thoughts, the pale-skinned, red-haired Cassandra quietly announced, "Cousin Webster visits me sometimes, mother, and he calls me 'Flame'." Smiling with innocence, she continued, "because of my red hair. He says that he called Grandmother Flame also, when she was with him in New Orleans."

"What kind of a name is Flame?" asked a now indignant Miles, who did not appreciate his mother's story being interrupted. "You are such a child, Cassandra."

"I am not," she pouted, looking to her mother for support. "Tell Miles not to tease me."

Actually, Hannah was, for the moment, very curious. Her mother had never told her that Webster Mayne had called her by such a name, nor had her grandmother, Diana. But then again, Carrie didn't like to talk about Webster, a man she had known as Junius Wade, so it was doubtful she would have shared such an intimacy as a pet name with her daughter. She would have to remember to ask her mother about it when she and her father returned from San Francisco. Perhaps she should stop telling the very impressionable Cassandra the tales of ghosts in residence at Rourke House. "Enough of the stories," announced Hannah, clapping her hands. "Go on downstairs and do your morning chores, Miles. Cassandra—" The child turned to face her mother. "Aunt Mariette said she would French braid your hair this morning. Comb out the tangles before you see her."

"Yes, mum," answered the slim child, curtsying the way her proper English grandmother Carrie had taught her.

She watched her children go, feeling Miles slipping away from her in the moment that his footfalls sounded on the narrow attic steps. He would be moody and unfriendly once again, and he would soon treat her like a stranger, rather than his mother.

Alone now, with only the spirits of the old house for company, Hannah allowed the past to sift through her memories. Her dear husband had been dead for nine years now, and at times she still felt a little bitter that he had left her to care for their two children alone. She felt, though, that she'd done a fair job of being both mother and father, as Miles and Cassandra were good children who seldom caused trouble. They were courteous and devoted to their studies, and got along well with the other residents of the house. And, of course, they had good male role models in their Grandfather Drew, and in their uncles, Noble and Bundy. Sometimes, too, Michael was attentive to them, though much more attentive to the pretty girls about town. But Roby . . . well, that rascal was another matter!

In addition to Hannah and her children, Hannah's twenty-three-year-old sister, Mariette, also lived at the house, as well as Michael and Roby, the twin sons of her uncle Noble. Also in residence for the summer was Lara Seymour, the granddaughter of Penley Seymour, who had been her mother's guardian, and his wife, Anne. Michael had taken an interest in the young English woman, but Hannah had noticed Lara's eyes straying to the rebellious Roby. At thirty-five years of age, neither twin had shown much of an interest in taking a wife, until the precocious Lara, only seventeen years of age, had appeared on the scene. Hannah predicted trouble between the brothers over the teasing flirtations of Lara, since they frequently got along as well as prowling tomcats.

But her thoughts were straying from the source of her momentary discontent; Cassandra's innocent declaration. She had always been a child who acted much older than her physical years, a sensitive child who thought about things that probably never entered the minds of other children. Cassandra liked her ghosts, but until now, she had not admitted that Webster Mayne, whose evil had spanned four decades, was one of them.

Yes . . . perhaps she should taper off with the stories of

spirits giving life, and character, to the staid old house against the historical backdrop of Philadelphia.

At the moment, ghosts were the least of Cassandra's worries. She sat before her mirror, tugging the comb through her waist-length locks of flame-colored hair, worrying that Aunt Mariette would not undertake the intricate braiding if even one tangle remained.

She was still tugging when the shadow emerged from the far corner of the room and entered her line of vision across her mirrored image. She smiled up to the black-haired man, resplendent in dark waistcoat and white jabot—proper attire, she imagined, for the latter half of the previous century—his buckled shoes clicking upon the planked boards surrounding the plush, oriental rug upon which her canopied bed was perched. "Good morning, Great-grandpapa," she greeted, turning on the vanity stool, her slim palms covering the velvet folds on either side of her hips.

Cole Cynric Donovan, his fingers linking at his back, shook his head in gentle scolding. "I told you, lass, that you were not to tell your mother of Webster's presence. Din't I tell you I would take care of it and keep you safe?"

Her eyes dropped, her feelings hurt by the man she had grown to love very, very much, a man she had never known in life. She might not have known who he was had it not been for the portrait of him and her great-grandmother, Diana, hanging in a place of honor over the parlor hearth. "But he's not been mean to me, Great-grandpapa. He says he is very sorry for the bad things he did, and I really believe he means it."

"Bah! You're young, Cassandra. You din't know what you're talking about."

She looked up now, tears welling on her lower lids. "Please, Great-grandpapa, do not scold me. My auntie is going to braid my hair very soon, and if she sees that I have been crying, she'll want to know why. And—" She shrugged, a slim finger flicking at the tears now forging paths down her pale cheeks. "Aunt Mariette doesn't like to hear about you and Webster and . . . Claudia. She thinks I'm just a lonely little girl inventing friends."

Claudia, a very eccentric servant of Rourke House for her entire eighty-two years, had died two years before. Cole suspected that she had a lot to do with Cassandra's familiarity with the ghosts of the house, much more so than his granddaughter, Hannah. Bending to his knees, so that he would be eye-to-eye with the seated Cassandra, Cole dropped a gentle hand to her slim shoulder. "I can think of worse friends than ghosts, lass. Just be happy . . . that is what matters in life. Like love. One day, lass, in ten or twelve years, you will find love, and you will know right away if it is a destined love, like the love your great-grandmama and I still share."

"You are waiting for her, aren't you, great-grandpapa?"

Cole smiled sadly. "Aye, lass, of course, I am."

Cassandra snickered. "You'll have a bit of waiting to do. She's as spry as a new Spring kitten." Then a thought came to Cassandra, and she was almost sure that if he had, her Great-grandmother would have mentioned it to her. "Haven't you visited her, Great-grandpapa?"

"Aye, lass, every day." Anticipating her question, he continued, "But she doesn't see me as you do."

"Then I am special," quietly reflected Cassandra, her gaze returning to her pale image in the mirror.

"Aye, lass," he spoke affectionately. "Very special."

"Is there a heaven, Great-grandpapa?"

He shrugged, looking away. "I suppose . . . but I din't know for sure." He rose now, the emotion thick in his throat. "And I'll not find out until my lass is beside me. Sometimes I think this house is trying to cling to my dear Diana's soul. She belongs to me, aye, that she does." Coughing, then turning back, he again issued the warning to the youthful Cassandra, "If Webster comes, you must tell him you do not wish to speak to him."

"But I wouldn't want to hurt his feelings."

"Bah! He has no feelings!" Cole Cynric Donovan began to move, slowly, silently, turning in the shadows to give Cassandra one last word, "Remember, lass, your great-grandpapa is looking out for you."

Then he was gone. Cassandra, turning back to the mirror, began tugging at the final tangle in her hair.

Ghosts! They were just like adults! Always giving orders!

Part One

One

Adam Cassidy was so angry he knew that if he gritted his teeth they would shatter beneath the pressure. He stood in the small waiting room of Bertrand Redding's clinic, listening to the moans of the fellow he'd found shot outside of Philadelphia. And now, having brought him in to town, he felt responsible for him.

This was the farthest east his wanderings had brought him. He preferred the west coast, California and Washington, and journeying into Canada when the mood struck him. But he had a special reason to be here in Philadelphia. In Kansas City he'd agreed to work for a lawyer whose brother's child had been kidnapped by the obsessed nanny who had been discharged the week before. He had tracked the woman to this fair city, and the child, a handsome, brown-haired boy of six, was now with a reliable escort, being returned to his father in Missouri. He'd been paid a modest fee for the job, but he hadn't really wanted to take it.

He'd been on his way out of town when he'd come upon the wounded stranger.

Being in Bertrand Redding's office brought back old memories that he'd tried to distance himself from these past seven years. He didn't want to think about Emily and Beth . . . and he didn't want to remember how inadequate he had been, and still was. But the past held on with vicious pincers, and he knew he would never be able to escape, not if he lived a thousand years.

"You're welcome to sleep in the alcove there."

Adam's tall frame jerked to its full height of a fraction over six feet. Eyeing the tired, but still friendly, features of Dr. Bertrand Redding, a fourth generation physician from an old Philadelphia family, Adam's thoughts snapped back, the anger instantly gone. "Yes . . . thank you" he replied, turning his back in an effort to staunch the flow of further family histories. He now knew more about the talkative Bertrand Redding's family than he knew about his own. And, he couldn't help being intrigued by the years of intertwined history the Reddings shared with another local family, the Donovans. Perhaps after a night of long overdue sleep, he'd be willing to hear more.

For now, he preferred to move toward the proferred sleeping quarters. Dr. Redding had returned to tend the unfortunate fellow whose identity was unknown, so Adam dropped heavily to the small, comfortable cot and stretched along its length. He'd decide what to do tomorrow about the lack of funds for the stranger's medical expenses should the doctor expect him to pay them; perhaps he'd be able to pick up a job around town, enough to buy the blasted horse to take him out of town. He hated public transportation, which was dirty, uncomfortable, and cramped.

He also liked to travel alone; he didn't deserve the pleasure of decent people's company.

* * *

Mariette skirted the mess the puppy had deposited to the kitchen floor. Flinging back her loose, waist-length hair, she clucked her tongue, her eyes scanning the soiled area with firm disapproval. She had told her niece *not* to bring the puppy inside and leave it unattended. *Where was the sloppy little beast hiding,* she wondered.

Catching her reflection in the shiny copper bottom of one of the hanging pans, she thought at once that her moment of anger had hardened her features. With some degree of deliberation, she unpinched her mouth, then chased away the tiny lines from between her brows with a somewhat shaky smile. "Cassandra is only ten," she reminded herself. "She probably forgot that the little mutt was inside."

Hannah entered the kitchen, her nose crinkling in reaction to the disagreeable smell. "Cassandra let the puppy in?" she queried, immediately adding, "I'll clean up the floor, Mariette. Cassandra is brushing her hair in preparation of the braiding you promised her. And—" She smiled, the scolding of her younger sister not really intended as such, "Don't fuss at Cassandra about the puppy." A small, canine whimper suddenly echoed from beneath the corner cabinet. "I'll put the creature in the pen outside," added Hannah.

"I've got the brisket on," said Mariette, shrugging, flinging off her apron and smoothing down the crinkles in her mauve skirt. As she exited the kitchen, she mumbled, "Why couldn't the child have brought home a kitten? Puppies! They grow up to be yapping, growling, biting, smelly, disagreeable nuisances!"

From the kitchen she heard Hannah call out, "I hear you fussing, little sister. Hush this minute!"

Mariette smiled, drawing in a deep breath as she began to ascend the stairs. On the platform above, she stopped to survey her appearance in the oval mirror overhanging a small trestle table. Her cheeks were pink with the anger she had felt; she placed her cool palms to them, feeling the warmth instantly subside.

When she entered Cassandra's room moments later, her temperament had returned to some degree of normalcy. The child's quick smile chased away the annoyance she felt with the undisciplined little cur hiding in the kitchen below.

She thought at once that a moment of mischief had skittered across Cassandra's pale, youthful features. "What are you up to?" she asked, sternly, and yet with the hint of a smile touching her mouth. When Cassandra lowered her eyes, Mariette added, "Haven't been talking to your ghosts this morning, have you?" So pretty was Cassandra, sitting quietly in the light spilling from the window, in her pink dress with its scalloped lace trim, that Mariette immediately regretted bringing up the subject of the ghosts. She had, after all, fussed at Hannah for keeping the subject alive for her children. Even their parents, Andrew and Carrie, disapproved. A limber bounce now advanced her toward Cassandra and a handful of russet curls soon filled her right hand. "All the tangles out, Cass?" Vivid blue eyes graced by delicate lashes lifted, and a tiny smile compelled Mariette to say, "I think we're ready for the braiding. There isn't a single tangle."

An enthusiastic Cassandra drew up a silver filigre brush. "Oh, yes, Auntie . . . and I've chosen blue and pink ribbons to match my dress. Will you tie them in a pretty bow at the end of the braid?" As Mariette began the rite of beautification, lovingly tucking in every stray whisp of coppery hair in the process, she allowed her thoughts to wander away for a moment. Her parents, Andrew and Carrie, were in San Francisco on business, and she missed them dearly. Instinctively, her eyes lifted, meeting her own reflection in the mirror. She was more like her mother, flame-haired, emerald-eyed, and "as feisty as a she-cat," her father often teased her. Her sister, Hannah, on the other hand, older by thirteen years, was dark-haired like their father. The child, Cassandra, sitting so patiently having her hair braided, looked more like she should be Mariette's child, rather than Hannah's, and often Mariette thought of her as such. Hannah had left written instructions that should she die before they were grown, she wanted Mariette to be guardian to her children. Cassandra would be no problem but, Mariette shuddered, feeling instantly guilty for it, Hannah's boy would be more trouble than she could handle. He was spunky and always causing mischief in the house. And Hannah, thinking him to be such a saint when she was well aware of his temperament. Oh, how blind was a mother's love.

An echo rippled through the dark corridor outside the door. Their English visitor, Lara, granddaughter of old family friends, the Seymours, giggled in response to a low, masculine voice. Mariette listened, instantly assessing the voice as belonging to Michael, son of her uncle, Noble. He was enamoured of the seventeen-year-old Lara, though he was more than twice her age, and Mariette could scarcely believe that he could not see beyond her fickle, narcissistic personality. He saw only the waving auburn hair and chestnut-colored eyes, not the hardness of a heart no true emotion could penetrate. Mariette hadn't said so, but she was anxious for the little tart to return to London. Lara had set her sights on Roby, Michael's twin, whom she was ardently pursuing. The distant Roby had scarcely given her more than a glance since she'd arrived in Philadelphia three weeks before.

"Aunt Mariette, you're not paying attention."

Mariette startled, the child's gentle voice managing to shock her from her thoughts. "Oh? Is something wrong?"

"I was trying to show you my arm." With childlike innocence, she now offered the arm, her right sleeve pushed up. "See? I've got an ugly rash."

Mariette's brows arched into a severe frown. "So you do," she responded, scrutinizing the red, mottled area. "How long have you had this?"

"Since Saturday, Aunt Mariette."

Since you brought home that ragged little cur! thought Mariette, responding instead, "Well, I think a little trip to Dr. Redding's office is in order. We'll have this seen to." The braid, now completed to Cassandra's waistline, was ready for the ribbons, which were offered to her. Tying them carefully, then clipping the ends with scissors so that they'd be even, Mariette's hands now closed over her niece's shoulders and she viewed her appearance in the mirror. "See how lovely you look?"

Cassandra smiled. "Will Dr. Redding give me some hard candies?" she asked, meeting Mariette's gaze in the mirror.

"I think that he will," laughed Mariette, withdrawing. "Now . . . let me change into something suitable. In the meantime, you run down and show your arm to your mother, and tell her that I'll take you in to see Dr. Redding."

"While we're there, we should pick up Aunt Liddy's medicine."

Liddy was Noble Donovan's second wife, the daughter of a late Rourke House servant who had been something of a character. Liddy had been born blind, but Mariette suspected she could see as well as any of them. Certainly, she could see the problems the visiting Lara Seymour was causing between her stepsons, Michael and Roby.

"Yes, we'll do that," answered Mariette after a moment. "Don't let me forget, all right?"

Mariette took little time in changing, tying back her hair and sending the upstairs maid to direct that a carriage be made ready for their journey into town. Within moments, she was downstairs, assuring Hannah that the rash was nothing serious, and coaxing the excited Cassandra to the waiting carriage. Cassandra had all but forgotten about the rash; rather, her thoughts were on the large jar of hard candies Dr. Bertrand Redding kept for his special patients, the children he often referred to as "his own."

The slamming of the door at mid-morning caused Adam Cassidy to jerk to full wakefulness. He heard a child giggling, and he was suddenly flooded with memories brought back from his past. With sadness, he listened to the child being greeted by the genial Bertrand Redding. Just as he would have pressed the pillow to his head in an attempt to recapture his peaceful sleep—and crush the painful memories—a voice, soft, lulling, beautifully female, caught his full attention. Rolling to his side, he propped his head on his right palm, attempting to gain a better view through the slightly parted curtain separating the alcove from the waiting room.

At first he saw only the fullness of opulent, rose-colored fabric forming the careful folds of her skirt. Then . . . an hour-glass waist, her three-quarter length jacket of rich satin hugging its small size. She was wearing a bonnet trimmed in cream lace, satin rosebuds and ribbon with metallic stitching. He wanted to see her face; leaning toward the edge of the cot, he fought to gain a better view.

Thud! Adam Cassidy suddenly felt himself hitting the floor. As he attempted to save himself from further humiliation, his hand caught in the curtain, ripping it down from the doorway. Gaining his momentum, he looked up, immediately meeting the severe frown of the most beautiful woman he'd ever encountered. He had the good senses to immediately notice that no band of gold gleamed on the ring finger of her left hand.

Her cheeks and lips were blushed in soft rose, and even from here, he could see the emerald specks in the richness of her eyes . . . livid, dancing, disapproving eyes.

Adam might have been embarrassed to hell if the pretty child with the woman had not suddenly snickered. Cassandra moved a step closer to Adam and said, ever so politely, "You look silly, sir."

Remembering a similar one, his fingers lightly touched the small, angelic face, then withdrew quickly. A cockeyed grin, eyes briefly cutting from the stern features of the woman, he responded, "Suppose I do, young lady," then dragged himself to his feet and attempted to extricate himself from the folds of the dismantled curtain.

He knew he looked a mess. Sweeping back his unruly silver and blond hair, then making a half-attempt to tuck in his shirt, he moved slowly toward the Philadelphia beauty. Extending his hand, he introduced himself, "Adam Cassidy."

Mariette was amused, her eyes sweeping down his long, lean form. He was certainly not from this area, and she imagined that he might look the part of the cowboys she had read about in various works of fiction. Offering her hand, she said politely, "Mariette Donovan. And this—" Her left arm swept across the shoulder of her young relation to draw her close. "This is my niece, Cassandra."

"Where do you live?" asked Cassandra, tucking her hand into Mariette's.

"Here and about," he responded, his gaze skittering to the bemused features of Bertrand Redding.

"I would imagine more like 'there and away'," offered Mariette, retrieving her hand from the overly warm one of the cowboy.

"Don't you have a home?" asked Cassandra.

He shrugged boyishly, never taking his eyes from the narrowing ones of Mariette Donovan. "I have a house back in California, but I haven't been there in quite a while."

"That's on the other side of the world!" Cassandra's woeful eyes lifted to her aunt's. "He's so far away from home, Aunt Mariette. May we take him home with us?"

"I think we'll reserve that privilege for lost puppies and wounded pigeons," offered Mariette, smiling shyly. Her gaze now leaving his intense one, she looked to Dr. Redding. "Will you look at Cassandra's arm? She has a rash." Politely, she said to Adam, "Will you excuse us?" Momentarily, she moved into a small alcove to the left, where she showed Bertrand Redding the area of concern beneath Cassandra's sleeve.

Bertrand's brows pinched; he had a way of pursing and lifting his mouth so that it almost touched the tip of his nose. Then he said to Mariette, "Speaking of lost puppies . . . has our little lady brought home any lately?"

"I'm afraid she brought home a cur Saturday last."

"Well, what we have here is a ringworm that's been scratched by someone's little fingernails."

"I told you not to keep it, Cassandra!" scolded Mariette without thinking. "Now see what the little runt has done?"

"A worm? I've got a worm in my arm?" immediately

wailed Cassandra, at which time the candy jar was brought down from the shelf. The tears were staunched almost as quickly as they had begun and a candy of each color carefully chosen.

In the following moments, the stout, middle-aged man cleansed the area with green soap, then applied an ointment containing sulphur. Presently, jars of each were placed in a brown bag and handed to Mariette. "Clean the area as I have done several times a day and apply the ointment. It'll clear up in no time."

"Will it kill the worm?" asked Cassandra, accepting the brown paper from Dr. Redding in which to wrap her candies.

"There is no worm, Cass," he offered in his most professional tone. "It's a frightful fungus that jumps on pretty little girls. But—" He took her hand and patted it with paternal affection, "we'll have to do something about the puppy."

Tears gathered anew, flooding her lower eyelids. "Will you have to shoot him dead?"

Dr. Redding laughed, "I don't think that'll be necessary." To Mariette, he suggested, "Bring the puppy to me this afternoon. I'll keep it in the pen and treat the ringworm." To Cassandra he said, "And then you can take it back home."

Mariette softly mouthed the words, "Couldn't you find another home for it?"

"I heard that, Aunt Mariette," scolded Cassandra with youthful flourish. "That's *my* puppy! Mama said I could keep it."

"And Mama probably has a ringworm, too," fussed Mariette, "since she is the only other one who has touched it."

"Miles touched him, too," pouted Cassandra, then

with more inflection, "and I hope that old worm gobbles him up all the way to his toes."

Rising, taking Cassandra's hand as he did so, Bertrand Redding escorted the two ladies into the waiting area. There sat Adam Cassidy, who came to his feet as they made their appearance.

In a tone that almost boasted pride, Cassandra announced, "I've got a ringworm."

To which Adam replied, "I had one, too, when I was a youngster. Sorry to announce that it won't eat your brother."

Cassandra liked the tall, dark-eyed stranger with hair the color of her sterling silver bracelet. Tucking her fingers into Mariette's, she entreated, "Can he come to supper this evening, Auntie? He doesn't have a home."

Mariette flustered. "Well, I'm sure that Mr. Cassidy has other things to do—"

"Actually, I do," he immediately responded.

"What other things?" Cassandra demanded.

"Well, I—" Staring into Cassandra's upturned eyes, Adam fought for some excuse. He could not tell the child that he avoided the company of beautiful women and children . . . and other men, for that fact. He liked to be alone.

Cassandra sniffed accusingly, "See, you don't have anything else to do. You just don't like us, do you?"

The way her mouth pressed, producing two little dimples in each corner, tore at his heartstrings. "Your aunt has probably warned you many times," he said in a quiet, even tone, "that you must be wary of strangers. Some men are evil, and it's very hard to tell which ones are not."

Mariette thought him ruggedly handsome, his eyes warm and friendly, though a bit tired-looking, and his clothing was dusty from his travels . . . he certainly was not from the region. A bath and a change of clothing would surely be an improvement. Now, becoming aware of his polite gaze,—a gaze that made her feel uncharacteristically giddy inside—she made a decision. "Do come to dinner, Mr. Cassidy. You'd be most welcome."

"Well, I don't know—"

"Please," implored Cassandra.

Mariette said, "You do look fairly harmless, Mr. Cassidy. And I'd imagine you don't know many people here and about."

Cassandra moved toward Adam, compelling him to lower his head to her level, then whispered something in his ear. He looked up to Mariette, smiling, the secret safe in his heart as the child moved back to her aunt. "I'd be honored," he said after a moment.

"We dine at six, Mr. Cassidy," announced Mariette. "Do be prompt." To Bertrand Redding, she said, "Will you add the visit to our bill?"

When he had replied, "Of course," she turned toward the door and the bustle of activity on the street outside.

Then Cassandra pulled back on her hand. "Don't forget Aunt Liddy's medicine." Immediately, Bertrand Redding retrieved the readied potion from a narrow shelf, approached and tucked it in with Cassandra's medicine. Taking Mariette's hand, Cassandra moved to her side.

But before they could exit, the warm, masculine voice of the stranger caused her to halt.

"Where do you live?" asked Adam.

"Dr. Redding will tell you," she said, firmly grasping Cassandra's hand to hurry her down the short flight of steps and the carriage.

*   *   *

He'd merely shrugged his shoulders, agreeing some-what reluctantly to drive her into the country. Yet, Lara viewed Roby's commitment this morning as a victory of sorts. Since her arrival at Rourke House three weeks ago, he'd scarcely spoken a complete sentence to her . . . but those few words had sent her hopes and expectations bubbling through her veins. Now she chose a long, flow-ing dress of lavender jacquard from her wardrobe, pin-ning a cream-colored cameo to the high, lace-trimmed collar. Sweeping her hair up, then gracing it with tiny faux pearls, she joined Roby at the carriage house just as Mariette and Cassandra were returning from town.

Lara didn't like the way Roby had been described to her by some in the household . . . a dark, somber, brood-ing troublemaker. He had left the family several years ago to discover his Indian roots in Florida. But he'd been ostracized by the Seminole tribe to which his grandfa-ther—a renegade killed almost seven decades before by Cole Donovan—had purportedly belonged. Roby had returned to Pennsylvania, a bitter, difficult man, jealous of his favored twin, Michael, who conformed to their fa-ther's plans. It was this dark, brooding indifference that Lara found so compelling.

Lara smiled as Mariette hopped down from the car-riage, then assisted Cassandra to the ground. A little sternly, Roby said, "Why didn't you let the man drive you in, Mariette? There is no reason for a woman to be managing the carriage alone."

Mariette now turned, scrutinizing the dark eyes of the man she considered her cousin, despite the lack of familial blood, then drew the child's hand firmly into her own. "I've told you before I can manage the carriage quite well. And as I've told you before, the *man* has a name . . . John."

"You called to me, Miss Mariette?"

Mariette turned, watching the aging gentleman who took care of their horses and carriages exiting into the morning sunlight. Mariette had never been as trusting of John as had the others of the house. For that reason, she redirected her attention to Roby. "Where are you going?"

Lara bubbled forth, "He's agreed to drive me into the country this morning."

"Can I go, too—"

"No!" Lara had cut off Cassandra's entreaty so quickly that her gaze lifted to Mariette's with a somewhat apologetic smile. "I mean . . . what I mean is that I'm not sure when we'll be back."

With a gentle hand at Cassandra's back, Mariette said, "Go on to the house with the medicines and give them to your mother." As soon as a skipping Cassandra was out of sight, Mariette drew Lara aside. While Roby unharnessed the bay Mariette said to Lara, "What are you doing? You know how Michael feels about you? You'll cause trouble between him and Roby."

"Oh, Michael! Michael!" Lara fussed in a harsh whisper, her chestnut-colored eyes flashing toward Roby. "Michael is as boring as . . . as baked beans!"

Pressing her mouth in an attempt to staunch her anger, Mariette studied the tall, slim woman who had not yet reached eighteen. She was ordinary, though still pretty, her face a little too thin, her mouth a little too full, her eyes forever flashing mischief and contradiction. Mariette imagined that Roby was a perfect match for the wild, rebellious English girl-woman, but he'd shown no interest in her beyond tolerance, at least, not until this morning. Michael, on the other hand, had brought Lara fresh flowers daily, taken her to the best restaurants in Philadelphia, and on long drives in the country. That she was more attracted to Roby, possibly because of his indifference to her, had not yet sunk into the lovestruck Michael's brain.

"You ready, Miss Lara?" Roby had drawn his booted foot up to the carriage step; his left hand was dangling across his knee.

Mariette watched the Englishwoman put distance between them. Shortly, she placed her hand into Roby's and hopped into the carriage seat, scooting across the plush leather to allow room for him. As a masculine "click" eased the mare into movement, Mariette watched their departure, the tall, dark-skinned, broad-shouldered Roby and the petite Lara snuggling against him. *She's going to cause trouble,* Mariette thought, drawing a deep sigh, then lifting her skirts slightly as she moved toward the carriage house. In the dark interior, she found John seated on a small stool, mending harnesses. He stood, slightly nodding his head. "John, would you mind taking the puppy Cassandra found in to Dr. Redding's office some time today?" She warned him of the ringworm.

"No, ma'am. Be happy to."

Following polite amenities and small talk, Mariette resumed her journey to Rourke House. Stopping a moment to sample the beef intended for their evening meal, and telling Hannah about her daughter's rash, and the unexpected guest, she now moved up the stairs before Hannah could begin one of her sisterly interrogations. Pausing on the platform, her gaze moved among the portraits, and she remembered all of the conversations she'd enjoyed with her mother and her grandmother, hearing the fascinating story of their family for generations past.

There was nothing she didn't know of them, nothing she hadn't wanted to know. Hannah, on the other hand, was not interested beyond "creating" ghosts for the chil-

dren, and usually heard bits and pieces of the family
stories in passing. She knew, of course, about her abduc-
tion as an infant, and was vaguely familiar with the more
reknowned members of their clan, but Mariette absorbed
tales of the family skeletons with something of an obses-
sion. She had frequently joked to her sister that one day
she would put it all in a book.

Now, here she stood before the portraits, enthralled by
their history once again. Momentarily, her gaze settled
upon the portrait of the original Cole Cynric Donovan,
who had built the house in 1685, his wife, Emilia, who
had died giving birth to a daughter, also named Emilia.
There were portraits of Emilia and her husband, Moss
Rourke, who had renamed his father-in-law's house after
his death. Before his death, Emilia's father had contemp-
tuously hated her intended and had cursed his daughter
and her new husband. For eighteen years Emilia had
conceived no children. Then, miraculously, she had given
birth to a son, Standish, who was Mariette's great-grandfather, and two years later, to a daughter, Jocelyn. Standish Rourke's only daughter, Diana, had married a far,
far distant Scottish relation, also named Cole Cynric
Donovan, to whom Andrew, Mariette's father, had been
born. But the rich history of the Rourkes and Donovans
might have been rather mundane, had it not been for
Webster, born of Jocelyn's marriage to Phillip Mayne. In
order to maintain their residence in the rich old house,
following the frail Jocelyn's natural death, both Webster
and his father had kept her mummified remains—since
she was the only one with true rights to the house—in her
private chambers on the second floor of Rourke House for
thirteen years, until the grisly discovery was made by
Diana, Mariette's grandmother. In the fire that had consumed the wing of the house where Jocelyn's remains had

lain, morbidly cared for by a simple-minded servant named Claudia, Webster had been presumed killed. Only his severed left hand had been found in the debris.

Then, more than thirty years passed without incident. When Mariette's father brought his wife, Carrie, to Rourke House, the hideously deformed nemesis, Webster, amnesiac for those thirty years, had followed his "Flame," the kidnapped woman he had purchased at a white slave auction in Haiti, back to Philadelphia. Then, for Diana, the horror had returned from the ashes, for in the ensuing drama she had seen Andrew's and Carrie's first daughter, Hannah, kidnapped on Christmas morning and taken into the Alleghenies. Webster had been killed that day, and save for the grace of Providence, the family might have forever lost the infant Hannah. But the young couple, traveling the mountain trails, in whose arms Webster had placed the child, had reluctantly returned her to her grieving parents in Philadelphia.

And now, here they were, thirty-six years later, still living with Webster's evil in the form of the "ghost" Cassandra swore was her friend. She hated it when Hannah took the children to the dark, spooky attic to tell them those hideous stories and keep this monster from their past alive for them—

"Aunt Mariette?"

She startled, swirling so quickly on the platform of the stairs that she might have lost her balance. "Miles—you frightened ten years' growth from me."

"You had a frightful look on your face," the precocious twelve-year-old remarked, skipping past her on the stairs.

"Thank you . . ." said Mariette, only now reclaiming her ability to smile. "For the compliment."

She resumed her journey upstairs, pausing to study the portrait of the stern, gaunt Webster Mayne painted in his youth, before the fire had disfigured him. Even then, he had been ever so thin, unattractive, with narrow cruel eyes. His mouth had smirked menacingly, his left hand, later accidentally lopped off during the fire, raised, fingering the pristine cravat immaculately tucked into his coat. Just as she would have turned her eyes away, the mouth seemed to take on a rueful expression, compelling Mariette to quietly remark, "You don't frighten me, Webster Mayne."

Then, as she stepped onto the planked floor of the upper corridor, she wondered for the hundredth—no, the thousandth—time why the family kept Webster's portrait hanging in such a place of prominence. She would have to remember to ask Grandmother Diana when she visited her this evening in her private suite on the third floor of this gloomy old house.

Two

Roby didn't like the way Lara was clinging to him. He felt a little like a parent being smothered by a frightened child, and all his efforts to dislodge the clinging arm were met with high-pitched giggles and continuous, aggravating launches into stories of her pampered childhood. As far as he was concerned, she was still a child, an assessment that had to be reconsidered when he noticed the swell of womanly curves straining against the tight fabric of her gown. The gentle aroma of her, like lavender in bloom, affected him in ways he fought by instinct. She was a white woman; he a halfbreed, though his looks, dark, somber, and hardened by misfortunes, hinted very little at the white blood coursing through his veins.

"Tell me about your childhood, Roby."

Concentrating on little more than the countryside passing them by and his own dark thoughts, her voice caused him to startle. Momentarily, he replied, "Not much to tell."

Leaning into him, she half-whispered, "There must be something. Tell me about how your parents met." She noticed at once his moment of hesitation. And in that moment, she found her thoughts spanning three-thousand miles of ocean, a gentle, rolling English country-side and flying, like the wind, through the doors of Holker Hall, the great manor house where she had been born. She had been blessed with grandparents who loved her, though they had frequently expressed disappointment in her wild, rebellious ways. She had lived in grandeur, her every whim met, her education accomplished by the best private tutors, and her moods tolerated with some degree of familial endurance. Lara was fairly certain that had there been a military school for girls, she would have been shipped off early in her youth. She knew that when the Seymours had approved her trip to America, they had done so with the heartfelt hope that the months away would quell her rebellion, that she might return "the proper English lady" that her mother, Rebecca, their only daughter, had not been. But these first three weeks in America had done nothing to quell her rebellion; rather, this land, so unlike her stuffy England, had fed it, like a strong wind swelling the currents of an ocean hugging the coastline.

"They grew up together in the Appalachians."

She startled, momentarily lost from her thoughts. "What? What are you talking about?"

His look questioned her sanity. "You asked about my childhood—"

"Oh, yes," she cooed in her sweetest tone. "I must have drifted off somewhere. Yes, do tell me about how you came to be here . . . in Pennsylvania."

He shrugged, not really wishing to talk, but feeling the obligation. He had, after all, agreed to drive her in the country—though for the life of him he didn't know why—and now, he was duty-bound to engage in small talk. "My father and Andrew and my mother Jolie, the daughter of a man named Zebedee Ward, took over the trading post on Wills Creek before I was born. My mother died in childbirth."

"So did my mother," said Lara, her voice lowering in deference to the sad occasion. "I always felt responsible."

"You were responsible," Roby said immediately. "Just as my brother and I were responsible for Jolie's death. It is a way of life."

Her features lowered, tears suddenly springing to her eyes. "But, I didn't ask to be born. What brought me here was not my fault."

"I didn't say that it was. I merely remind you that had we not been born, our mothers would not have died." Roby slowed the carriage; when the horse halted, he turned to Lara, his strong, burly fingers settling beneath her chin to turn her eyes to him. The hardness in his voice did not match the gentleness with which he touched her. "Don't pout. Only children pout!"

Why he thought of his boyhood at that moment, he was not sure, but the image of a boy at his school came rushing back to haunt him. He remembered being taunted as a "breed," a taunting that had never included Michael and that he himself had joined in. Michael had always fit in with the other boys, because his heart was white. Their tauntings had managed to turn Roby into a hellion who could not be controlled by either the schoolmasters or his own family. Had he not been a brooder, seeking solitude wherever he went, he might have shared the likeable personality of his twin. As it was, he rebelled against his roots in white society, his family, and most of all, his brother. Roby would never forget that Michael had taunted him enough to make him hate. Though Michael had matured, apologized for his childish behavior, and begged Roby's forgiveness, he needed the hate in his own heart enough that he had refused Michael's entreaties.

"What are you thinking, you halfbreed monster?"

His thoughts snapped back, his dark gaze settling uncomfortably upon the young Englishwoman's pretty features, and her teasing smile. He had no chance to reply, for . . . without warning, she flung herself into his arms, nearly dislodging him from the carriage seat. "You called me a child, Roby Donovan!" Grabbing his hand, she settled it upon her left breast, noticing at once that he did not withdraw it as she had expected. "Does this feel like the curve of a child? I think not!" And in that moment she remembered her promise to spend the day with Roby's boring brother, Michael. But Lara could not imagine the soft, limp hand of Michael hugging her swelling breast as the wild, wonderful Roby now did without abandon.

All of Roby's instincts to avoid this woman flew away with the wind. Against his will, he began to massage the fullness of her through the crisp jacquard of her gown. When she offered her pouting, youthful mouth to his own, he claimed the kiss completely, as would a man teetering on the brink of brutal passion.

They were alone, at a clearing next to the river where few travelers ever passed, and he could tell by her lusty movements, that she was offering more of herself than his good senses forbade him to take.

Michael Donovan had been late this morning getting away from the shipping office. He'd felt obligated to stay around until his father, Noble, and his Uncle Bundy had boarded one of their ships for Savannah, Georgia. Now, he hopped down from his horse at the carriage house, careful not to spill the bouquet of red roses he had purchased from Mr. Maxwell in town. He had promised Lara that he would drive her to the country and picnic on the banks of the river.

John approached from the dark interior of the carriage house, carrying the stray puppy, the drawstring of a small burlap sack tied loosely around its neck, so that only its head was visible. Before Michael could question him, John said, "Ringworm. Miss Mariette wants me to take it to Dr. Redding for treatment." Spying the bouquet of roses he was attempting to shield at his back, John added, "She's not here, Mr. Michael. Gone off in the carriage a couple hours ago with your brother."

Michael's hand suddenly opened, the roses falling to the ground. "She went off with Roby? Miss Lara went off with Roby?" The June morning was suddenly too warm for comfort. And the years of living with Roby suddenly rushed upon him, tormenting him and making him hate his brother in a way that he had not hated in many years. He and Roby had shared equally in the privileges of growing up at the trading post on Wills Creek with their father, Noble, and their stepmother, Liddy. But the animosity had started early in their youth, as Michael could recall a bloody nose when he and Roby had turned three. While Michael had been the sensible, studious son of Noble Donovan, Roby had been the devil-be-damned one. While Michael had been the one taken into the family business at the age of twenty-two, at that same age Roby had fled Philadelphia with a chip on his shoulder, determined to find his roots among the Seminole Indians of Florida.

Michael remembered that Roby had located the tribe their grandfather, Oclala, had belonged to, and despite the vicious memories the elderly village people had of the renegade, they welcomed Roby warmly at first. Then he had begun to show his true colors, laying claim to a maiden already betrothed to the chief's son. The maiden, taken by force by Roby, had committed suicide, and Roby would have been killed by the tribe had he not escaped into the mountains. A party of young men had trailed him through the Appalachians and into Kentucky, where Roby had continued to elude them. Then he had returned to Philadelphia even more bitter than when he had departed more than two years before. He had allowed the chip on his shoulder to double in size and become an insurmountable obstacle between himself and the rest of the family. Now, he was pulling one of his old tricks: claiming a woman another had shown interest in.

Michael pulled at the collar of his shirt, dismissing his recollections. When John, slowly nodded the answer to his question, Michael asked, "In which direction did they go?"

"Off to the west," answered John, climbing into the saddle of the old gelding he favored. As he turned his mount, he halted, asking Michael, "Do you want me to take care of your horse?"

Rather than reply, Michael remounted. The old gentleman, puppy in tow, coaxed the gelding down the drive, soon entering the road toward town. He knew he might have caused trouble, but he tried not to think about it. The "boys", as he called the thirty-five-year-old Michael and Roby, were forever quarreling.

Cassandra encountered her great-grandpapa the moment she entered her bedchamber. He was seated in the wicker rocker, his hands twisted over the knotty arms. "I've been awaiting you, lass," he said, arising. "Where have you been?"

Cassandra was a little annoyed. It was bad enough being constantly drilled by the adults in the household, now she had to answer to her great-grandpapa's ghost. Still, she remembered that she had been raised to show only respect for her elders, whether they be dead or alive, and somehow managed a small smile. Approaching, leaning against his knee, she pulled up her sleeve and somberly announced, "I've got a ringworm. Aunt Mariette took me to see Dr. Redding."

"Impossible! Redding's not still alive."

Cassandra drew in a small sigh. "Dr. *Bertrand* Redding, Great-grandpapa. I'm sure he's not the same Redding you remember."

"Indeed, he isn't." Cole Donovan rose to his full height so suddenly that Cassandra was taken aback, her eyes widening curiously. "You must go downstairs, lass, and tell your mother there will be trouble between the lads—" He turned, lowering to her level, his hands gently covering her shoulders. "Tell your mother that Michael must be stopped before he gets to the river where Roby is. There'll be trouble—"

"What do you mean, Great-grandpapa?"

"You needn't know, lass. Just go tell her."

An exasperated Cassandra threw her hands out with childlike drama as she turned, dropping into the chair at her dressing table. Now she looked back, her pert chin dropping to the back of the chair, a hardness that compelled her to tuck her hands between chin and chair. "And how can I tell Mum, Great-grandpapa? Shall I say, Mum, the ghost of my great-grandfather has told me to come downstairs and tell you that Michael is going to cause trouble with Roby at the river?' "

The direction of the child's logic left Cole Donovan in awe. He knew that his offspring were certainly not dolts, but this child was especially intelligent . . . and mature. He imagined that in ten or twelve years she would break some poor fellow's heart. . . . He could almost see the wild rebellion of the child in the spirited dancing of her eyes as she watched him, anticipating his response. He could see his beloved Diana, the way she had been many, many years ago, reflected in the child's lovely gaze. His heart panged, even as his first words were stern. "Perhaps, Cassandra, you could explain that you 'have a feeling'—"

"A feeling?" argued the child, her chin rising from its comfortable position against her hand.

Cole became a little aggravated; turning, roughly straightening his cravat, he cleared his throat with a balled hand pressed to his mouth. "You've got a mind, Cassandra, I'll give you that. Don't be a pest. Just do as I've asked."

Drawing in a long, steady breath, Cassandra climbed to her feet. "Very well, Great-grandpapa. But if I get in trouble, it will be your fault."

"If you get in trouble, I'll tell you the story of my encounter with Oclala—"

"Roby and Michael's grandfather, the awful, terrible, vicious, murderous renegade you had to kill?"

"The same, lass." He turned back now, smiling. "You do like my stories, don't you, little Cassandra?"

"Yes, Great-grandpapa," she responded, without enthusiasm, and quite without a smile, an accomplishment in itself since the encounter with Oclala was her favorite of all her great-grandpapa's stories. "I'll return in a few minutes."

Cassandra slipped into the wide corridor, closing the door behind her. A dark silence hung all around her, and as she moved toward the stairs, her shadow twisted, stretched and distorted along the hallway, snagging, it seemed, against the portraits of her relatives who had passed into eternity . . . well, most of them, that is. She met no one in her descent of the stairs, and when she entered the kitchen, her mother stood at the stove, seasoning the half-baked potatoes she would soon return to the oven. Her mother smiled, momentarily easing the tension hanging painfully between Cassandra's youthful shoulders.

"If you're worried about the puppy," said Hannah, "you needn't. John is taking it into town and Dr. Redding will take care of it, making it all well."

"I'm not worried."

The shallow sound of her daughter's voice now caught Hannah's attentions full. The bottle of seasoning settled, with a metallic tinkle, upon the stovetop. "Is something the matter, Cassandra?" Hannah approached, stooping before her daughter to take her hands.

"I'm to give you a message," she responded demurely, hoping the pain she forced into her eyes might staunch any motherly lecture. "Great-grandpapa says Michael must be stopped from reaching the river or there will be trouble between him and Roby—"

"Great-grandpapa? You mean Cole Donovan?" Drawing up once again, Hannah continued to firmly hold her daughter's hands, shaking them as she talked. "The stories I tell in the attic are just that, Cassandra . . . stories. They're not real, simply meant as entertainment for you and Miles. There are no such creatures as ghosts. Do you understand me?"

"Yes, Mum. There's no such things as ghosts." She grinned now, cutting her eyes to the doorway, then slowly bringing them back to her mother's stern features. "But perhaps you'd better come up to my room and tell Great-grandpapa that."

Annoyed, Hannah dropped her daughter's hands. "That's enough, young lady. No more stories." And— little lady, if I believed in that kind of punishment—it would be off to your room without your dinner."

Cassandra sighed. She knew she'd get in trouble. With impudent boldness she asked, "What is my punishment, Mum? I'd like to begin it quickly so that it can be over with."

Hannah drew a calm breath. How exasperating the children could be! And Cassandra . . . she was usually the good one. "I'd go on up to your room now, Cass, if I were you, before you feel the spatula against your back skirts."

Cassandra turned, exited the kitchen, then crossed the wide expanse of the parlor and began to descend the stairs. At the platform, she paused before the portrait of Webster Mayne and gave him a small, shy smile. "You haven't been around in a few days, Cousin." Though she was sure that the pressed mouth in the portrait had turned up in the slightest smile, she treated the silence as a lack of response. She continued to her bedchamber, soon closing herself inside.

Now, she settled onto the full pillows of her bed, tucking her hands beneath her flaming red hair as she contemplated the words she would say to her grandfather, so that he would feel especially guilty for getting her into trouble with her mother once again.

Mariette entered the kitchen just as her sister was putting the pan of potatoes back into the oven. "Was that Cassandra's voice I heard just now?"

Hannah sighed deeply. "It was, indeed!"

Hannah's sharp response prompted Mariette to ask, "What was it this time?"

"She said that her great-grandpapa told her to come downstairs and give me a message. What am I going to do with that child?" asked Hannah, turning now, dropping her hands to her hips.

Mariette began tying on a large white apron. "And whose fault is it the child sees ghosts?" Turning now, placing her palms upon the table as she relaxed against it, she smiled broadly. "I think, big sister, it is *your* fault, and no one else's."

"Well—" Hannah knew she was guilty. "Miles hears the stories, also, and he doesn't see ghosts."

"Or perhaps—" Mariette turned to begin rolling out the biscuits. "He's just too smart to *admit* it, seeing as he's witnessed Cassandra constantly getting into trouble because of the ghosts." The rolling pin dropped heavily into the dough. "What was the message she brought you from Cole?"

"Apparently, he told her Michael and Roby are going to get into a scene at the river."

The rolling pin dropped; Mariette turned to Hannah, her features ashen now. "What? Does Michael know that Roby is with that little English snip?"

Hannah shrugged. "I saw Michael come in and talk with John. I imagine John mentioned it."

"Dear Lord . . ." Mariette snatched at the ties of her apron, ripping the garment off and casting it aside. "I'd better ride out and see if I can prevent an encounter. Michael cares deeply for Lara, though I have no earthly idea why, and if Roby does anything to—" She halted her narration, lifting apologetic eyes to her older sister. "I'll be back as soon as I can to help with the cooking. Don't forget that Mr. Cassidy is coming."

Mariette did not bother to change. Though her gown was not suitable for horseback, the skirts were wide enough to allow for riding astraddle without exposing her legs. At the stable, she coaxed her mare from the stable, hastily threw on the English saddle and cinched it. When the mare resisted the bit, Mariette fussed, "Not now, Gypsy . . . I don't have time to worry with you." As though the mare understood, the bit slid between the short, wide teeth and within moments, Mariette was coaxing her down the drive and onto the road toward the river.

Please . . . please, Michael, don't cause trouble with your brother. But she knew that if the two brothers came together, and there'd been any question of Lara's indiscretion, there would be trouble.

With the moist heat of Roby's kiss still upon her mouth, Lara jumped down from the carriage. As he watched, his eyes a strange mixture of humor and passion, she danced in a wide circle, slowly peeling away the clothing she had suddenly found too stifling. The jacquard jacket caught in a cluster of blue wood aster, her bonnet, suddenly caught on a heady wind, settled at the edge of the river. As Roby watched, his tongue slowly tracing a path around his full mouth, Lara's undressing soon left her naked and running, childlike, toward the water. He watched her dive in, the pale, ivory form of her now shadowed by the murky depths.

"Come out of there, Lara," called Roby, painfully aware of his body's reaction to her nakedness. "You'll catch your death. And you'll be the talk of the gentlefolk if you're caught like that in the company of a man."

"The water's wonderful," she called back to him. "I rode out here the other morning and in the three hours

I stayed, nary a soul ventured by. Don't be such a baby, Roby. Come in . . . the water is wonderful."

The English vixen was sure to get him in trouble, Roby thought with a smirk. Her tawny hair floated on the surface of the water, fanning out in all directions . . . her slim, youthful form distorted in the swirling of the current, but still he could make out her alluring curves of womanhood.

Gritting his teeth in outrage, he could not keep this distance between them. She was a woman, for God's sake, a young, and very beautiful one. Slowly, his booted feet touched the earth and his long, masculine strides took him to the water's edge, where he crouched, picking up a twig to drag through the damp earth. Again, he said, "Come out, Lara."

"In my altogethers?" she cooed, her slender arms fanning the water's surface. "Why don't you skim down to bare flesh and join me?"

That was an invitation hard to resist. He could well imagine the soft curves of her brushing his taut skin beneath the cool water. He could imagine her arms possessively easing across his shoulders to hold him close. He could taste the sweetness of her kiss boldly touching his mouth and . . . God! Where he found the courage to say simply, "No!" he would never know. He didn't even know the resistance was part of his nature, but now he found himself rising to his full height, spreading his feet and dropping his hands to his slender hips. "I said 'get out of the water.' If you don't—" Christ! Why did she pout like that . . . so pretty . . . so alluring . . . so, damn . . . inviting? Quickly, lest the courage leave him, he turned his back and began retracing his footsteps to the waiting carriage.

Suddenly, a wet, naked Lara Seymour was at his back, her arms moving quickly around him. Momentarily, he found her fingers linking in a soft, feminine lock, and though it would have been nothing to break her hold, he found that he was not willing to do it. Rather, he turned to face her, his hands rising roughly to grip her shoulders. "You're a damned vixen, Lara Seymour! What the hell do you think you're trying to do to me?"

Rather than respond, her long, tapered fingernails eased beneath the lapels of his shirt and ripped it down. Ravishing kisses sunk into the downy black matte covering his chest and though his good senses warned him to cast her away, the maleness of him pulled her closer. Dragging up her chin, his kisses brutally ravished her mouth.

With aggravating impatience, he began to drag her toward a patch of clover in a stand of linden trees. There, he dropped to his knees, taking her slim, naked form with him. He became like an animal, his eyes narrowing, darkening with need, his hands so roughly claiming her that her brows pinched in pain. And yet, she rubbed herself against him, dislodging his clothing further, her slim hands boldly easing beneath the tight band of his trousers. Then, as she claimed that aroused part of him, his senses returned full force, and he scooted on his buttocks away from her. His breathing deep and painful, he slowly rose to his feet, straightening his clothes and turning from her.

As he began to put distance between them, she hissed, "You halfbreed bastard . . . how dare you!" The crisp, tutored English accent was gone; she could have easily been a Cockney whore.

As his long strides stretched the distance, he called, "Collect your clothes, Lara. . . . We'll be returning to the house now."

Just at that moment, Michael rounded the bend in the

road, halting, his surprised gaze instantly connecting to the one of his brother.

The naked and unaware Lara boldly moved into the clearing to collect her clothing. But Michael's gaze was only for his brother, and slowly, he dismounted his horse.

Lara Seymour had never before pulled on a gown in such haste. As Michael moved slowly toward Roby, so much black rage in his eyes that he would surely kill, Lara moved against him, attempting to halt his progress. "Nothing happened, Michael," she whispered frantically. "It was my fault. Roby did nothing. I swear, Michael . . . I swear!"

But he would not be stopped. Slinging her away from him as though he'd suddenly found her repugnant, he moved within half a dozen feet of Roby, then, with an outraged groan, leaped upon him from that distance. Both men fell to the ground.

Lara was horrified. Without thought or the rest of her clothing, she jumped into the carriage, then turned the mare toward town. Scarcely had she rounded the bend in the road before Mariette was forced off the road by the speeding carriage.

Lara had never driven a carriage before and she knew that she'd lost control of the harness horse. Releasing the reins, she clung to the carriage seat, weakly calling out, "Help . . . help me . . . I can't stop——"

Mariette, immediately regaining control of her own spooked mare, muttered an expletive, then coaxed her mount into a run. The rampant carriage stirred up so much dust that she could not see it, though she could hear Lara's screams gaining in clarity.

Three

Dr. Redding linked his fingers beneath his stubbled chin. Narrowly watching the lean, gaunt features of the gravely injured man the stranger had brought in, he thought now that certain things about him were vaguely familiar . . . his eyes deepset, his brows whispy and feminine, his mouth much too full for his thin face. His right temple beneath the bandage was swollen and mangled; the graze of the assailant's bullet had done considerable damage.

Redding was troubled, not so much by the unconsciousness of the man that was, in itself, a bad sign when assessing his chances for full recovery, but by the resemblance he bore to some soul from Redding's past. This was a man whose very presence made the blood run both hot and cold in his veins . . . his was a face that might be capable of malevolence. . . . Bertrand could almost picture a half-cocked grin and treacherously narrowed eyes.

But why, for God's sake! He'd never laid eyes on the man before last night. He might be someone's thoughtful husband . . . the beloved father of half a dozen adoring children . . . he might be the son of proud parents awaiting his return . . . he could be a man of God . . . or a disciple of the devil. All of Bertrand's inner instincts told him the latter was closer to the truth . . . and he felt guilty for assessing the character of a man who could not defend himself.

Bertrand now eyed the portfolio Adam Cassidy had found with the man. The leather was cracked and dry, the clasp tied down with a short length of twine; would it yield the identity of this man who, for reasons known only to the God of Jehovah, might compel a gentle-hearted physician like Bertrand Redding to press a pillow to his face and snuff the life out of him? His watery gaze held the portfolio, his hands twisting the edge of the blanket he'd earlier draped over his unconscious patient.

"I think we should take a look."

Bertrand Redding jerked up from the chair, a crimson tide of shame rushing into his features. "Mr. Cassidy, I thought you were fast asleep." He turned, a brief smile managing to alleviate the guilt. "Take a look? What do you mean?"

A long, masculine finger pointed toward the portfolio. "There, let's take a look at the contents. We need to know who the fellow is." Actually, Adam was surprised neither he nor the kindly Philadelphia doctor had not already done so. The fellow's identity was in question, and if he had kin nearby, the portfolio might yield clues. Now, Adam approached the table where the valise rested, his hand dropping casually to it. "Well, what do you think? Should we take a look?"

Adam did not await Redding's permission; he had found the man bleeding on the side of the roadside, and that in itself gave him the right to study the man's belongings. Untying the fragile length of twine, Adam soon dragged a stack of papers from the portfolio. In it were decades worth of newspaper clippings in varying stages of rot and age, letters written by a variety of hands, birth announcements, death announcements, prescriptions for medicines and doctor's orders scratched across crisp, aging paper.

Though Bertrand Redding was crawling with curiosity, he forced his attentions to the gravely injured man. He was fevered, his skin hot and flushed, and a tick occasionally jerked his right hand away from his body. Bertrand's gaze cut to the small table, now scattered with various papers, and he attempted to read some expression in Adam Cassidy's features. Adam had now opened a brown folder and from it spilled still other clippings carefully cut from newspapers.

Stirring against the back of the chair, Adam asked, "Do you know a fellow named Webster Mayne—?"

"Mayne!" Bertrand spun about, stunned to hear the name of the nemesis that had terrorized three generations of Rourkes and Donovans. "Webster Mayne, son of Philip . . . indeed, I know of him! But—why would you ask?"

Adam swept back his hair, oblivious to the wretched curl returning immediately to his forehead. "If I am reading all this information correctly, that fellow there is Webster Mayne's son—"

"Impossible!" The single word caused wind to gather in Bertrand's cheeks, puffing them out like those of a pouting child. "Webster died without issue, years ago—" But even as he argued, his gaze narrowed in its return to the man's features. Yes, yes, of course, this thin, gaunt, mean-spirited face was identical to the one in the portrait at Rourke House. He had seen it several times when he'd made house calls, usually to treat one of Cassandra's frequent illnesses. Yes, he had seen those features there; a wretched scar on the history of the house. He'd never understood why the family allowed the portrait to hang there, tormenting the family even after Webster Mayne's hideous death on the cobbles at the front of the house.

God! How many times had he listened to his grandfather tell that story. Webster had been presumed killed in the fire that had swept through the west wing of Rourke House, but had turned up thirty-five years later, a grotesquely deformed man calling himself Junius Wade. Ironically, he had purchased a white slave in the Caribbean and brought her to his brothel in New Orleans at about the same time Andrew Donovan, Noble, and Noble's half-brother, Bundy, were docking their steamboat there. Carrie, Junius Wade's slave, had been kidnapped from the shallow waters of the Isle of Wight in the English channel, and in New Orleans had been sold for a night of pleasure to the charming Andrew. Thereafter, she had stowed away aboard his steamboat, *Donovan's Dream,* and Junius Wade had followed her up the Mississippi, determined to recapture his lost prize. Injured in a fight in one of the Philadelphia taverns, Junius had suddenly regained his lost memory and had thereafter secreted himself in the attic of Rourke House, his domestic needs filled by the simple-minded servant, Claudia, and his sexual ones by her blind daughter, Liddy. On Christmas morning in 1822, he had taken Andrew's and Carrie's daughter, Hannah, and fled into the Alleghenies, leaving her with a couple traveling into the interior. Webster had been killed when he'd fallen onto the cobbles from a second floor window, before he had been able to tell them what had become of the infant Hannah. In the weeks that had followed, Andrew and Carrie had tried to come to grips with the probable death of their daughter, but she had eventually been returned to Rourke House by the couple.

They had all thought the evil had ended that night. Now, lying upon the small cot in Bertrand Redding's clinic lay an extension of that evil . . . that poison . . . that despicable monster who had tried so desperately to destroy the happiness of Cole Donovan and his family.

In a voice hushed by horror, Bertrand said, "We'll have to be sure, beyond a shadow of a doubt, before we inform the family."

"And what family is that?" asked Adam, drawing up to relieve the tension in his back.

"You met two of them this morning, Miss Mariette Donovan, and her niece Cassandra."

"Indeed? And why not inform them now?"

"Blasted, man, didn't you just hear the story I told you?"

Adam raised a quizzical brow. "All I heard was the silence after I told you who I suspected the man was and you said that his father died without issue."

Bertrand looked askance. Of course, Mr. Cassidy did not hear his thoughts. But they had been so loud, so ringing clear inside his head, that he was sure they had reverberated and scattered into broken fragments for Mr. Cassidy, and all of Philadelphia for that matter, to have heard.

Now he looked to Adam Cassidy, feeling the utter fool, and dropped into a small chair beside the man's bed. "If you're around long enough," he eventually said, "I'll tell you all about Webster Mayne."

"Or perhaps he will," said Adam, nodding toward the bedridden man.

"We'd all be better off," Bertrand softly reflected, "if he silently passed into eternity."

*   *   *

Weeping now, Mariette pulled Michael's bloodied head into the folds of her skirt. She could not see his horse; Roby must have taken it when he'd fled, leaving his own twin brother wounded upon the roadway. She could not see visible signs of life in this man she considered her cousin; Roby had sought his vengeance well. But who had ridden out here with vengeance in mind? Michael! Dear God, her thoughts were running amok through her brain. She couldn't think clearly. But wouldn't Michael have ridden out to seek a sensible solution? And wasn't Roby the hot-blooded one whose nature alone spoke the old adage, "Shoot first and ask questions later?"

Mariette's trembling palm rested against Michael's cheek. She could feel the warmth of blood there and with her other hand took out the handkerchief, ever present in the pocket of Michael's coat, to wipe away the mixture of blood and perspiration. She spoke his name, "Michael," so softly that she was sure no sound had evolved, and yet he slightly responded to her voice. She said, "Michael," once again, and his hand came up to firmly grasp her wrist.

"Lara?"

Oh, that English tart! She was not good enough to have her name form upon Michael's lips! "No, it is me, Michael . . . Mariette. Hush—hush, we need to find help for you."

Her eyes cut along the roadway in this sparsely populated area beside the Schuylkill River. *Why couldn't Mr. Pittman visit his elderly sister on Cherry Street this morning? He and his lumberous wagon frequently traveled this way. Where was the morning coach of the Allegheny Coachline? Wasn't it overdue . . . or had it already passed through?* Dear Lord, Michael might be dying in her arms and there was no one nearby to help her.

Then her brain began to explode with expletives. *How*

could Roby have left his own brother on the roadway like this? How could he have hurt him so badly? She knew that Roby and Michael were constantly at odds—and even more so since Lara had come to the house—but, she'd never imagined that even the hotheaded Roby could beat his brother badly enough that death might be imminent. She felt so helpless . . . so utterly helpless. Why wouldn't someone come by?

Though tears popped into her eyes, she could still see the gentle currents of the Schuylkill, the deepening green of the patches of clover and the stands of elms bearing new leaves. She could see the scatterings of Lara's clothing, that which she had not dragged on in her haste to get away from the men who were fighting over her. Blast the English tart! She should have remained in England!

A wagon rumbled nearby, the groaning of its wheels hinting at a heavy load. Mariette watched the roadway until it appeared, a freight wagon drawn by four draft horses. Rising so quickly that she spooked her horse nearby, she now waved her hands frantically, waiting for the wagon to pull to a slow halt beside her. A large, full-whiskered man looked down at her. "Had some trouble, little lady?" he asked, his travel-stained features nodding toward Michael.

She did not go into details. "Thank the Almighty you've come by. Please help me. I need to get him to Dr. Redding's clinic on South Eighth Street."

The man flipped a seaman's cap back from his forehead. "A bit out of my way, little lady. I'm crossing the river up at the bridge."

Tears popped again into Mariette's eyes. Her outstretched hands now moving slowly to her face, she looked down, her head of flame-colored hair flinging from side to side. She wasn't sure which way to turn, toward the man with the hopes of imploring some sympathy, or toward the now groaning Michael who was steadily growing weaker. "What will I do?" she muttered softly.

"Say, ain't you from that big house on the hill . . . Rourke House, is it?"

She slowly nodded. "Yes, I live there."

"Tell you what—" The big, burly man hopped down from the wagon seat with the agility of a cat. "I'll take the two of you back there . . . won't be fer outta my way. Then you can send a servant in for the doctor."

By the time the freight wagon pulled up in front of Rourke House, Michael had lapsed into unconsciousness. Within moments, the house was in an uproar, a nervous John saddling up once again to fetch Dr. Redding, Cassandra crying in fear that Michael would die, the normally calm Hannah furious to the point of screaming because Roby belonged in prison somewhere, Lara locked in her bedchamber, refusing to come out, and Mariette trying to be the calming influence in the household.

Things hadn't improved much by the time John returned. Hearing the clip of horses' hooves, Mariette crossed the foyer, pulled open the door and ran down the stairs toward the carriage house where she expected to meet Dr. Bertrand Redding.

But she stopped abruptly, her pale hands more firmly gripping the folds of her gown that she'd held up in her haste to reach the carriage house.

Alighting Dr. Redding's horse was the man she had met that morning. Raising a quizzical eyebrow, she waited for him to make eye contact, then asked, much more sharply than she'd intended, "What are you doing here? Where's Dr. Redding?"

"He's with an injured man," Adam responded huskily, politely removing his hat.

"That answers part of my question. So what are you doing here?"

"I've had some medical training," he replied. "Redding thought I could be of help."

"Medical training? What do you mean by that?"

Dark eyes met emerald ones in an instant clash. He would not admit that he was a doctor, and once upon a time quite a good one. He didn't like the way she looked at him, narrowly and wary, trying to contain her curiosity, but flashing it like lightning in her gaze. He couldn't believe that he'd admitted his profession to Dr. Redding, nor that he'd agreed to come here to Rourke House. And now, the very lovely, very alluring Mariette Donovan held up her chin in a haughty manner, trying to back him into some invisible corner.

"Mariette, come quickly."

She spun rapidly at the echo of Hannah's voice. "Well, come on, Mr. Cassidy, and bring your medical training with you. I suppose you have a little black bag?"

He drew one from the other side of his saddle, holding it out to her. "One of Redding's. It'll do, won't it?"

"I don't like you, Mr. Cassidy," she blurted out, turning when Hannah again spoke her name. As she moved toward the house, with Adam slightly to the right and a step behind, she tried not to feel the penetrating bore of his eyes upon her profile; she could see it from the corner of one eye, she could feel its heat, but she refused to respond to it. Actually, she was wondering what had transpired to make the fellow who'd fallen from the cot this morning trying to get a better look at her suddenly become such a stuffed shirt. His last query, *It'll do, won't it?* had been aggravatingly condescending.

As she stepped into the foyer and turned to face a stern-faced Adam Cassidy, she said, "I suppose it's just as well you're here in a medical capacity, Mr. Cassidy. You're still welcome to stay to dinner . . . if you don't mind a round of sullen faces."

"Dinner is the last thing on my mind right now, Mariette." He deliberately called her by her Christian name to see her reaction. After all, a woman who claims to dislike you wouldn't appreciate the intimacy of first names. He was disappointed that she simply raised a quizzical brow. "If you'll show me to your cousin's bed?"

Hannah entered, expecting to encounter Dr. Redding. "Who is he?" she asked, eyeing the handsome stranger before her.

Mariette turned toward the stairs. "A doctor of sorts, I suppose, Hannah. Dr. Redding has a gravely injured patient and couldn't come."

Adam Cassidy had been told that Mariette had a sister named Hannah. He was surprised by the contrasts between them . . . Mariette flame-haired and emerald eyed, with the graceful curves of a goddess . . . Hannah extremely thin, tired looking, and yet still pretty, her wispy brown hair pulled back in an untidy bun. The obvious difference in their ages showed in the features of the elder sister.

The house they shared with other members of the family seemed something of an enigma. He could easily see that efforts had been made over the years to update the centuries-old dwelling, and yet there was still something dark, sinister, and foreboding about it. The place seemed to close in and smother its occupants, even as the large rooms were painting in pale, sober colors and light gauze curtains fluttered at the open windows. Where there should have been sunshine and fresh air, he sensed shadows and muskiness. Then he began to ascend the stairs on the heels of the lovely Mariette, his eyes catching the images of past generations, and on the platform of the stairs he paused, surprised by the vision of the man whose portrait seemed larger than all the others.

Damned if it wasn't an exact image of the man lying in the small back room of Bertrand Redding's office!

Was this family in for a hell of a surprise!

Only now did he become aware of the tapping of Mariette Donovan's toe upon the corridor floor a dozen steps above him. He looked up, catching the blinding rays of her flame-colored hair against the light of a single dome-shaped window. "We haven't time to look at portraits, Mr. Cassidy . . . or is that *Doctor* Cassidy?"

He slowly ascended the steps, stood beside her and frowned beneath dark, hooded brows. "Actually, I prefer Adam . . . and if you don't like that, *Honey* will do."

Mariette remained undaunted, because she was sure he was trying to intimidate her, though for the sake of her she couldn't understand why he would. Resuming the short walk to Michael's chamber, where his stepmother, Liddy, was taking care of him, she casually responded, "I imagine the kind of women who call you 'Honey' get paid well for it."

She wasn't really sure why she enjoyed bantering insults with him, perhaps because he was handsome and very cocky about it. He was probably acutely aware that women would turn twice to look at him.

They stood beside the door at the end of the east-end corridor. Gently, Mariette knocked, then called, "Liddy, it's me. I've brought someone to look at Michael."

The woman within called, "Come in, Mariette," then

stood when she and the man entered the chamber. She could tell he was very tall by the long strides he took, and she knew he was not the short, stocky Redding.

Adam smiled to the older woman, then instantly noticed that she was blind. But she seemed to know her way around and soon stepped aside, allowing room for him at Michael Donovan's bedside.

Adam made a cursory examination, checking his pupils, pressing his finger and thumb to his wrist to take his pulse, then using a stethoscope, which he took from Redding's black bag, to check his heart rate.

Mariette gave him sufficient time before asking, "Is it serious?"

"Very serious," shortly responded Adam. "This man needs to be in a hospital."

"We take care of our own!" snapped Mariette. "I'll bring in whatever—and whomever—is necessary to take care of him."

"Who the hell would beat a man this badly?" Not expecting an answer, Adam began to issue orders, "Bring gauze or strips of cotton, we need to get his ribs wrapped. He'll need to be kept very still; I suspect a concussion. Keep the draperies drawn and give him plenty of liquids when he comes to. When I return to Dr. Redding's, I'll ask that he send laudanum for his pain—"

"We have morphine in the house—"

Adam instantly cut Mariette short. "What the hell for? It's addictive and not to be toyed with."

Mariette instantly wondered at the source of his hearty objection to such a common household medicine. "And did I say we were toying with it?" she snapped, linking her fingers so firmly that pain shot into her wrists. "We had it on hand for one of the horses this past winter, to keep it quiet while a pulled ligament was healing."

An apologetic smile eased into the corner of his mouth. "Oh . . . sorry to have snapped at you—" Liddy, who had stood back against a bureau, now came forward, stumbling against the chair that Adam had inadvertently moved into her path. Again, but directed to Liddy, he said, "Sorry," then put his fingers beneath her elbow to lead her around the chair. She smiled prettily, easing the tension Adam felt being here . . . at playing the role of doctor . . . a role he had sworn never again to play.

The day Beth had died.

The handyman, John, sat upon the small stool in the tack room, preparing to make the necessary repairs to Michael's favorite saddle. He'd been asked to perform the chore weeks ago but had always seemed to be too busy. He held the small saddle upon his lap, the pick in his right hand tapping gently against the smooth leather.

His deeply lined features grimaced, his mouth pressed so tightly that only a thin line remained. Narrowing his eyes, he muttered beneath his breath, his lips moving nervously and failing to form sensible words.

The pace of the pick steadily built, until the frenzy of its attack upon the saddle filled it with smooth, deep holes.

But it did not stop there. No emotion moved the man's features as the pick eased across the leather and began to stab into the flesh of his right thigh.

Blood trickled from the wound, then began to spread in a wide pool upon the coarse fabric of his trouser leg.

An hour later Adam was sitting in the wide, spotless parlor of Rourke House, alone except for its unseen spirits. Exhausted, placing his head against the overstuffed divan and his forearm across his eyes, he did not see the person who entered, but he could tell that it was the child, Cassandra. Easing his eyes open beneath his sleeve, he watched her quietly move across the oriental carpet, then ease into the Queen Anne chair several feet from him.

When he allowed his hand to fall, Cassandra asked, "Are you a doctor?"

Adam sat forward, his hands now hanging across his knees. "I am," he whispered huskily, "but it'll be our secret . . . all right?"

Cassandra smiled. "I like secrets. Shall I tell you one of mine?"

"Is it a secret to keep . . . or a secret to share?"

Cassandra gave him a quizzical look. "Isn't that a contradiction, Mr. Cassidy? If it is shared, then it is no longer a secret." Then she hastily added, "But a secret can be shared between two people, and not any more than that."

"I see—" Putting on his sternest expression, he said, "Then let's share your secret, Cassandra."

Her slippered feet slid to the floor. Slowly, she crossed the carpet, then drew up to the divan beside him. "The ghosts of the house talk to me. That is my secret."

Raising a pale eyebrow, Adam replied, "And that is a much better secret than mine."

Cassandra liked the tall, distinguished gentleman very much. She thought he looked much too young to have silver in his blond hair, and she thought he had kind eyes and a gentle voice. Cassandra imagined that her father might have looked very much like him, though she couldn't remember him and there were no portraits of him in the house. She imagined that Mr. Cassidy would make a good father, but she knew that he had noticed her beautiful aunt, Mariette, and not her mother, who acted old and rarely had fun, except when she told stories to her children in the attic. No, if Mr. Cassidy had an eye for one of the women in the household, it would surely be Aunt Mariette.

"Would you like to get married, Mr. Cassidy?"

He smiled instantly, staunching his surprise at the question. "And what makes you think I don't already have a wife?"

"Because, Mr. Cassidy," she laughed, easing into the plush fabric of the divan, "if you did you wouldn't have looked at my Aunt Mariette as you did in Dr. Redding's office this morning."

What a thoroughly charming child, and so astute, Adam thought. "You're right, little Miss Cassandra. . . . I don't have a wife, and I have to admit, I *did* look at your Aunt Mariette. One day a man will look at you that way—"

"What way?" Mariette entered the parlor, crossing the divan to share a look between Adam Cassidy and her niece. "Cassandra, you weren't bothering Mr. Cassidy, were you?"

"Oh, no!" she said haughtily, jumping off the divan to ease her hand into Mariette's. "We were sharing secrets . . . weren't we, Mr. Cassidy?"

He came to his feet. "That we were," he remarked, his gaze holding her own. "That's quite a little charmer there."

"Yes, she is." Absently, Mariette grasped Cassandra's hand, then drew it fondly to her. "You'd better get washed up for dinner, Cassandra."

The little hand withdrew. Pausing in her retreat, she asked, "Are you going to stay, Mr. Cassidy?"

"I'd imagine," he replied, "that with your aunt's permission, I'll stay the night to keep an eye on Mr. Donovan." As a gleeful Cassandra skipped from the room, Adam asked, "Is that acceptable to you?"

She did not immediately respond. Rather, her gaze held his own for a moment, then briefly scanned his appearance from head to toe as though inspecting the attributes of a horse she intended to purchase. She knew that it embarrassed him, which was her intention. A woman could tell the character of a man if she could see such a reaction in a full assessment. Crimson had eased into his bronze features, and she could tell that he wanted to look away, perhaps concentrate his attentions on something beside her.

Having elicited the proper effect, she replied, "I'd be most grateful. You shall certainly be compensated for your services."

Adam had never been looked at so completely by a woman as beautiful as Mariette Donovan. She had certainly flustered him. "I don't need your money," he countered, gaining momentum. "I care about people, though sometimes I don't know why."

How could a woman so lovely be so outrageously intimidating. Her bold scrutiny, the way her mouth turned up in a somewhat mocking smile made him want to take her in his arms and shake her . . . want to feel the heat of her body against his own . . . want to feel the moist caress of her mouth pressed to his seeking one.

Had Hannah Gilbert not called from the dining room, "Dinner's ready," he might have done just that.

Four

Adam had surprised himself. It was not like him to insinuate himself into the lives of others, especially a beautiful woman's like Mariette Donovan. Yet Mariette was as alluring as Emily had been . . . and she might very well be as poisonous and self-destructive . . . beautiful women usually were. Women like Emily plunged daggers into their hearts.

But now he sat across a wide, spotless, linen-covered table from the flame-haired beauty. At the head of the table sat her sister, Hannah, beside Mariette was the young Cassandra, and beside Adam sat a sullen Miles. The blind woman, Liddy, was taking supper at her stepson's bedside, and two plates, set at the table by habit, must have been intended for Michael and Roby Donovan. Lara Seymour's plate, as explained to him by an eavesdropping Cassandra, was deliberately not set at the table, a delicate hint that she was not welcome to dine with the family.

From Cassandra he had learned much about the history of this family that Bertrand Redding had not told him. The child had filled in the missing pieces as if, by instinct, she knew what the doctor would not have brought up. Absently looking toward her, he imagined that half of what she had told him she had fabricated, though she had instantly explained that her "Great-grandpapa" had told her many things that no one else in the house knew, and that her mother wasn't to know about her little chats with the ghost. He smiled when she looked to him, and he was instantly reminded of a little girl in his past who had been dear to him, who had once been his reason for living. A wretched ache grabbed at his heart and he quickly looked down, filling his fork with a healthy portion of potatoes and meat.

No explanations had yet been given as to who had started the fight. Adam discovered that though Michael was the one who had initially sought the confrontation, he was normally not a fighter, and used the power of the spoken word to reason out disputes with his brother. Roby, however, was hot-headed and would just as soon kill a man as look at him a second time. The general consensus was that Roby had instigated the fight, and he was the one who would be held accountable. Besides Michael, the only other person who had a firsthand account was Lara, and she wasn't talking to anyone . . . including the Philadelphia marshal who had appeared at the house a couple of hours ago to investigate the situation.

Adam hadn't met the woman, but as young as Cassandra had said she was, she would probably pout for several days before addressing reason. Women in their teen years usually did.

Lara was hardly pouting. She lay on her stomach on the wide, lace-covered bed, her pert chin dropped to her stacked hands. Night had fallen, a favorite time in her life when she could dream and wonder about important things; Roby, and where he was this very minute.

She was pleased with her day's dramatics; hadn't she so often told her exasperated grandparents that she had the makings of an accomplished actress? She liked the excitement of what the day's activities would do to the aggressive, and yet moody, Roby Donovan. She liked to think that she had alienated him from the family and that he would seek refuge in his wild past. She liked to think that when again they met, he would not hesitate to make her his woman. He would not walk away from her again. She liked to think that at this very moment he hated her as he'd never hated any woman before; after all, love and hate went hand in hand, and if she wanted his love, she would have to seek it through the barrier of his hatred.

She turned to her back, flinging her hands out. "Oh, Roby, you deliciously wicked man!" Then her thoughts suddenly turned to that despicable stable boy back at Holker Hall. She hadn't really cared that much for him, though he had been good for a rollicking tumble in the hay now and then. She was well aware that her grandparents had sent her to America to get her away from him, but how could they possibly know they had merely sent her into the arms of a man who was as wild and angry and impossible as the fiercest of storms, a man who made the stable boy look like a saint? She wanted Roby Donovan as much as she had wanted the diamond brooch now pinned against the material which scarcely covered the cleavage of her bosom. Absently, her fingers caressed its coolness, then traced a path over the gold filigree framing the priceless mass of stones.

The diamonds were as indestructible as her newfound love for the irascible Roby. They glittered with the secrets of the ages, just as her eyes glittered with images of herself in Roby Donovan's arms. She loved the wildness of him—the unpredictability of him. . . . She melted in her tormenting thoughts of him . . . and prayed . . . oh, how she prayed, that he would open his eyes and see her as a woman . . . with womanly passions waiting to be reawakened.

So, she was only seventeen! She was a woman nonetheless! Roby was a man . . . and surely he must want her as she wanted him! She would believe nothing else.

Though she tumbled childishly over the bed, she was still careful not to crush the velvet folds of her dress. She had chosen it especially for this evening, the gloriously rich colors of the floral print fabric comprising the bodice, the simple elegance of the black velvet of her full gown. She thought the colors complemented her gleaming wheat-colored curls, her creamy complexion, warmed by a petal-soft blush. She thought that Roby would like the cool color of her eyes framed with her sweeping lashes.

"I am deliciously beautiful," she murmured in the silence of the chamber, then giggling wickedly. "I am deliciously beautiful . . . all over, Roby Donovan . . . if only you will take what I offered you this morning."

"I will take it now—"

Startled by the deep, resonant voice emanating from the shadows of the room, Lara spun onto her stomach, then pushed herself forward. Roby moved into the pale glow of the lamp, his knuckles locked over a coiled length of braided twine. "Roby," she whispered. "What are you doing here?"

"I have come for you." He harshly whispered the words. "Isn't that what you wanted?"

Pushing herself to a seated position on the edge of the bed, she took a moment to reassess her earlier declaration. The man should, logically, pose a threat . . . but that is not what she felt was making her heart beat so wildly. That same logic warned her to flee, but instinct dragged her slowly up and deliberately into his embrace. Only when her slender arms surrounded him did he smile, and then it seemed malicious. Dragging his own arms up, he went over her head and to her back, still clutching the coiled leather braid. "What will you do with that?" she cooed, resting her chin against the expanse of his chest as she attempted to gaze into his deep-set black eyes. "Take your rage out on my hide?"

"The thought did occur to me," he responded. Dropping his arms now, he stepped back, ordering, "Let me see your wrists."

With a small giggle, she offered them. Roby wrapped the coils around them before she could usher a protest. Just as she opened her mouth to do just that, a clean white handkerchief filled her mouth, instantly being tied at the back of her loose hair. Now, she was furious, and as she began to thrash against him, he picked her up as though she were weightless and threw her across his shoulder.

He said nothing, but with the same stealth, exited the room through the window he had entered just moments before, made his way along the edge of the roof covering the veranda and down the trellis. With the slim, youthful Lara thrashing, panting in her exhaustion to free herself from his brutality, he soon eased into the saddle of his horse, threw her across the pommel and spurred the horse into the darkness.

"I heard a horse," Cassandra said, cutting her gaze toward the window overlooking the veranda.

Before Mariette could respond, Adam gently chuckled,

"For a prim and proper little girl, you have quite an imagination."

"No," she argued demurely. "This horse was right outside the window. And why wouldn't prim and proper little girls have imaginations, too?"

Adam set his fork aside, his gaze sweeping to the charming child. She had now puckered her lower lip and was blowing at the wispy locks of pale hair that had settled onto her forehead. It appeared that she might have forgotten about the horse for a moment.

"You haven't said, Mr. Cassidy."

He now looked to Mariette Donovan, who had also placed her fork aside and had dropped her chin quite charmingly onto her raised and linked fingers. "I haven't said what, Miss Donovan?"

"You haven't said what you do for a living," Mariette diverted. "Are you a doctor?"

Cassandra had asked him the same question half an hour ago but Adam would not give Mariette the same answer. "I've had medical training, enough to care for your kin until Dr. Redding can appear on the scene."

Voices reached them from the foyer. Momentarily, the man, John, stood in the doorway. "Don't mean to disturb your dinner, Miss Mariette," he said, holding his hat protectively in front of him. "But thought you'd like to know Roby just rode away from the house with Miss Lara all trussed up and thrown across the front of his saddle."

"Oh, dear," said Hannah, unconcerned that, once again, she had been overlooked as the lady of the house in favor of her younger sister.

Mariette rose so quickly that her chair fell backward, hitting the rug with a dull thud. "Are you sure, John?"

"Ol' eyes are gettin' bad, Miss Mariette, but I seen 'em

sure enough. He was a headin' west, I s'pose, into the mountains."

Mariette set her chair right, returning immediately to it. "I suppose if she was trussed up, then she didn't go willingly."

"Didn't look like it to me, Miss Mariette," John replied. "Do you want me to bring her back?"

Her eyes cut slowly to Adam Cassidy, and she said nothing for a moment. Then she smiled a small, shaky smile, dropping her palms to the table at either side of her plate. "We take care of our own, Mr. Cassidy. I'll send one of our men—"

"Which one?"

Her eyes narrowed then; her mouth puckered, then pressed into a thin line. "We've got plenty of men." She halted, thinking, geographically placing each man in her family still young enough, and able enough, to track Roby Donovan into the mountains. Her father was with her mother in San Francisco. . . . Noble and Bundy had left for Charleston on business just that morning. . . . Michael was lying gravely injured in his chamber upstairs. . . . While she considered John family, he was needed at Rourke House. . . . And there was Miles, who would be so willing to go in pursuit, but who was much too young.

"I repeat . . . do you want me to bring her back?"

She really wasn't sure where the anger came from, but now she was once again on her feet, her foot tapping, her arms crossed and her gaze looking past him for a moment, then coming back to Adam Cassidy's somewhat passive features. "Why would you waste your time doing a favor for my family, Mr. Cassidy? You've already given considerable time to tending my cousin's serious wounds. For what reason? Are you being paid by Dr. Redding? Or do you simply find me so charming that you're willing to go out of your way for me?"

Adam sat back, slumping lazily, his dark gaze raking boldly over her slim form. Not only did he find her charming, beautiful, and alluring . . . but she made him feel like a man again . . . a man who for the past seven years had taken what he wanted from women without feeling, freely paying for their services, and walking away without so much as a look back. But Mariette Donovan! She made him forget his hatred . . . and his pain . . . at least for a moment. . . .

He smiled as he came forward to look at her with slightly raised brows. "Actually, Miss Donovan, I find you anything but charming. You're boring and a bit too taken with yourself to suit my tastes. I was thinking that this seemed like a job that might bring a damn good fee."

Cassandra snickered, and Hannah, coming to her feet, took her hand and merely dragged her from the table. While her mother shushed her, Cassandra protested, fibbing that she hadn't finished her dinner.

Now that she was alone with Adam Cassidy, Mariette calmly repeated his insults, "I'm boring? I'm taken with myself? What right do you have to judge me?"

"I wasn't judging you . . . merely stating my observations."

"Your observations are not appreciated."

"The truth never is." He imagined that if the table was not between them she would be at his throat, tearing out his jugular vein as viciously as any mountain lion he'd ever encountered. She was slender and tall, very delicate in appearance . . . and yet he knew somehow that she would be able to hold her own in a fight. The fire in her emerald eyes held an untamed rage and the strength in her curled hands could probably deck him as completely as any saloon brawler. When her silence continued, Adam asked, "How much will you pay me to bring the English tart back to Rourke House?"

"Don't call her an English tart!"

"Why not? Everyone else in the house does . . . including you."

"Hannah doesn't! And neither will you! She has a name—Lara Seymour! And her grandfather is a duke!"

"Very well. How much will you pay me to bring back Lara Seymour whose grandfather is a duke?"

The condescending tone of his voice made the blood race through her veins. "You are a bastard."

Rising, arching his back, he clicked his tongue. "Such language . . . and from a lady, at that." Turning, he put a few feet of distance between himself and a very charming, furious young woman. "I'm too tired to banter insults with you, Miss Donovan. When you have your answer, I'll be sleeping on that cot in your cousin's room. If you want me to go after the Englishwoman, let me know before dawn. I'll leave then, and I'll need to borrow one of your horses. Mine is lame."

He had just reached the stairs when he heard a shattering of glass. *How childish!* he thought. *She could have taken better aim.*

Hannah rushed to the dining room just as Mariette dropped to her knees on the planked floor. "What happened?"

She was thinking that the arrogant Adam Cassidy might have thought she'd thrown something. She wouldn't waste her energy. "I turned away from the table and knocked a glass onto the floor. I'll pick up the pieces."

"I thought you'd thrown something at him," Hannah

said, bending to help her. "I could see that he was getting to you. And if I could see it, he could, too." Laughing then, she sat back on her knees, cradling the pieces of glass carefully in her palm. "You have met your match, little sister. I do believe Adam Cassidy is the man for you."

"What I would like to do to him, Hannah, would end his bloodline!"

Hannah laughed again, finding a place for the broken glass at the edge of the table so that her hands would be free. Standing, she took the shattered glass from Mariette and placed it with the rest. Then guilt flooded her, and when she had offered her hand to assist Mariette up, she said, "I shouldn't be enjoying myself. Michael is gravely injured upstairs and I could act appropriately for the situation."

"Michael loves your laughter," Mariette said as she gathered the broken glass in a napkin for the trip to the kitchen. "I've always suspected that he would have shown a romantic interest in you if he hadn't considered you family."

"We are family," she agreed. "But we're not blood. I've always been fond of Michael. I can't say I would have rebuffed romantic intentions since my husband's death, if ever he had shown them. But . . . well—" She shrugged as she entered the kitchen behind Mariette, "He likes women like Lara, young and flighty, without a single sincere bone in their bodies."

"And Lara has almost gotten him killed!" Mariette argued. "Perhaps he'll look toward more sensible women now . . . a woman like you, Hannah."

"I doubt that," said Hannah. She had prepared a tray and now picked it up from the kitchen table to hand it to Mariette. "Will you take this up to Grandmother's room? She asked about you earlier."

Mariette took the tray. "How is she today?"

"Her usual mood. All her talk is of Grandfather Cole and the old days and the adventures they had together. She thinks he is waiting in the house until she dies, so that they can be together in eternity."

"And I'm sure Cassandra keeps her up-to-date on the little chats she claims to have with him on a daily basis. You really must talk to the child, Hannah. She's beginning to believe she *really does* talk to 'Great-grandpapa Cole.' "

Hannah sighed heavily. "I hope she'll grow out of it soon."

With a single "Harumph!", Mariette turned, hoping she would not encounter the irrascible Adam Cassidy in her ascent of the stairs.

When she did not encounter him, she wondered if the pang catching inside her soul was disappointment.

He had stirred for the first time since he'd been brought in. Bertrand Redding bent slightly over his patient and watched the heavy movement of his eyes. Then they opened and Bertrand jerked back as though he'd been struck. "Who are you?" the man growled the whisper. "And where am I?"

Bertrand climbed up from his chair; instinctively, his gaze drifted to the small cabinet where he kept a loaded pistol. "I am a doctor," he replied. "You were apparently shot on the roadway outside of town."

He tried to rise, but could only manage to lift his head from the pillow before grabbing it between both his hands. Immediately, his finger dug beneath the clean white bandage. "I remember . . . some fellow stopped me on the road, wanting to know if I had money. When I told him I had none to give away, he pulled his weapon and shot me."

In these days and times, Bertrand wasn't surprised. There was so much crime in the region that he wasn't sure it could get worse. But that was the least of his worries, at the moment. "You're Webster Mayne's son, aren't you?"

His patient shot him a look filled with surprise. When his hand lowered to draw the covers across his chest, he politely replied, "My mother knew him as Junius Wade, sir. But . . . yes, I have reason to believe he was my father. I came here in hopes that I might garner further information about him." His confession went no further. The documents he'd been sent from the fellow in Philadelphia had indicated his father's reputation had been in doubt. He would not volunteer information, but only answer the doctor's questions.

Bertrand was surprised that a man claiming to be the son of Webster Mayne would politely exercise calm and control. Through the gossip he had heard, Webster had been a foul-mouthed man not above murder and mayhem. But was this man simply hiding his true nature in order to gain information? Bertrand could not take any chances with the lives of the Donovans, whom he loved like family. "You have come a long way for nothing, sir," Bertrand said after a moment. "Webster has been dead for thirty-six years."

"I am aware of that. I am hoping there will be family remaining here."

"There is no family left," Bertrand replied without pause. "The house burned years ago—" That was only a partial lie, since there had been a fire. "You really have no reason to remain in Philadelphia." As an afterthought, he asked, "What name do you go by?"

"Justin Laszlo." A short pause interrupted their conversation. Drawing in a breath to gain momentum, Justin said, "I already know I've got family left here, sir. The Donovans, I understand. I don't know why you feel it is necessary to lie to me, because I mean no one any harm."

Bertrand had always been a kind man, and one who gave a man the benefit of the doubt. But that same consideration could hardly be advanced to a man who claimed to be the son of a treacherous beast like Webster Mayne. He remembered the stories his father and his grandfather had told, and he could still feel the shudder of revulsion rocking through his spine. Now, linking his fingers above the space between his knees as he bent forward, Bertrand continued, "The Donovans are good people, Mr. Laszlo. Don't cause them any distress. If you want to know them, go about it without larceny in your heart. They will extend the hand of friendship and welcome you into their family, if you show your sincerity."

Justin's mouth pressed into a thin line. Guilt caused his gaze to cut away from the small, dark eyes of the doctor. He would not tell him that his initial reason for coming here was to avenge his father's death. Perhaps his own inner conflict held the confession back, because Justin still was not sure why he felt the need to avenge a father he had never known.

Presently, he said, "I know how to conduct myself, doctor. You needn't worry about the Donovans." Then, "Am I well enough to leave?"

Bertrand rose and turned away. "I'd rest until tomorrow, Mr. Laszlo. Your wound is healing nicely." As he moved toward the door, he said a little curtly, "I'll have a healthy meal brought to you. I'm sure you're hungry."

Justin's "thank you" was said to an empty doorway.

* * *

Justin Laszlo felt sick at heart. He was a good-natured man, had always made friends easily, and yet couldn't befriend the first man he'd met in Philadelphia. Because he was the son of Webster Mayne, the man had felt compelled to distrust him and lie to him about his existing family.

Easing from the cot, he retrieved his portfolio, finding the moment to feel annoyance that the hands of other men had gone through it. How else could the doctor have known who he was? Now, he began to remove the papers that had been his father's . . . the layout of the large, three-story house with hidden passages and chambers he had constructed from his "hidden" memories . . . newspaper clippings that had been sent to his mother in New Orleans only last year by a man who had identified himself as "Oliver Purvis." A corrected mistake in the man's signature, however, had indicated to Justin that this was not his true identity. Why had the man lied about something so mundane?

Skimming through the documents, he encountered once again the yellowed accounts of births and deaths and social events surrounding the lives of these people called the Donovans. If the lengthy letter of the informant, Mr. Purvis, was to be believed, his father, a good man by nature, had suffered vicious abuses at their hands. But that characterization contradicted the one given him by his own mother. He had to find Purvis and speak at length to him. His heartstrings were tugged by the depths of his own true character—the man everyone liked—and he was afraid he would not have it in him to seek the vengeance his father might possibly deserve.

He couldn't help but wonder why this man Purvis had been interested enough in the Mayne and Donovan families to have gone to such lengths to find him. What could

have kept a stranger interested in the affairs of the Philadelphia family for so many years?

Justin Laszlo did not yet know that he was the image of
his father, Webster Mayne. The only vision he had of him
was his mother's description of a gruesomely burned and
disfigured, one-handed man with the personality of a
cold-blooded killer.

From the papers Purvis had sent, Justin had learned
that his father had also killed a preacher in western Pennsylvania, stealing his horse and leaving his body to rot in
the wilderness. He was alleged to have abducted an infant
on Christmas morning.

But was this man Purvis making up these stories for
reasons Justin did not yet understand? He had to meet the
family and decide for himself. He had to talk to Purvis and
learn his motive. He was close to people who might be his
family for the first time in his life, and he was obsessed
with the quest he had begun as a child . . . to know his
roots, fully and completely, even if they were roots a man
could not be proud of.

Subtlety was the key here if he was to learn everything.
He wanted to make himself a part of the Donovan family,
win their trust, assure them of his loyalty and love. If it
took a year or two or three, he would be patient. And if
he learned that his father had been wronged, then he
would avenge him.

His thoughts abruptly ceased, changing direction.
Why, he wondered, would he even care about avenging
a father he had never known? Was it because of the hard
life he and his mother had lived in New Orleans? Would
their lives have been different if his father had not returned to Philadelphia, where he had been killed?

Though weak, his abdomen wracked by hunger, Justin
Laszlo managed to write down a few thoughts while they

were still fresh in his mind, a few questions that he would have to remember to ask someone in the Donovan family.

He hoped his father had truly been a wicked man so that he could end his lifelong quest for vengeance in his name.

Five

The sun was setting over San Francisco. He sat in a high-backed, leather chair in front of a window overlooking the garden, his gaze following the withdrawal of light from the camellia blossoms as the shade took up residency there. Occasionally, his hands would flex, his long, slim fingers caressing the smooth leather of the well-worn arms. If he listened closely, he could hear the surf breaking against wave-washed rocks; she had liked it there, and they had frequently walked, hand in hand, adoring, masculine chuckles echoing along the beach with petite giggles that had endeared her to him completely.

His days of weeping had ended abruptly; now, he sat, staring out the window, his face like chiseled marble, without expression . . . without hope . . . without ambition. She had taken his life away from him. She had destroyed all that was precious to him.

Slim, ivory arms swathed in gauze suddenly slid across the back of the chair and attempted to ease beneath the lapels of his shirt. Catching the heady, familiar whiff of her perfume, he jerked to his feet as if shot, spinning to glare at her with contempt and revulsion. Tears filled her eyes; normally, a woman's tears tore at his heart; now, they made his gaze narrow lethally, his mouth press into a thin line to cease its tremble of rage.

"I am your wife, Adam," she tearfully pleaded. "You cannot continue to punish me. For God's sake, I am your wife!"

"Yes," he said sullenly, refusing to see the tragic beauty of her, refusing to acknowledge her tears of grief . . . refusing to yield even a single emotion of his own in respect of the years he had spent with her. "Yes, you are my wife, Emily.

Adam awakened suddenly, then rubbed his eyes so hard that pain slid across them. The visions that had filled him were the reasons he did not enjoy sleeping. Always he dreamed of her, and always the vision nurtured his hatred like nothing else in his life. Why did she continue to torment him? And why did he continue to make her so vital a part of his life that she ruined his every sleeping and waking moment? Would he ever forget her? Would he ever stop hating her?

He now became aware of his surroundings and looked toward the bed where the man, Michael Donovan, was sleeping. He did not seem to be in any pain; his breathing was strong and even. Sitting forward in the cramped, uncomfortable chair, Adam dropped his hands into the cup of his palms for a moment. The night was warm; someone had opened a window at the far end of the room and the slightest breeze washed against him, cooling the perspiration that had gathered along the fringes of his hairline.

Then he saw her standing there, her gown so dark that she had easily made herself a part of the heavy midnight hour. She must have been the one to open the window, and when he had awakened, she had pressed herself to the wall, hoping, perhaps, that he would fall asleep again without noticing her.

Adam said, "Thank you for opening the window. It was hot in here."

She wanted to know who Emily was, the name he had spoken in his sleep. "I know," Mariette replied. "The whole house is stuffy. It's the night, settling heavily over everything. We could use a bit of rain, I suppose." Moving from the darkness, Mariette paused at the door. "Could I bring you something cool to drink?"

"You probably won't have what I'd like," he replied.

"A whiskey?" She imagined that a man as tortured as he seemed to be, who murmured the name of a woman lost in his past, might want something to take away the pain. "My uncle Noble keeps brandy in the liquor cabinet, if you'd rather."

Linking his fingers, Adam settled his chin upon them. "Actually, I was thinking that I'd like a cold glass of milk. But I'm sure you wouldn't have that on such a warm night."

"There might be some in the cold cupboard. I'll check."

He looked toward her now, a little suspicious that she was being pleasant. The last time they had spoken, they had bantered insults. But now she stood in silhouette against the dim light of the corridor, and she was much too lovely to fight with. He felt a tightness in his shoulders that immediately traveled into his spine as her womanly curves defied the barriers of her gown and robe—or was it his imagination—and when she suddenly moved from sight, he wanted to order her back . . . so that he might take her in his arms and gently hold her.

He listened to the retreat of her footsteps, quiet and slippered, betrayed only by an occasional creak upon the ancient, planked floor. In the quietness of the old house, he took a moment to wonder what he was doing here, to wonder why he wasn't a hundred miles away, making it back toward the west, as he always had. He thought of the house in San Francisco he had left, wondering how the gardens looked after years of neglect, whether the paint was cracking and falling from the once smooth, blue-washed sides of the Victorian structure. He wondered if the swing was still hanging at the end of the front porch, and whether the rains had washed the mortar from between the bricks on the front walk. He wondered if sparrows had nested once again in the attic. . . .

"Here is your milk. I hope it's cold enough."

Looking up, Adam took the glass. Had enough time passed for her to have journeyed to the kitchen and back again? "Thank you," he said, taking a sip. "It's perfect. You should have brought a glass for yourself."

"I don't drink milk." Quietly, she took a chair beside him, then leaned back. "It does terrible things to my skin."

"You have an allergy," he said. "Milk is one of the most common foods to cause allergies."

"Milk is not a food—"

"Oh, but it is . . . one of a child's most important foods. And for most people, it is good all through life."

From the silent darkness of the high-backed chair, Mariette studied the profile of the man who had been a stranger until this morning, until chance had thrust them into each other's lives. "You *are* a doctor, aren't you?" When he did not answer, she continued, "It's an honorable profession. I don't see why you won't admit it. Or—" She wanted to ask him if he had done some terrible thing for which he'd lost the privilege of practicing medicine. Perhaps he had killed someone in surgery. Perhaps he had simply lost the nerve—

"Or what?" Adam looked toward the light of the corridor, taking small sips of the milk.

She immediately recognized the defense rising in his voice. "Or what?" she echoed his words. "Oh . . . I was only going to say that perhaps—" She shrugged, settling comfortably into the chair. "Perhaps you're a very private

person who does not wish to speak of his past . . . or his
occupation."

"Speaking of the past does not change it," he whispered harshly. "A man should worry only about today,
and tomorrow—"

"And a woman?"

"Men should spend less time worrying about
women—"

"I meant, shouldn't women also worry about today and
tomorrow?"

He was glad she could not discern the moment of
embarrassment coloring his cheeks. "Oh. Yes . . . women,
too. Dwelling on the past is destructive."

"And what in the past, Adam Cassidy, has destroyed
your life?"

He wanted to feel angry that she so boldly attempted to
pry into his privacy and his past, but he'd put enough
energy into anger for the day. Instead he shrugged, then
set the glass of milk on a small side table. Looking toward
her, he caught the pale glow of the lighted corridor
beyond the fringes of her flame-colored hair. She looked
wild and untamed, and still every bit a lady. She hugged
her robe to her slender flame as though she expected him
to be undressing her with his eyes.

But he was not . . . he saw beyond the primitive needs
of man . . . he saw what he knew was intelligence and wit
. . . determination . . . yes, these were the things he saw
in Mariette Donovan, the woman who now looked toward him with narrowed eyes and a mouth pressed into
a firm line of disapproval. Had she misread the direction
of his thoughts?

Mariette liked the way the rangy Westerner was looking at her, as though he were assessing her without boldly
and lewdly using his imagination to determine her anat-

omy beneath her full, loose robe. She hadn't known she could be charmed by men like this Adam Cassidy . . . men who lived in a tortured past and who needed to be rudely dragged into the present and the future . . . men who were rugged and soft-hearted, and had redeeming qualities . . . men who were polished, and yet could hold his own in a bloody good fight now and then, as she was sure he could.

"The silence is killing me. I am curious as to your thoughts."

Only now did Mariette match his gaze. "My thoughts? Really, a man such as yourself would find them quite boring." When his mouth curled into a cocked smile, Mariette continued with haste, "I've decided that if Michael is well enough in the morning, and if your price is within reason, we will go after Roby and Lara—"

Adam came to his feet now, his hands finding a place on his slim hips to lightly settle. "What do you mean . . . we?"

"You and I . . . Mariette and Adam . . . what do you think I mean?" Even in the semi-darkness of the chamber she could see his eyes narrowing thoughtfully. "Surely, you didn't think I would let you go after Roby and Lara by yourself."

He shrugged slightly, though he really wasn't sure why he wasn't offended by her question. "It never occurred to me when I made the offer that you would want to come along. If you want the girl back . . . and back fairly quickly . . . I could travel better without company."

"Could you indeed?" Mariette had hoped that she could get through this moment without becoming angry once more. She remembered Hannah saying that if a man could so easily move a woman to anger, then he had to mean something to her, even if they were little more than strangers. For that reason, Mariette forced a moment of calm into her voice as she continued, "Mr. Cassidy, this is my family. . . . Roby is my family . . . and I care about him." She paused before quietly adding, "You don't."

Adam Cassidy turned, pressing his palms into his back for a moment, then looked toward Mariette Donovan. "You're right, I suppose." When he began to retreat toward the door, Mariette delicately coughed. He turned again. "If you're going to sit with your cousin for a few minutes, I need to get outside for a while. I'm not accustomed to being cooped up these days."

"Ah, the wild and reckless outdoors."

He caught a whiff of sarcasm in her statement. "I won't rape and plunder the premises while I'm out of your line of vision, Miss Donovan. I love the wild and reckless outdoors, as you put it, but that doesn't mean I am wild and reckless myself. Of course—" he paused, his voice now touched by subtle sarcasm, "if you would like to tag along, I'll try to be a gentleman."

She smiled, though she didn't imagine that in the dim light he would have noticed. He might have been a stranger to her, but she was beginning to know him probably better than he knew himself. He tried to be evasive, aloof, to annoy her when his heart really wasn't in it, but she could see beneath the rugged exterior and he was as refined and proper a gentleman as she had ever met in the historical halls of her beloved Philadelphia. This was no backwoods, uneducated rogue. . . . Adam Cassidy, as tortured and as cryptic as he seemed to be, was a man who could match her, wit and bone, as well as any that had ever crossed her path.

"I trust you not to rape and plunder the household,"

she remarked. "Of course, you know we have ghosts here who protect the inhabitants."

He smiled, stepping into the doorway. "So I've heard."

All of a sudden, Mariette did not want him to leave. She enjoyed bantering with him, she enjoyed the musky, manly scent of him, and she was intrigued by the mystery surrounding him. She pushed herself up from the chair and approached, her arms linked against her waistline. "If you're going outside, why don't you look over the horses. You might want to pick one out so that we can get an early start in the morning."

"You insist on going along then?"

Rather than respond to his cryptic inquiry, she said, "The white-faced sorrel is mine, the dapple is lame, but you can ride any of the others. I wouldn't recommend the black . . . he's a bit headstrong and unpredictable. Father will probably trade him off when he returns from San Francisco." The way his eyes immediately flashed took Mariette by surprise. "Did I say something wrong?

Adam did not wish to admit that she had mentioned his hometown—a place he had not seen in more than two years. "No."

"When you pass through the kitchen you might look in the cold box. I'm sure there are leftovers from dinner."

He smiled now, patting his waistline with his right palm. "Watching my weight, Miss Donovan." Turning, taking his hat from the mahogany rack beside the door, he slipped his head beneath the wide rim. "Don't mean to be rude, wearing my hat in the house, but if I should encounter a ghost, I don't want to be tempted to throw it in his face. Best durn hat I ever had."

Then he was gone, and Mariette settled back into the chair, listening to his footfalls as they descended the stairs.

Soon, she heard a door open and close . . . and she suddenly wished she was beside him in the pale glow of the midsummer moon.

Adam paused on the lawn, leaning against one of the large, twisted oaks. Instinctively, his fingers rummaged in the front left pocket of his shirt, though they did not find what they sought. He'd only smoked cigars for six months before quitting more than a year ago, but sometimes he forgot and sought the comfort of the habit.

Women were usually the reason he forgot—beautiful women like Mariette Donovan . . . women he tried not to encounter in his travels. . . .

Mariette's background was too much like Emily's . . . rich, spoiled, pampered, accustomed to getting their own way, and being relentless in pursuit of that which they desired. Though thoughts of Emily were black thorns in his heart, he smiled nonetheless, thinking of Mariette Donovan condemning herself to a saddle for days on end. He wondered if she was an experienced rider, whether she would ride sidesaddle, whether she would whine and want to stop to rest every half-dozen steps. He wondered if she would wear sensible clothing, and whether she would complain about mosquitoes and chiggers and ticks.

He smiled; he had no doubts she was strong, stubborn, and . . . hadn't he decided earlier on that she wouldn't hesitate to slug him if she felt he deserved it?

A horse whinnied, instantly interrupting his thoughts of Mariette. Pushing himself up from his slumped position, he moved toward the dim lantern light in the overhang of the carriage house. Pausing at the entrance, he looked down the line of stalls on either side of the long walkway, listening to the muffled stirrings of horses in their individual stalls. Slowly, he began to move, first to the left, where he paused at each door to look over the fine animals. At the third stall, he saw why Mariette had chosen the sorrel. A fine, sleek thoroughbred turned to the doorway to have its head scratched, then nibbled at the back of Adam's fingers.

"Sorry I don't have any sugar for you, girl." Then he continued his inspection of the horses, crossing the walkway at the end of the stable to make the trek back down. At the second stall he paused, unable to see little more than a movement of thick muscles in the blackness. Then a fiery beast came forward and he jerked back as the body hit against the stall door. Adam drew his hands to his hips and stared at the stallion as though he could not believe his eyes. He could hear a narrow, shod hoof striking the ground . . . one, two, three . . . one, two . . . one . . . as the small head nodded at the air. A grumbled whinny finally drew him back and his hand moved toward the bolt. "Well, I'll be damned—" The gate cracked and Adam took several steps back as the Arabian stallion moved into the walkway, stood for a moment, then eased toward Adam and dropped his chin across his shoulder. Immediately, Adam's arm circled his neck. "I didn't think I'd ever see you again, old boy."

At the moment, Adam did not care how the Donovans had come into possession of his horse. He cared only that after a two-year absence, the stallion he called Charlie was unmarked and appeared well-fed. He cared only that Charlie remembered him and the little games they'd played and that he was more than anxious to play those games now. With a soft nudge at his back, Adam found himself moving toward the dark lawns of Rourke House. There, he moved ten paces, at which time the horse moved ten, then turned in a circle, once to the left and twice to the right—several times they went through the routine, and when Adam attempted to return Charlie to his stall, he budged. Shrugging his shoulders, Adam turned toward the house. He knew that Charlie wouldn't go anywhere now that they were together again.

Halfway across the lawn, though, Adam heard the horse coming up behind him in the dark. Charlie paused at the kitchen door when Adam entered, but would not allow the door to be closed in his face.

"All right, Charlie," laughed Adam, leaving the door open so that cool air would be allowed into the stuffy chamber. "You go back to the stable when you feel like it."

He had his horse back; it had to be Divine intervention after all this time. Tomorrow, he would ask Mariette how her family had come into possession of him.

He didn't imagine that they'd stolen him, as had the nefarious gentleman he'd encountered outside St. Louis two years before.

He had really missed Charlie, and now, he was as excited as a child with a new toy, so much so that it took him more than thirty minutes to fall asleep. He had heard the case clock chime the hour of two, and it was the last sound he would recall when he awakened at dawn.

Something stabbed into his ribs. Adam jerked his forearm from its resting place across his eyes and looked toward the source of the assault. A flame-haired beauty stood beside him, one slim hand resting lightly on her hip and the other tapping a riding quirt against the arm of the divan.

"We need to get under way," she said. "Dr. Redding arrived a while ago and thinks Michael will be all right.

You and I have some riding to do." Mariette turned to walk away, then pivoted back. "Oh, by the way, when Hannah entered the kitchen this morning there was an unspeakable mess on the floor. Did you have a horse in the kitchen?"

"No!" he growled, swinging his booted feet to the floor. He wanted to tell the pretty Mariette Donovan that her family were nothing but horse thieves, and claim ownership of Charlie after these two years of life without him.

He smiled. If he did that, she would know that he had made the discovery, enjoyed a few carefree moments with the horse in the predawn hours and had, indeed, been careless enough to leave the door open so that he could get into the kitchen. He was already on pretty shaky grounds with the younger Donovan woman. Best to wait to cast aspersions upon her family.

When he did not respond beyond his abrupt answer, Mariette said, "Well, someone let a horse in and Hannah is quite upset about it." Then she moved toward the kitchen, the odor left by the horse replaced by the aroma of freshly baked bread and pepper-hot eggs scrambled just the way she liked them.

At half past the hour of six, the two riders were under way. Mariette was surprised that Adam had chosen the very horse she had suggested that he not, though she imagined that was precisely why the choice had been made. And, she was a little surprised that the horse was acting civil, something it had never before done. The ornery, mean-spirited stallion had bitten and kicked a fair number of Rourke House occupants.

They had left the hill overlooking Philadelphia five miles behind, and as they moved onto a trail leading into the Alleghenies, Mariette watched the tall, proud stance of the man riding ahead of her. He had given her little more than a perfunctory glance since they'd left Rourke House, and she imagined that he was still a little annoyed that she'd insisted on going along. She hoped that by the time they reached the trading post on Wills Creek by tomorrow afternoon he would have grown a little more tolerant. Perhaps he was simply waiting for her to prove her worth, though she wasn't sure how she was supposed to do that. Perhaps if she managed to stay in the saddle, didn't complain about the mosquitoes, and didn't get bitten by a snake, he would realize she was not like other women of her breeding.

But why should she care what he thought? She was going along on the trip regardless of his feelings about it, and she was dictating the rules here, not him. But why was she trying to justify herself? She didn't have to—

"I'll take this horse in payment of my services."

She startled for a moment. "What?" Coaxing her mare up beside him, she said, "What did you say?"

"I said I'll take this horse as payment. I'll need a good mount when I leave Philadelphia."

"The horse is worthless."

"The horse is a prize," he argued, choosing once again to withhold the information that the horse was his. "Since you consider the horse worthless, I see no problem with my accepting him." He turned now, his coppery gaze meeting her own. "Do you?"

She shrugged, casting her gaze upon the ground. "I suppose not. But if you wanted a horse in payment, we have better ones."

"This one will do." He clicked his tongue, and the horse he called Charlie surged forward on the trail, outdistancing the slim mare Mariette rode by several lengths.

They were entering the woods with which Mariette was so familiar . . . the small evergreens and silver birch and poplar thickets . . . through the long, low valley to the right lay a clear mountain pond in which she'd swum at the beginning of the summer. She, Hannah, and the children, escorted by Michael, who'd put aside duties for the day, had journeyed there to picnic and swim and enjoy the lazy day away from the hustle and bustle of Philadelphia.

They moved quickly. Now, the small pond was behind her. She coaxed her mare onto the trail winding through hardwoods and conifers, into the warm July morning and onward, deeper into the mountains than she'd been in well over a year. Only now did Mariette realize how reckless she was being, riding in the company of a man she had met only the day before, a man whose only redeeming quality thus far was the compassion he had shown for her wounded cousin. But was it, indeed, his one good quality? She'd heard gentleness in his tone, even when he'd tried so hard to be cryptic and annoying. She had seen the flash of humor in his eyes, even when his words had been harsh and unkind. She saw good breeding in his mannerisms, even as his attire put him in the company of more common men. . . .

She sighed deeply, resigning herself to the silence of the mountain trail. Occasionally, a rabbit would dash into the ground cover or a doe, flashing her white rump, would flee into the distance . . . and the hours passed . . . one, two, three . . . Mariette knew noon was approaching because her stomach was protesting its emptiness. As the sun hung brightly over the timberline, she coaxed the mare up behind Adam Cassidy.

"Are we going to stop for lunch?"

He halted abruptly, dismounted the stallion and, flipping his hat back from his forehead, moved off the trail into a damp, narrow glen. Dropping to a fallen tree, he asked, "What do we have?"

He had reacted so quickly that Mariette still sat atop her mare on the trail. She dismounted and moved into the glen to join him.

Adam drew his hat forward and peered at her from beneath the rim. He had said nothing upon viewing her attire at the carriage house, but now he watched her, studying her discreetly. He had never seen a woman wearing britches before, and wearing them so becomingly. The gun hanging at her right hip was twice as big as her hand. He couldn't resist the temptation to tease her. "Can you use that thing?"

She had clipped a line to her mare's bridle and now secured the other end to a small strapling. "The gun, you mean?" she queried, patting it as she dropped to the same log, keeping several feet of distance between them. Then she looked around, shielding her eyes from the sun. Spying the fluttering of wings, she removed the sidearm from its holster and asked, "Do you see that cardinal over there?"

He, too, looked toward the woodline. "Yes."

With a small smile, she took aim. "Watch it carefully, Adam Cassidy."

In a low, growled voice he said, "You shoot that cardinal and you'll eat it."

She lowered the gun, then turned to stare at him. She tried not to smile and betray her moment of humor, but it was quite difficult in view of the hard set of his jaw. Of course, she wouldn't in a thousand years kill anything deliberately, especially something as beautiful as the cardinal now sliding through the air, its jeweled wings catching the sun's rays as its much less glamorous mate joined it in its flight. She had simply been curious as to his thoughts on life . . . and who and what had earned the privilege of enjoying it. She was very pleased with his response, though she wouldn't let him know it. So, she successfully pouted a reply. "You were just afraid that I'd be able to hit it from this distance."

"If you want to show off, aim at a leaf or something." He settled back now, crossing his arms against the expanse of his chest. As his booted foot came to rest on the log, he said, "Now, what the hell's for lunch?"

Six

The morning air hung serenely still. Not so much as a bird soared in the sky or a leaf fluttered through the forest. It was as if time itself had stood still.

Mariette and Adam sat atop their horses on the trail and took it all in. Neither had spoken a word for several minutes, and their mutual surveyance of the forest seemed to have occurred simultaneously and by instinct. Now, in the void of time, Mariette took a moment to think about the past twenty-four hours she had traveled with Adam Cassidy. She thought of the night, of her bedroll separated from him by a span of twenty feet, of the sounds of the dark night ricocheting through her head, and of his rhythmic breathing that had calmed the rapid pace of her heartbeat. Of course, she would die before she admitted that she feared the forest at night, as well as the treacheries that lurked within, and she had been thankful for his nearness and his protection.

"What are you thinking?"

She startled, at once angry that his words had interrupted the peaceful morning. "Thinking?" She really didn't know what to say. "I'm thinking about the trading post on Wills Creek and seeing Hester again."

"Hester?"

"Yes, Uncle Bundy's wife. You'll like her. And her daughter, Dora, and Dora's husband, Cawley. They're nice people."

"And I suppose there'll be a dozen chattering youngsters."

"Dora and Cawley have seven sons, but the youngest is twenty-six . . . and none of them married as yet."

"Strange," he mused, offering his first smile of the morning. He knew he'd been an old bear since arising at dawn, but he had a crick in his back and all he wanted was a good, hot meal. "I suppose all these adult children are hanging around this trading post of yours being supported by their parents?"

Her mouth pressed into a grim line. She thought of Jake, the eldest, spending fourteen hours a day in his workshop making furniture which he sold throughout the region. She thought of Armand, a traveling preacher, who took the Christian religion to the Iroquois. Then there were Griffin and Guy, both educated and teaching school for the children of the Alleghenies . . . and Sabin and Jesse, who trapped and sold furs, showing up at the Wills Creek Trading Post only once or twice a year. Then, of course, there was Isaac, who helped his parents in the trading post despite the fact that scarlet fever as a child had left him chronically ill.

Becoming aware of Adam's narrow-eyed scrutiny, Mariette responded, "I'll let you meet the ones who might be at the trading post, and you decide for yourself if they are worthless.' Then she coaxed her mare ahead of him on the trail and refused to look back.

* * *

Moses Macardle had heard about Bertrand Redding's strange patient. This warm July morning, he completed his column for the *Philadelphia Gazette* editorial page, then began organizing the papers atop his crowded, unkempt desk and gathering up those that had fallen to the planked floorboards. His editor, the critical, stony-faced Mr. Pitts, abhorred sloppiness, and Moses was well aware that if he were not an accomplished journalist, he would not still be with the newspaper.

He huffed as he rose from the chair, his rotund features beet-red, his belly flopping over the trousers hanging below his belly button. He could no longer button his cotton shirt, and the fabric of his coat strained against even the simplest movements. Wiping fat, perspiring fingers across his balding pate, he prepared to leave his desk for the morning.

Now, he began to pray, something he seldom did, that Bertrand Redding's strange patient was the man he had been waiting for. He had sent the nefarious fellow the portfolio of papers he had collected over the years, hoping it would compel him to these parts. From the description of the gentleman Moses had received from several acquaintances, he fit the mold he had in his head of the man who would be Webster Mayne's bastard son.

Of course, he could never let the man, Justin Laszlo, know that he had sent the portfolio. To entice a despicable man to Philadelphia—and surely, the son of Webster Mayne would have to be—would not set well with the decent citizens of the city. Moses had only to sit back and let things happen . . . things that he could write about, things that would set a record in newspaper sales . . . things that would compel the old man, Mr. Pitts, to promote him to the coveted position of first assistant editor, second only to Pitts himself. That was the reward Moses

wanted, and that was the reason he had enticed Justin
Laszlo to Philadelphia.

He would call on Mrs. Hannah Gilbert at Rourke
House, but under what pretense, he wondered as he entered the busy street. He walked briskly toward Pine
Street where his horse was stabled. He would wait a few
hours, until the dinner hour. If Justin Laszlo had made
contact with the family, perhaps they could sit down to a
meal together for a nice, long chat, with Laszlo being
none the wiser.

Things were going to start hopping in Philadelphia.
. . . Moses Macardle felt sure of it!

Hannah was enjoying a few hours in the summer room,
by herself. It was a perfect time to repot the geraniums
and cut back the miniature roses. The children were with
their tutor in the school room and if Hannah knew Miss
Lee, she would keep them well past the usual hour since
she did not see them yesterday.

Hannah had tied on a large, white apron and tucked
her hair into her favorite floral bonnet. The summer
room floor had been swept that morning, and John had
cleaned the windows; she knew he had, because they
sparkled in the mid-morning sun whereas yesterday they
had been covered by a dull, dusty film. She wanted only
to think pleasant thoughts, to be free of the children's
whining and demands and not have to worry about Michael. Liddy was sitting with him, and John, escaping the
confines of the carriage house now and then, made frequent visits to the second floor to see if he could do
anything.

Hannah had just placed a repotted geranium on the

wire rack when John appeared at the garden entrance to the summer room. "Yes, what is it, John?" she asked.

"A man's askin' to see you, Mrs. Gilbert. Says it's real important."

"A stranger, John?"

"Yes, ma'am."

Dark eyebrows rose as she looked toward the groom. "Send him in, and—" she paused, lowering her voice, "stay nearby, will you?"

He bowed politely as he turned, then momentarily escorted Justin Laszlo into the summer room. Hannah had returned to her work with the plants and did not at first realize the man stood quietly near the doorway. Then she saw John moving along the garden path and turned to see who he had escorted to the summer room.

The sun was blinding beyond his tall stature; she could see only his outline. Then he stepped forward, shading himself against the potted trees she was preparing to prune this morning, and she was at once surprised by his noticeable frailty. She could see only half his face, the other half being hidden by the bandage surrounding his head beneath the wide rim of his hat. As he removed the hat, he stepped toward a potter's bench, asking, "Do you mind if I sit? I've had a bit of bad luck."

"Of course not. Do sit." Seeing John waiting on the garden path, she waved him away, her brief smile hinting that she did not feel in any present danger. The man, after all, could scarcely walk. Pulling up the rocker, Hannah, feeling quite nervous in the stranger's presence, tried to settle into it. "Sir, what has brought you to Rourke House?" He seemed familiar, in a way, and when Hannah found herself staring at him she politely looked away.

Now, the gentleman was opening a portfolio upon his

lap. "I believe we're related, Mrs. Gilbert," Justin Laszlo said.

"Related? On whose side of the family?"

"Your father is Andrew Donovan?" When Hannah nodded, he continued, "And his mother's maiden name was Diana Rourke?" Again, she nodded. "And her first cousin was Webster Mayne, son of Philip and Rosalyn Mayne?"

"You seem to be familiar with our family, sir. And what, may I ask, is your connection?"

Justin Laszlo smiled now, though the smile did not linger beyond a moment. "My name is Justin Laszlo. My mother's name was Topaz Laszlo, and my father was—"

"And your father was?"

"Do you think I could have something to wet my lips? Water perhaps?"

"I'm sure a little refreshment can be arranged, sir. You were about to tell me who your father was."

"My father, Mrs. Gilbert, was Webster Mayne."

Hannah felt the color drain from her face and when she spoke, her voice was dry and measured. "You are surely mistaken, sir. Webster Mayne died without issue thirty-six years ago. What is your age?"

"I am thirty-five. My father died before my birth."

Hannah rose gracefully, then linked her fingers and pressed them firmly, trying to compose herself. She was sure this stranger sitting before her could see the rapid pace of her heartbeat against the fabric of her dress. "And where were you born, sir?"

"New Orleans."

"To whom, sir?"

"To a man then calling himself Junius Wade . . . and a woman named Topaz Laszlo."

Feeling that she might faint, Hannah returned to the

rocker, locking the fingers of her right hand over the smooth wood. "And suppose I were to accept that you are Webster Mayne's son—which I certainly do not profess to do—what do you want here? This house is my family's house. It was never Webster's house, nor his father's—"

"I don't want the house, Mrs. Gilbert. I simply want—"

Tears filled Hannah's eyes . . . tears of fear . . . fear that came from so deep inside her soul that she was not sure how far it had journeyed, or its strength now that it was here. She knew only that if this man was, indeed, the son of Webster Mayne, then the evil had returned . . . and the evil would destroy them. "You simply want what, Mr. Laszlo?" she asked thickly, now burying her balled hands into the folds of her apron.

He wanted to avenge his father, he tried to convince himself, but he could not make himself unwelcome by voicing any degree of suspicion or aspersions on the Donovan family. "I want only to know my father's family, Mrs. Gilbert. That is all I want. Just to know my father's family."

He sounded sincere, even reverent, in a way, his voice dry, droned, unaffected by emotion, though she would have expected it under the circumstances.

Hannah was certainly at a loss. It was not completely her decision as to who stayed at Rourke House, though she did seem to be the only conscious adult in the household for the time being who had easily adapted to the role of decisionmaker. Liddy was too trusting of everyone, and usually did not make important decisions. Since her parents, and both her uncles, were away on business, as was little sister Mariette, chasing after the elusive Roby, then it was up to her. But what was she to say? *Yes, of course, Mr. Laszlo, make yourself at home in Rourke House. After all, your father tried to murder everyone on the premises, but it was such a little sin.*

"Mum?"

Hannah turned sharply in the rocker, seeing Cassandra standing sedately in the doorway. "Why aren't you in the school room, Cass?"

"Miss Lee has the jitters," she explained ruefully, fully expecting to extricate herself from guilt that, perhaps, she might have helped cause it. "She told Miles and me to take an hour to get the mischief out of our bones." Then, entering the summer room to stand beside her mother, she said quietly, "I know who he is."

"You do?" asked Hannah.

"Yes," she answered, smiling. "He's cousin Webster's little boy."

Justin Laszlo returned Cassandra's lingering smile, a little amused at hearing himself referred to as "little boy" by the child. And what a pretty thing she was, pale and slim, her hair the color of a forest fire. Her pinafore was pristine, the cutwork on its front highlighting the deep green, floral dress underneath. Sitting forward, he offered his hand, around which the trusting Cassandra wrapped her small fingers. "I'm glad to meet you, Cass."

"Only mum calls me Cass. The name is Cassandra."

"My name is Justin Laszlo . . . and, yes, Webster Mayne was my father."

Discreetly, Hannah took Cassandra's arm and drew her back against her. "Pay no attention to Cassandra," she went on to explain, "She's a child."

He didn't like the way the woman had cast a dubious glance his way. "You don't believe me madame? You think I come here to your house with lies? Tell me, what would be my motive in telling you Webster Mayne was my father?"

With a sudden flare of vexation, Hannah shot to her feet, her hand moving out as she ordered, "Go on, Cass . . . go find Miles and stay with him. I'll fix you both something to eat in a little while." When Cassandra did not immediately move, Hannah ordered her. "Go, now!"

Cassandra turned, sulking, shuffling from the summer room with her fingers linked at her back. But the mood did not linger, for when she was out of sight Hannah heard her sing a happy tune.

Justin Laszlo had risen, placing the portfolio in the chair he vacated. "I don't mean to cause trouble," he said. "But please . . . please, Mrs. Gilbert, what could be my motive? I will tell you . . . my motive is only to know my family. I did not know you existed until several months ago, and now that I am aware of you, I want to know you . . . all of you. Then I will return to New Orleans, knowing my roots and, perhaps, who I am as well."

"Webster Mayne was the black sheep of this family. He was evil and he did everything possible to destroy this family. There is nothing you could not learn here that would not hurt you deeply. Is that what you want, Mr. Laszlo?"

He thought the lady had grown frighteningly pale. Approaching, his long, bony fingers closed for a moment over the sleeve of her right arm. "Please, Mrs. Gilbert. I do not ask for lodgings here. Though I am low on funds"—The thief who had waylaid him on the road had overlooked a small purse tucked into his portfolio—"I can pay for boarding in the city for the length of time I plan to stay. I want only to visit here occasionally and to talk to the members of my family. I swear—I swear that I will cause you no trouble."

A peculiar set of emotions curled in her stomach. She knew that part of it was fear, part compassion . . . but what of the rest? She looked into the one eye of the man she could see that was not covered by a bandage, and thought he looked sufficiently humble. His mouth pressed, neither into a smile nor a frown. He wanted only to know his roots. If she denied him access to what had once been his ancestral home as well, would she be completely devoid of compassion?

"Save your money, Mr. Laszlo," she heard herself saying. "If you don't mind a chamber accessed only from the outside, you may stay on the third floor. I do hope you'll take your meals with the family."

A smile touched his mouth. Closing the distance, he took her hand and held it firmly, despite her efforts to immediately withdraw it. "Thank you . . . thank you so much, Mrs. Gilbert. I'll be a respectable guest. And I'll look forward to meeting the family."

Hannah responded, "Most of the men are away." She had deliberately said *most* so that he would believe—just in case he had ulterior motives—that there was a healthy male member of the family to protect them in the event it became necessary. "Please, enjoy the summer room while the maid does some dusting in the rooms you will occupy. In the meantime, I'll prepare a tray of refreshments for you, and then try to locate the key so that you can lock up your rooms when you're away. They are not accessible to the main house from the interior—"

"So you said," Justin responded. "It is all right." He managed a small laugh as he added, "Perhaps *I* don't trust *you* either."

She, too, laughed, though it wasn't in her heart.

Great-grandpapa Cole was furious. Cassandra sat impudently upon the stool, tapping her toes together beneath the hem of her dress as she listened to his lecture. Her arms were crossed, and her bottom lip was pushed out to display her displeasure.

"What is your mother thinking?" Cole fumed, pacing back and forth on the carpet, his hands flinging out to add emphasis to his ire. "If this—this Justin Laszlo is, indeed, Webster's son, then someone should take a dagger to his black heart!"

"For heaven's sake, Great-grandpapa . . . you're being silly. He was very nice. I just think everyone is being mean to poor Webster, and to poor Webster's poor son."

"Poor . . . poor . . . poor! We're not talking about poor relations here, Cassandra! We're talking about evil . . . pure and simple! You were not there, Cassandra, when he tried to destroy our family!"

"I've heard the stories," moaned an indulgent Cassandra. "But it was hundreds and hundreds of years ago."

Cole ceased his pacing now, turning to face the child with a humored smile. "Scarcely hundreds and hundreds of years, though it might seem so to a lass as young as you, Cassandra. Now . . . we must be rid of this Justin Laszlo—"

Cassandra studied Cole Cynric Donovan for a moment. She had never thought about it before, but she wondered how tall he was. She wondered if he ever changed his clothes, or if he had to trim his hair. Did he have to get up every morning and bathe and shave? Did he have to eat meals to maintain his strength? She wondered if he ever had to go to the—

"Of course not, Cassandra!"

Now, the crimson was upon her own youthful cheeks. She smiled, to alleviate her moment of embarrassment, and her eyes, no matter how hard she tried, could not lift to his critical gaze. She didn't like it when her great-grandpapa read her thoughts. She was just about to pout, to make him feel terrible for eavesdropping on her thoughts when he knelt beside her and his strong fingers went beneath her chin. "I din't mean to yell at you, Cassandra. I'm worried . . . you are my family, and I am worried that you—all of you—are in danger." Withdrawing his fingers, he stood to his full height, then turned slightly away. "And, blast it, I'm powerless to help."

"Please don't worry," responded Cassandra, hopping from the stool with youthful agility. Approaching, she slipped her hand into his own. "Aunt Mariette will be home soon, and—she has a gentleman friend."

"I saw him," said Cole. "He seemed a decent sort."

"He's very nice, and quite handsome."

Cole shrugged. "I suppose. As far as men go, I imagine he could hold his own—"

"Cass?"

The child jerked back, turning toward the door, beyond which her name had been spoken. "Yes?"

The door opened. Hannah Gilbert moved into the wide, spacious room, then looked curiously about. "Who were you talking to, Cass?"

Stepping into the long, narrow beam of light stretching from the window, Cassandra retrieved her bonnet from the back of a chair. "Nobody, mum . . . I was going to go out in the garden and gather some flowers for Miss Lee. I suppose Miles and I were very bad this morning and flowers will make her feel better."

Hannah had been looking around the chamber, though she wasn't really sure who, or what, she had been looking for. Now, she turned her attentions toward Cassandra, gently smiling. "Yes, that would be nice. And do be on time returning to the school room. You know that Miss Lee demands promptness."

"Yes, I will," said Cassandra, tucking her hand into her mother's warm one. As they moved from the room, she looked back, seeing the twinkling eyes of her great-grandpapa, who stood in the alcove where her small desk was located. She smiled for him, then lifted her free hand to wave farewell . . . for the moment.

By mid-afternoon, a moist wind had risen. Masses of gray-black clouds rolled across the horizon, toward the clearing into which Mariette and Adam now passed. Momentarily, their weary horses dragged up to the wide porch of the trading post, and as they dismounted, Hester flew from the interior and hugged Mariette just as both her feet had touched the ground.

"I wasn't expecting you!" the older woman laughed. "Why didn't you send word that you were coming? I'd have called the family together."

"It is an unexpected trip," Mariette responded, stepping back and taking Hester's hands fondly between her own.

"Roby?"

Mariette gasped, "He's been here then?"

"He and the English girl—came dragging in at dawn this morning and left shortly thereafter."

Adam had now joined them. "Which way did they go?"

Hester arched a graying eyebrow, her gaze darting between Mariette's and the tall, blond and silver haired stranger.

"He's all right," assured Mariette. "He's helping me track them so that we can take Lara back to Philadelphia before her grandparents find out what's happened. Was he—?" Mariette hesitated to continue, "Was Roby being kind to Lara?"

"He was treating her like a sack of potatoes." As she spoke, Hester's head shook from side to side. "And she was spitting oaths such as I had never heard before . . . even when Cawley dropped the andiron on his foot had I heard such language! She's quite a lady, isn't she?" Hester smiled up to Adam Cassidy, then returned her gaze to Mariette. "I'll bet the two of you are starving." As she moved into the trading post, she turned occasionally to chat. As they settled into the comfortable living quarters in the back they were joined by Hester's grandson, Jake, the furniture maker, by daughter and son-in-law, Dora and Cawley Perth, and by Isaac, her youngest grandson, who helped in the trading post.

Adam joined right in, as though he were family himself. Mariette watched him, deeply engaged in conversation with Jake at a small table on the back porch, and wondering what they were discussing. Only when her name was spoken sharply, did she redirect her attentions to the occupants of the kitchen.

"What?"

Isaac was grinning at her from beneath a wide-brimmed hat, which Hester immediately snatched off his head. "Awe, ma, Mariette'll see my bald spot."

"You're losing your hair?" teased Mariette, rising, her hands landing against both his ears to pull his head downward. "Let me see, Isaac."

Playfully slapping her hand away, Isaac grabbed the hat from his mother and placed it back on his head, pulling it firmly over his ears. "Ain't nobody goin' ta see my scalp . . . 'ceptin' maybe the Injun that lifts it off me!"

Mariette's laughter did not linger, her attentions returning to the man beyond the window who was her traveling companion. She didn't know what he was discussing with Jake, but the subject had made both men laugh occasionally. *Women!* she supposed. *What else would men discuss with such devotion?*

"Are you sure it's the horse that was stolen from you in St. Louis?" Jake asked, leaning back and taking a swig of the ale from his glass. "I can't imagine my Uncle Andrew purchasing stolen property."

"I'm sure it's Charlie," replied Adam, casting a glance toward the kitchen and the occupants within. Then he dragged a palm up beside his mouth and whispered, "I'm sure the women think we're discussing women."

Jake laughed, "Then let's not disappoint them." He was a big man, tall and muscular, and he had not removed the leather apron he'd been wearing in his workshop that day. Now, he sat back, soon tucking a burly hand into a pocket to remove an augur, which he carelessly tossed to a cluttered corner of the porch. "Women," he mused after a moment. "My mother wonders why not a single one of her seven sons has taken a wife. As for me, I haven't found one who doesn't think like a woman and act like a child."

Shrugging, dragging his fingers up and linking them atop his head, Adam drew his booted feet to a chair. "Sorry . . . I can't share your low opinion of that delicate breed. I've a lot of respect for them—" He chuckled, "As long as they belong to someone else."

"And Mariette?"

His gaze narrowed now. "What about her?"

"You allowed her to tag along."

"I said 'no.' She said, 'yes.' With no deciding vote cast, she declared herself the winner."

"You don't seem the sort, old man, who would allow himself to be pushed around by a woman."

Again, Adam grinned. "I didn't say I didn't let her win." He leaned across the table, his voice lowering as he continued, "What is she to you . . . as kin, I mean?"

"A cousin . . . sort of."

"A cousin, sort of," he repeated Jake's words. "And what do you see when you look at this cousin, sort of?"

"I see the face of an angel . . . the form of a goddess . . . and the disposition of a trapped she-cat. What do you see?"

"I see—" Adam grinned wickedly, casting a glance toward Mariette, who was looking back at him. His gaze returned to Jake as he mumbled, "A woman I couldn't bring myself to say 'no' to."

Seven

Mariette strolled toward the wide, clear mountain pond to watch the sunset. The pink of the horizon soon changed to the color of pale flames, then darkness descended, like a veil covering a mourning face. Folding lazily to a patch of clover, she drew up her knees beneath the wide hems of her skirts and wrapped her arms carelessly around them. A movement in the pond caught her attentions and she watched a beaver move onto the bank on the far side. She remembered the story her father had told her, of her mother being dragged into the pond by a sudden, fierce storm, and how she had been sucked into one of the beaver mounds. While everyone at the trading post assumed that Carrie had drowned, Andrew had continued searching through the night. The mound had long ago rotted into the pond.

Mariette lifted her hair away from her perspiring neckline. The night was sweltering, scarcely a breeze blowing through the forest. She dropped back to the lush, clover-blanketed bank and stretched her arms out. She watched the dark sky; the stars seemed to pulsate . . . she watched an owl skim across the treeline and find a perch. . . .

Were it not for the events that had brought them to the

trading post, the day would have been one of the best she could remember. Adam had fit exceedingly well with her relatives at the trading post, and had gotten along especially well with Jake. The two men had talked of everything through the afternoon, including fishing and hunting, two of Jake's passions, and Jake had given Adam a lesson in furniture making. Two hours after the men had entered Jake's workshop, Adam had proudly returned to the living quarters of the trading post to show off a newly made chair of unstained oak. They had all had a good laugh when one of the legs had promptly come loose and fallen to the floor with a clatter.

Then the family had been joined by Hester's friend and her children. They had taken supper together, all thirteen of them, and had enjoyed Hannah's and Dora's wonderful meal of barbecued pork shoulder, baked beans, ginger beets, corn sticks, and jam cake for dessert, washed down with freshly drawn milk from their old speckled cow.

All the while Mariette had watched Adam Cassidy . . . the way he had joined in and hung on every word, no matter how mundane, as though it was important to him, how he had enjoyed being with a happy family and holding the small children on his knee, to tell them stories of his home in California. Family seemed to be something he had missed . . . something he had refused to talk about . . . and a subject brought up by Mariette which had prompted him to seek the solitude of the woods. She was sorry she had attempted to pry, because they'd been having such a wonderful time.

Adam Cassidy was an enigma. She loved being with him and that frightened her. She loved their banters and insults, the way he brushed against her in passing. Though she argued with him constantly, she enjoyed his company. She enjoyed the way her heart beat quickly when he spoke her name, with just that small note of sarcasm he knew would prickle her nerves.

He was the first man she'd ever met who consumed her thoughts by day and her dreams by night. She thought if she could ever love, it would be a man like Adam Cassidy.

She was frightened to the core by that revelation. Adam Cassidy had probably never stayed in one place long, certainly not long enough to nurture a relationship with a woman. She was usually so strong, and certainly perceptive enough to see that a man like Adam should be avoided at all cost.

Was she growing weak? Was she letting down her guard?

Yes, she thought so.

She remembered a time her mother had once again repeated the story of her first meeting with the man who would become her husband. Theirs had been a happy ending, and Mariette could not imagine that such a life was her destiny.

She thought of her sister's short-lived marriage that had produced two children, and how her life now consisted of being "residential maid" at Rourke House.

She thought of Cassandra, living her life through the ghosts of the house.

She thought of Roby, wanting only to be happy, but doing everything in his power to prevent it from happening.

Her family . . . how they exasperated her! How she worried for them, and wept for them, and longed for normalcy! Sometimes she thought Rourke House was an asylum and every resident a lunatic, she among them. Sometimes she wished she could go far, far away and never see them again . . . make a life for herself and never

have to settle controversies and petty arguments and
. . . and . . .

The long squeal of a nightbird overhead jarred her
back to the present. She looked up; the sky became a blur,
the stars magnifying, the treeline scarcely discernible from
the darkness beyond, and only then did she realize that
tears filled her eyes. They fell down the sides of her face,
joining the perspiration that had dampened her hairline
. . . her mouth trembled, and a great ball of emotion grew
inside her chest. Turning to her side, she drew her head
to the fabric covering her bent arm and wept gently.

Adam Cassidy had made himself a part of the dark
woodline. He had approached the pond through a leaf-
strewn cove, to demand to know why the search for Roby
was being interrupted by the family reunions. Now that
he looked down on her weeping form, he could not imagine how she hadn't heard his approach. He grew a little
angry then; any manner of threatening beast could have
walked right up on her, and she had exercised no caution
whatsoever.

Still, foremost in his thoughts was that she was weeping,
and that she was very sad. He wondered if it was his fault;
he hadn't been especially kind to her these past two days,
though he hadn't thought that she'd have taken notice of
it. Their aloofness had been mutual. Was she weeping
because he had hurt her feelings in some small way?

And didn't she know that she was breaking his heart?

His hand eased up, his fingers curling over the twisted
vines of wild wisteria circling a pine. The heady fragrance
of honeysuckle filled the forest air, mixed with the pun-
gent odor of ragwort. But they had not drawn him to the
forest as powerfully as had the alluring scent of Mariette

Donovan's perfume commingled with her natural essence
. . . an essence that had been like a magnet . . . and that
had made him rude and cryptic and aloof these past two
days so that he would not betray that she was affecting
him in ways he did not wish to admit. She was the most
delicate flower this wild evening forest could yield and he
wanted only to lie against her, draw her into his embrace
and kiss away the tears falling into the rich depths of her
hairline.

But the sight of her weeping so delicately caused
thoughts to hover at the fringes of his memories. He had
once turned his back on a woman's tears, had told that
same woman he had once loved above all else that he
loathed the very sight of her, and then had walked out on
her, leaving her alone in a world that was already hostile
toward her. He wondered if things would have been different had he stayed . . . but could he have looked at her
day by day after what she had done?

Adam Cassidy shivered despite the heat of the night,
the icy threads of his memories melting in the boiling pot
of his hatred for that woman who had taken everything
from him.

And hardened his heart toward every woman he had
met since.

Mariette Donovan must be among them.

He stepped from his hiding place in the forest shadows,
a line of utter distaste pressing upon his mouth. When she
sat forward, then turned to stare at him as though he'd
lost all his gentlemanly manners, he gave her a wry smile.
"I wondered where you'd gone off to," he stated. "Should
you be out here alone?"

"I don't see why not," responded Mariette, turning
from him to discreetly flick away the tears. "You forget
this is a second home to me. I've spent as much time here

as I have at Rourke House. This is where I learned to ride, and to shoot, and to defend myself against male rogue animals."

He stooped beside her, his hand easing out to break off a long piece of grass. "Like me?"

His manner was light and teasingly affectionate; his moods were as quick to change as the weather, Mariette thought. She gave him a bold, rude stare, then attempted to shield her tear-reddened eyes from his close scrutiny. "Just don't think I've been crying," she said a trifle sullenly. "I got a speck of dirt in them . . . that's all."

"It never occurred to me that you might have been crying."

"Good . . . because I *never* cry."

"Bull pucky! Why can't you admit that you're human, that you are worried—"

"Worried about what?" she quipped, turning her critical gaze to him.

"Worried about the English girl, and about your uncle who took her away . . . worried about Michael and about Cassandra seeing her ghosts. I suspect, Miss Mariette Donovan, that you worry about everything . . . even whether you are going to get one of Cassandra's ringworms yourself!"

"Bull pucky!" She smiled now, her gaze lifting to his own, then sliding away politely. "I didn't touch the nasty little creature. There's only one thing I despise more than dogs—"

"Men like me?"

"No—" A chuckle rocked the still night air. "Spinach! I hate spinach!"

"So do I," he laughed, falling back, then bracing himself on one elbow. "The nastiest stuff I've ever tasted. Sun was always sneaking it into an otherwise tolerable meal."

Mariette looked to his firm profile against the infringing darkness. "Sun . . . what an unusual name."

"She was Chinese."

"Oh . . . I've never met a person of Chinese descent. She worked in your home, back in—?"

"I never said." The smile left his face and his eyes turned skyward, becoming lazy as they narrowed. "I could sleep out here—couldn't you?—beneath the wide open sky, with a warm breeze washing over us, the sounds of the night lulling us to sleep."

"Us?" She gave him a strangely thoughtful, measuring look. "Why, Mr. Adam Cassidy, I've never slept out in the open in the company of a man before in my life."

"I was speaking generally," he said. "I didn't mean you and me. I—hell, I suppose I don't know what I meant. Why, Miss Donovan," he mocked her gently, "I've never slept out in the open in the company of a woman before in my life."

Laughter slid from her full, sensual mouth, then became a faint tremor. "You know, for a man I really don't like, Adam Cassidy, I—well, I sort of like you."

Without thinking, he eased his hand out and gently caressed her arm through the silky fabric of her blouse. But her look, which in the darkness seemed to be one of disapproval, caused him to immediately withdraw the touch. Reclining on the summer-warmed ground beside her, he stretched his arms out, though not touching her. "Cassandra mentioned a relative named Webster Mayne yesterday morning. Tell me about him."

Mariette stared at him, surprised. Moments ago they had been talking about wide open skies, now he brought up the one subject that the family had avoided for as many years as Mariette could remember. Not only did mention of Webster Mayne cause Mariette's skin to crawl, but she could not possibly understand his interest. "Webster Mayne?" she echoed the name. "He was my grandmother's first cousin and he died many years ago."

"Well . . . tell me about him—"

"But why?"

"I might want to write a story one day. He might make a good subject."

An anguished expression darkened her lovely features. "It would have to be a tale of horror and murder and mayhem. Tell me why you're interested," she insisted, her voice taking on an angry tone.

Adam thought for a moment. He had been intrigued by the man he had brought into Bertrand Redding's office. Going through his belongings with the doctor, they had gathered he shared a relationship to the Donovans, and especially to Webster Mayne. He wanted to know some history, but as he thought about the subject now, he knew that to tell Mariette Donovan what he knew would only cause her to worry and want nothing more than to return home to Rourke House. She had enough to worry about, trying to find her uncle and the English girl, and return the girl to Philadelphia before her English relatives could learn of her adventure. He simply couldn't worry her with an unknown relative now, especially one who might cause trouble for her family. So, he dropped the subject as quickly as he had brought it up. "Mariette," he said softly "I was simply curious."

"Well—" Looking toward the moon-washed pond, she said, "That's quite a strange thing to be curious about." Then on an accusing note, "You should have had *some* reason for bringing it up."

"Actually—" he grinned pleasantly, "your niece Cassandra has a way of telling a story that seems to breed curiosity. She's very intelligent, you know, and has quite an imagination. And—" Tucking his palm beneath his head, he continued, "she seems to know more about that old house than seems possible for a child her age."

"She listens a lot," said Mariette, "and Hannah tells her stories of the past that she learned from our parents, and they learned from their parents. We have had quite an interesting history."

"An unbelievable one," mused Adam, closing his eyes now as he savored the warm breeze rolling across the pond and touching them, simultaneously. "I suppose that we should forget the past, Miss Mariette Donovan," he said on a quiet note, "and find that uncle of yours . . . and the girl, before irreparable damage is done."

The irreparable damage to Lara had been done a couple of years before by a fresh-faced stable boy, when the granddaughter of Penley and Anne Seymour had been scarcely fourteen years of age. Now, she found herself unceremoniously deposited to a patch of clover a dozen miles from the trading post they had visited that morning and where she had thought she might be rescued from this savage kidnapper. Her wrists were bound, her gowns torn and filthy, and her temperament was that of a treed cougar. When the dark, brooding Roby Donovan approached her, a threatening scowl turning down his mouth, she kicked out at him with one well-placed boot, and immediately found her ankle being turned outward by his burly hand. She screamed, turning in the same direction that her foot was being wrenched, then felt his hot breath against her hairline. She had brought this attack on herself by calling him a halfbreed bastard, the most vicious insult she could speak.

"You backwoods oaf!" she hissed another insult, attempting to kick him once again.

His hand edged into her hair and jerked her head back. His mouth against her cheek, he whispered huskily, "Let's just see how much of a she-cat you are, Lara Seymour! Let's just see how much fight is really in you!" Then his mouth groped for her own rebellious one, and she was immediately assailed by the stench of whiskey he had been swigging all afternoon as they'd rode through the woods, keeping off the trails. Then she bit him hard enough to draw blood, and he drew back, yelping. "God-damned she-cat!" Holding her head down with one firm hand, his other hand now pinched a hard path up her inner thighs, ripping her skirts as they traveled. She cried out, the pain of her hair being torn out, and the pain of his groping now bringing sobs from deep within. All the while she cursed him, spit in his face and tried to bite his cheek as it edged unwarily near her mouth. Then his fingers were painfully probing her and as her screams died into whimpers, his bleeding mouth was again upon her own. "You know you want me, Lara—" His voice was now a husky whisper, almost calming, his hand now plying a gentle caress back toward her knee . . . and the buttons of his trousers.

"I—I hate you—" she whimpered, her fingers clawing at his shoulder to tear down the fabric of his shirt. Then she was aware of her torn underthings, his exposed masculinity, and the probing of him against her below. Instinctively, her knees fell apart to allow for him, and she gasped as he entered her, "You bastard!" then began to rock with him in the same moment.

He was drunk and clumsy and she could easily have overpowered him if she'd been so inclined. A rock lay overhead, and though her wrists were bound, she could swiftly have brought it down to his head. But she did not. She liked the way his dark eyes gleamed in a mixture of drunkenness and lust, the way his tongue traced a path around her full, trembling mouth covered with blood from the wound her teeth had cut into his lip. She loved the way his stuperous state caused him to almost withdraw from her at every exit, and he cursed the separation. She liked the musky, unwashed odor of him, the way his dark, shoulder-length hair dragged across her sweating features in his throes. She liked the way his hips ground against her, commanding, but clumsy, seeking his own enjoyment even as he bordered on the brink of unconsciousness. She liked to think that he wanted her badly enough to stall the effects of the whiskey, though his torso was heavy enough against her own to smother life from her.

When her bound wrists suddenly circled his neck, his movements ceased and he lifted his head from its cradle against her shoulder to warn, "Whatever you're thinking . . . don't!" then continued to take the treasure he had stolen to its ultimate heights. His hands wrapped tightly into her riotous, unkempt hair and he held her head still as he stole a dozen kisses.

Lara could tell that he was weakening, and suddenly she could not bear the thought of his erotic movements ceasing, failing to reach the pinnacle of pleasure, both for himself and for her. Hot coals burned in her abdomen and every time his hands touched her flesh, she was sure he had left a searing path upon her. Now, he had stopped moving, his cheek rested heavily against her own, and she feared that the rascal had fallen asleep. "Ouf! How dare you!" She raged, her hands landed heavily upon his back, again and again, until he weakly lifted his head and uttered, "Huh? What the hell?"

Instinctively, he began to move again, and Lara pressed her thighs firmly to his hips, laying her ankles across his knees, so that if he considered sleep again, he would feel a painful jab. But now, he hardly seemed to be considering sleep, as his hips moved so quickly they were like a blur to her own feasting, lusty gaze. As his seed scattered within the delicate spread of her hips, she held him close, passion and sweat commingled, until he toppled upon her, only barely conscious.

He fell asleep then, still a part of her, and she whispered with humored passion, "You scoundrel . . . you rotten, halfbreed scoundrel—"

Under normal circumstances, the night would have been unbearably hot, with scarcely a breeze alleviating the heat that shimmered in visible waves, even at this dark hour. Mariette had fallen back to the patch of clover and her gaze swept the stars in the dark, cloudless sky. Though she tried to think of nothing but the beauty of it, she was only too aware of Adam Cassidy's light breathing several feet away. She had sneaked several peeks at him from beneath the fringes of her lashes, and each time had found his eyes closed. His hands were tucked beneath his tousled silver-tinged blond hair and occasionally a smile would turn up his mouth; she couldn't help but wonder what he was thinking, or whether the smiles were mere ticks as his mind sought sleep.

Adam smiled each time he caught her glancing his way, because he was sure she was unaware that his eyes were not completely closed. How could a man block out the beauty of a woman like Mariette Donovan, and still be considered to be in full possession of his senses? He had seen her frequently lower her lashes, as though to catch a little sleep of her own, but she seemed to be spellbound by the serenity of the skies overhead. He enjoyed these moments spent with her, though that was a confession he would never make. Undemanding, and yet sensual moments, as they shared an unspoken admiration for each other and labeled it, instead, loathing.

He knew in his heart that she didn't despise him. After all, hadn't she just said a while ago that for a man she didn't like that she *sort of liked him?* It wasn't exactly what he wanted from her, but it would do for now.

"What are you thinking, Adam Cassidy?"

His head turned; he saw that she was giving him a cool, assessing look. "Actually, I was thinking that for a woman I really don't like very much, I rather like you, Miss Mariette Donovan."

She smiled then, turning to her side and dropping her head against her palm. "Indeed?" When he said nothing further, she continued, "And what makes you think that I want you to like me . . . or even that I care whether you do or not?"

"I think it matters," he argued lazily. "But you're too stubborn to admit it." She laughed out loud, and he thought it a wonderful, melodious laugh. He, too, turned to his side, and before he could prevent it, the fingers of his left hand had spanned the short space separating them and lightly touched her hair. Though she not drawn back, she gave him a scathing look, compelling him to drop his hand and usher an apology, "I am sorry. You've got the most magnificent hair, Mariette . . . the color of pale flames, like the sky just as the sun was setting this evening. I watched the sunset from the tree line, and it was hard to tell the difference between the two . . . the sky and your hair. I imagine that you're beautiful . . . all over—"

Well, now that was quite a statement. Mariette turned

sharply, so that he would not see the crimson rushing into
her cheeks. He could be positively outrageous, and because she imagined that his spoken intimacy might be still
another challenge, she matter-of-factly asked him, "How
old are you?"

He was a little surprised by the question, thinking that,
perhaps, she would berate him for the intimacy of his
compliments. "Well, I just turned thirty-five this past
May."

"Oh, I see—"

"Any reason for your curiosity?"

"You're too young."

"For what?"

"To have so much silver in your hair."

"Hard living," he teased, a grin raking his full, masculine mouth. Then he again fell back, cushioning himself
against the clover now pressed to the earth by his long,
firm body. "At least it isn't falling out," he mused, tucking
his hands beneath his head once again. Then to more
fully explain, "My father's hair had turned completely
white by the time he was twenty-five, and his father's
before age thirty. It runs in my family, I suppose, among
the men."

Mariette drew to a sitting position, her eyes full upon
him, his slim form stretched out lazily beneath the moon-
light, catching the glittering strands of his thick hair, his
gaze tawny and relaxed for the moment, his mouth smirking occasionally, and his breathing scarcely noticeable
against the fabric of his tan shirt. She thought him the
most compelling man she'd ever met, and though she
hadn't planned it, she found herself easing across the
ground, until she kneeled beside him, her hands dropped
casually to her thighs.

She was content to just look at him, though she knew

that his eyes weren't fully closed and that he was aware of her beside him. Then her hand lifted from her thigh and fell lightly to the broad expanse of his chest. Though he made no other movement, his hand covered her own and his fingers squeezed gently, caressingly upon hers.

She whispered emotionally, "I don't know why I trust you, Adam Cassidy, but I do. I think if I had to make a decision at this very moment, that I would entrust my very life to your hands. Why is that?"

His eyes opened now and he slowly brought her palm up to touch a kiss to its magical warmth. "Because, Mariette, I've never given you any reason *not* to trust me."

"No . . . no—" she argued, "that isn't it. In all my life I've never met anyone I trusted as easily as you—"

"In all your life?" he teased. "What are you . . . twenty? Twenty-one?"

"I'm twenty-three, thank you," she quipped defensively.

"Why, you're just a baby, Mariette, compared to an ancient man like me—"

She smiled prettily, gently extracting her hand from his gentle grip. Just as she pondered an answer of sorts, his hand circled her neck and coaxed her down to him, his fingers lacing through her flame-colored hair. What he did not realize, however, was that she still maintained some measure of control, and when his mouth sought the intimacy of her own, she scooted out from beneath his hand and quickly disengaged his fingers from her tresses.

"I don't know what you think you're doing, Adam Cassidy, but I'm not one of the wanton women you have met in your travels. I am a lady—"

"And ladies need to be kissed, too," he argued dryly, undaunted by her self-control. "Especially ladies who have never before been kissed."

She gasped in surprised, her hands closing over her hips. "I didn't say I've never been kissed!"

"But your actions betray it," he argued, stifling the laugh tickling along his throat. "Why, Mariette Donovan, you're a virgin, aren't you?"

She huffed indignantly, "I believe that's none of your business!"

With one swift move, his hand went to her back and dragged her toward him. "And suppose I were to make it my business? And suppose I was determined to end your state of boring chastity?" She attempted to draw back, but his hand caught in her hair, holding her close despite her efforts.

Mariette instantly saw through his facade of roughness and insult. She smiled, at the same moment resting her elbows atop his chest as though she were prepared to get comfortable in this position. Then she sweetly replied, "Don't think I can't see through you, Adam Cassidy. Every time you think I've decided you're sweet and gentle, you get mean and ugly, in a rather rude attempt, I might say, to make me dislike you a little more. Well, it won't work this time. As a matter of fact—" Dare she continue on this course, and what would she do if her plan went awry? Well, she'd just have to take that chance. She was, after all, adept at protecting herself from male animals. "As a matter of fact," she continued again, "I've been looking for a man like you. I've bedded bankers and shippers and dock workers. I've bedded merchants and sailors and a soldier here or there. But, Adam Cassidy, I've never bedded a silvery-haired doctor from the west coast. You are a doctor, aren't you? And you are from the west coast?" The proper response was popping into the darkness of his eyes. She saw spitting anger beginning to deepen, and a thin line pressing upon his mouth. Even his fingers had loosened within the strands of her hair, and she could easily break contact, if she so wished.

Adam had never thought that such an ugly smirk could be accomplished by such lovely features. He didn't like being grilled about his profession, or the place he called home. He didn't like the sarcasm in her green eyes. And he especially didn't like to hear confessions more likely to be dropped from the gaudily painted lips of a boasting whore.

Did she think he had the brain of an idiot? Did she think he couldn't see through her, and knew exactly what she was trying to accomplish?

So, his grip tightened once again through her hair and his free hand raked beneath the lapel of her blouse and her chemise, finding a perch against a smooth, round breast before she could utter the first gasp of horror and surprise.

Eight

Of course, Adam Cassidy had stiffened his cheek, preparing for the slap she would immediately inflict upon him. And he was not disappointed. His face reeled from her blow, so powerful that she toppled backwards, which had the effect of ripping his hand from beneath her blouse. As she drew the torn fabric together across her bosom, she righted herself, then scooted several feet away from him to assess the damage to her clothing.

She was so angry that the night was spinning, like a child's toy, all around her. Giving him a venomous glare, she hissed, "You ever touch me like that again—"

When she stalled, he prompted, "What, Mariette? What will you do?" He refused to rub the stinging cheek, because he couldn't give her the satisfaction of knowing that she'd inflicted pain. Hell, the woman had quite a hand; he'd never been struck like that before.

"I'll shoot you dead," she said on a childish note. "Don't you think I won't."

"And I'll shoot you, dammit—" he shot straight back at her, "but not with a gun! That's not a threat, Mariette Donovan. That's fair warning . . . and a promise."

"You're crude and vulgar," she whispered, emotion

lacing her words. "I don't know why I ever try to get along with you. You're impossible." Rising, continuing the small chore of righting her clothing, she continued, "Take the mare back to Rourke House in the morning. I'll give you a letter directing Hannah to pay you fifty dollars for your troubles. Jake and I will bring home Roby and Lara—"

He rose so quickly that he nearly lost his balance. "No," he argued, closing the space existing between them. As his hands fell to her shoulders, and his silence compelled her to meet his gaze, he continued, "I said I would go after the man and woman, and by damn, I'll do just that."

"I won't give you the stallion," she threatened, attempting to throw off his roughly persistent hands. "Jake cares about Roby. He'll make sure he isn't harmed. I do not have that assurance with you."

"Look—if you want an apology for what I did just now, then . . . I apologize. It was uncalled for. You just have the damndest way, Mariette, of crawling under my skin like an itch."

"I just don't trust you."

"Yes, you do."

So, she shrugged, exasperated, she removed his hands from her shoulders. "You can tag along if you'd like, but I *will* ask Jake to accompany me."

"Good." He dropped back now, then covered his eyes with the back of his right hand. "We'll be a happy threesome, won't we?"

"I suppose that we will."

When she began her retreat, Adam Cassidy's smooth, mellow voice had the immediate effect of halting her, though she didn't turn back. "Jake told me a little while ago he's taking a wagonload of furniture to St. Louis. I wouldn't waste your breath asking him to take to the trail with you. He'll be gone before first light."

"He'll postpone the trip, if I ask him to," she said to Adam with confidence, though she didn't feel it inside. Jake never made those long, arduous trips to St. Louis to sell his furniture, unless he needed the money to buy a coveted thoroughbred before another buyer snapped it up. So when Mariette quietly repeated, "He'll postpone the trip," she knew that if there was a horse waiting nearby to be purchased there was no chance in hell that he would help her go after Roby.

Adam said nothing, but allowed her to drift away with the darkness. When, at last, the gentle fragrance of her had become part of the night, he dragged his hand from the cover of his eyes and watched the stars that had so mesmerized Mariette.

He really wasn't sure why he'd felt the need to molest her . . . perhaps to keep her on her toes, so that she wouldn't so easily trust men she didn't know. But, he very much liked the idea that Mariette trusted him, even now. And, he liked to think that she hadn't found his touch too terribly distasteful. Then, he grinned boyishly at the memory, his hand instinctively massaging his cheek that was still pink from her vicious slap.

After several minutes, he heard the door slam at one of the cabins, the one, he was sure, where Mariette Donovan would spend the night alone. He imagined that she had slammed the door so hard for just one reason . . . to further emphasize across this span of space her utter distaste for him . . . and the fury he had caused to surface within her. . . .

* * *

Mariette had instantly tried to catch the door before it slammed shut with such brutal force. She imagined that she'd awakened everyone in the trading post compound.

Her heart was beating quickly; her hand scooted along her sweating bodice and closed gently over the slim column of her neck. She hated what his intimate touch had done to her; she could still feel the searing heat of his hand roughly groping beneath her shirt. Oh, how dare he!

And how she wished he was with her, right now, though she was a little unsure what she wanted further from him. But a wonderful, though alien, warmth flooded through her, and she thought that a fire had been built inside her veins. She wondered if the feelings she had were desire, but if they were, why did it make her body ache so? Why had she left the open outdoors, and his company, to seek the solitude of the cabin where the unpleasant muskiness almost suffocated her? She was so confused that she felt she'd been bound tightly with string, then thrown into a vicious spin by a large, invisible hand.

How could she want to be with Adam Cassidy, when he was filled only of sarcasm and condescension for her? Why had her body responded so wantonly to his bold caresses, when her good senses warned her to fight him at every turn?

Grabbing her temples, Mariette turned and dropped to the small, quilt-covered bed, then fell backwards with little grace. She closed her eyes and tried to center her thoughts on Hannah and Cassandra and Rourke House, to recapture the good moments and hold them close to her heart for a moment. But they could not get near her heart; *his* fingers were wrapped brutally around it, and she could not shake him loose, no matter how she tried.

She realized she was trembling, as one whose flesh had been deeply penetrated by icy cold, and yet the warmth flooded her still. Why did thoughts of him—this bold, lusty male from the west—make her blood run both hot and cold in the same moment? How was it possible that he had reached in and made himself a vital part of her desires, because—God, yes—she wanted him to be with her this very minute, his hands massaging her flesh into passionate spasms, her body welcoming that which she had never before known. . . .

And why did she want these special moments with a man like Adam Cassidy? He could drive her half-mad with his vicious sarcasm, and yet make her desire him even as her eyes narrowed in lethal fury and every manner of atrocity fought to escape from her tongue. She wondered if he was aware of the feelings he caused to surface in her, or if he was totally oblivious to them. She wondered if he treated all women the same, or whether she was special.

Special, indeed! He delighted in tormenting her! He delighted in making her feel less than worthy, in treating her like a weakling and a woman who hadn't the sense to survive in the woods. She would show him, if it took all the strength and power she could muster! She could never let *him* get the best of her!

Turning on the bed, Mariette dragged a pillow beneath her head and sought sleep, smug in the satisfaction that she would show that male animal who was head boss on this trail!

The "head boss" hardly spoke a word to her antagonist for the following week of traveling, fighting the sweltering heat and sleeping beneath the skies in the long shadows of the Allegheny mountain range. A dozen miles from the trading post they had found remnants of Lara Seymour's clothing, and every mile or so a small patch of material that might have been torn from her petticoat. She was leaving a trail to be followed, though Mariette couldn't imagine that she'd rather be anywhere else than in the company of the brooding Roby Donovan. She imagined Lara was immensely enjoying the adventure.

Mariette could hardly bear the thought of another day of traveling with the sulking and silent Adam Cassidy. She didn't like the way he looked at her at times . . . one pale eyebrow quirking upwards and his gaze raking her as though he were considering her purchase at a slave auction. His thoughts were so shallow she could have read them through mud, and the harshness with which he issued orders. "Don't lay your bedroll in ants," "Wear your hat, you'll get sunburned," "Don't dawdle," "Don't run your mare." "Do this, do that, do, don't, do, don't, do, don't! Who did he think he was . . . king?

They had just pitched camp for the night. She was scouting a cool spot in a narrow cove, and he was seeing to the needs of their horses. She was trying to calm her disposition, after an especially exasperating day of traveling with him, and she was sure he was trying to forget that she even existed. That was fine with her; just as long as he kept out of her hair, the night would pass by without incident.

A fire lit the hazy midsummer darkness; he had made camp. As Mariette settled against the cool trunk of an oak, she watched him move through the dark dell toward a pond. He had become adept at fishing for their supper, and she knew from experience that she would have a few minutes to rest before she would be required to cook it over the fire.

She closed her eyes and thought of home. She wondered if her uncles, Noble and Bundy, had returned from

South Carolina. She wondered if a letter had arrived from her parents in San Francisco. She wondered how Michael was, but knew if anything drastic had happened that Hannah would have found a way to get a message to her.

She wondered if they were getting along well without her.

She wondered if anything exciting had happened in her absence.

Justin Laszlo sat in his room and looked through the large trunk Hannah Gilbert had asked the man John to bring up to him. It was filled with personal effects belonging to his late father, and his hand trembled as he removed each item . . . a blackened, misshapen pocket watch, its crystal shattered, that his father must have lost when he'd escaped the fire seventy years before, letters, documents, and jewelry that had belonged to his father and his grandparents, Philip and Jocelyn Mayne, and even a vest that had been his father's, still bearing a few continental bills that had been the currency of the day. At his feet, contained within the cedar sides of the chest, rested the complete history of the family he had never known.

He was grateful to the woman Hannah for sending his father's possessions to him, but suspicious as to her motive. He knew he made her uncomfortable, and that his presence had upset the normal routine of the household. She had given her children orders to avoid him, but to be polite, and the boy Miles had obeyed. The little girl, Cassandra, however, had occasionally crept past her mother's skirts, ascended the stairs at the west side of the house, and knocked on the door of his suite, announcing her intentions to visit. He liked the child; if the mother thought for a moment that he would do her harm, she was sadly mistaken. Cassandra knew too much about his father—much more, actually, than he would have thought the others of the house might have told her—and he enjoyed the stories she relayed and embellished with her youthful innocence. Just this morning she had told him, "and it is our secret," that his father was one of the ghosts who occasionally visited her when she was alone in her sleeping chamber.

"Oh, and does he know I'm here?" Justin had asked.

"Of course," had come her intentionally indignant reply. "Ghosts know *everything!*"

Now, he sat among his family's past, his fingers easing over words his father had written, over journals his grandfather had kept, over jewelry his grandmother had worn. He touched the smooth, mother-of-pearl cameo that looked as though it might have been lifted from the jeweler's tools just that morning . . . so fresh, unmarred and beautiful it was. He touched the face of a watch through broken glass that might have stopped at the precise hour his father had lost it. Then he found the newspaper clippings from the *Gazette,* and for the next hour and a half he read the daily accounts of the mystery surrounding his grandmother's death, the accounts of how she had lain for fourteen years in a private suite, her body mummifying and being tended by a servant who was too daft to realize the woman had been dead for years. He read the accounts of greed and murder and mayhem, as his father and grandfather had sought to keep control of Rourke House. To accomplish that means, they had caused to be killed Jocelyn Mayne's brother, Standish Rourke, and many months later, Webster had attempted to kill Standish's daughter, Diana.

He was intrigued, but sick at heart. His mother had told

him that his father had been evil, that Justin himself was a product of rape. But a little boy did not want to believe such aspersions on the character of the man who was his father, a man he had never known. So, his little boy's mind had created the vision of a man who had romanced his mother with roses and poetry, a man taken away by circumstances beyond his control. Justin had envisioned a man being held prisoner somewhere, pining to return to the beloved Topaz and take care of her. When boys had teased him about having no father, he had made up stories about his father that had been so convincing they had actually envied his good fortune to have such a wonderful man fighting all treacheries to return to him and his mother.

Then he had grown older, had watched his mother steadily decline from a sad, but beautiful young woman to a bitter, aged and haggard woman selling flowers on the corner of Bourbon Street, or making a penny or two selling herself to nefarious men coming in on the ships. Then, the wisdom of maturity had fought with the fantasies of childhood, and he had never been sure who had come out victorious. To this day, he chose to believe the best of his father, though he could not completely discount the truthfulness of his mother's tales of him.

When he had received the information from the man named Purvis, his teetering thoughts had accepted the evidence he'd needed to lean in his father's favor. These evil Donovans had made his life a living hell, and he had found the only way he could to fight back. For that reason, he deserved to be avenged.

He expected a visit from a man named Moses McCardle, a writer for the *Gazette*. He wasn't sure what the man's interest in him was, but he suspected that he might have been the one to send the intriguing information to him in

New Orleans. He was interested in finding out how the man had learned of his existence, and why he wanted him here in Philadelphia. The man had visited the woman Hannah last week, on the pretense of "gathering a little society news as fillers," but had left without much information. Justin got the impression that day that Hannah Gilbert was a very private woman, and didn't like her laundry aired to the public, even if that laundry was spotless. He imagined that she might be trying to keep secret the fact that her halfbreed "cousin," Roby Donovan, had stolen off to the Alleghenies with an English girl of questionable royal breeding.

The supper bell rang, though muffled by the thick walls of the house, easily heard by anyone in the vicinity. After several minutes, he arose, his fingers easing into the waist of his trousers, Justin kicked aside the papers that had held his interest as he moved toward the door. On the platform just outside, he saw the child Cassandra on the steps below.

"I didn't think you'd heard the bell, Cousin Justin," she said, smiling, tucking her hand into his when he descended to meet her. "Mother has baked a goose and sweet potatoes . . . and a cracker pudding for desert. Do you like cracker pudding, Cousin Justin?"

"I don't know," he remarked, moving down the stairs beside her. "I don't think I've ever had any." When they stepped upon the dirt, she tripped, and his grip tightened.

She quickly righted her footing, for now she skipped beside him as they skirted the house. "John let me help milk the cow," Cassandra bubbled forth, "and he squirted milk in my face right out of one of Lilly Bell's teats. What do you think about that?"

"Well, I think that wasn't very polite," he answered indulgently as they entered the kitchen. Hannah was just taking a pan of cornbread out of the oven. "Can I be of assistance?" asked Justin.

Setting down the hot pan, Hannah turned a curious gaze toward the man she had not known existed until a week ago. She didn't know why she was so distrustful of him; he'd been nothing less than a gentleman. But something lurked beneath the polite demeanor, something that very much frightened her. "No, why don't you go on in and find your place at the dining table. Michael will be joining us this evening. And Dr. Redding—"

"Oh!" He said nothing beyond that. When Cassandra attempted to take his hand once again, her mother called to her. "I'll go upstairs and escort Liddy to the table," Justin offered.

"That would be nice," said Hannah, and when Justin's tall, slim form had merged into the other room, she turned a narrow look of disapproval toward her daughter. "What did I tell you about Cousin Justin, Cass?"

She shrugged patiently, turning her gaze toward her mother. "You said to be polite, but not to be too friendly. But, Mum, he's so nice. And he tells me such amusing stories of N'Awleans." She had pronounced the name of the fair Louisiana city in Justin's natural drawl, causing her mother to stifle a smile. "Couldn't you try to like Cousin Justin a little better? I do think he could grow on you."

Well . . . that was certainly something Cassandra was repeating, though Hannah wasn't sure who in the household would be speaking up for Justin. As far as she knew no one really liked him that much, though he'd never given any cause thus far for his unpopularity. She was sure it was because he had professed to be Webster Mayne's son—the likeness was uncanny and, therefore, practically irrefutable—

and perhaps it was a little unfair to base a man's character on that of his murderous father.

Hannah gave the silently waiting Cassandra a small smile, bent to her level, then whisked the small, untidy curls back from her forehead. "All right, Cass, I'll try to like Cousin Justin, but you must promise me one thing." Small brows arched quizzically upwards. "You must promise that you'll never be alone with Justin, and that you won't go to his apartment. And you must promise that you won't tell him about your ghosts—"

"I won't, Mum." Actually, it was only a small lie; because her mother had made this request *after* she'd already told Cousin Justin about the ghosts. "May I go in to the table now?"

Hannah touched a gentle, affectionate kiss to Cassandra's cheek. "Yes, you may."

Cassandra bounced off and momentarily Hannah heard her voice commingled with that of Miles. She could tell by his tone that he was trying to "be tough." "I am, after all, your brother, and I must protect you." Apparently, Miles had overheard all or part of her conversation with their mother.

Hannah continued readying the plates and platters for the dinner table. Occasionally, and this was one of those times, she wished she weren't so stubborn. It would be nice to have someone in the house—a cook, perhaps—to help with the meals. But since the death of her husband when Cassandra was an infant, she had found comfort in kitchen duties. She didn't like thinking about her husband, and the manner in which he had died, and she didn't like worrying about things that she could not control.

Right now, she was worried about Mariette, much more so than Roby and Lara. Roby could take care of himself, and Hannah knew that he would not harm Lara. She suspected that he had taken Lara off to the mountains in a moment of rage—a state he frequently enjoyed—and when he'd gotten it out of his system he would bring the girl back. But Mariette! She was traveling with a man who was a stranger to the family . . . a man whose background and character they did not know. Mariette was usually a good judge of character, and that was the only thing keeping Hannah from sending someone she trusted after the pair. Adam Cassidy, a man who may or may not have doctoring skills, had been willing to sit with a critically injured man and see him through the crisis. Dr. Redding had told Hannah just that morning that whatever Adam had done that night might possibly have saved Michael's life. So that was definitely a plus when it came to assessing his character.

Soon, the family settled around the dining-room table. Michael, still bandaged and appearing a little groggy on his first trip from the sick bed, sat at the head of the table. Miles had taken the other end, and Justin, Cassandra, and Liddy sat at one side. Hannah joined Bertrand Redding after the last platter had been put on the table.

Now, they sat there, a solemn group who said very little. Only Cassandra seemed to be in a talkative mood, which was nothing unusual for the happy child. Hannah watched Dr. Redding from the corner of her eye, and was surprised by the frequent, vicious looks he gave Justin Laszlo. She wondered what had transpired between the two men when Justin had been the doctor's patient.

Cassandra, of course, could read a mood as easily as the newspaper. In a small, plaintive voice, she asked, "Dr. Redding, are you still angry at Cousin Justin?"

Dr. Redding gulped his food, then put his fork aside for

the moment. "I am not angry with your, ummm, cousin," he replied. "I do not know him very well."

"But I can tell," she insisted innocently. "The way you looked at him is the way mum looks at me and Miles when we've been bad."

"Do hush, Cass," warned her mother, "and eat your dinner."

Miles quipped, "Let her have her say," then cast Justin one of Dr. Redding's suspicious looks. "Perhaps Cousin Justin isn't what he claims to be. Perhaps he is an imposter."

Hannah gasped, "That's enough, Miles. You should speak only when spoken to. That is the rule at the dinner table."

"No, mother. That is the rule *only* when it applies to *me,* not Cassandra!" Giving his mother a narrow, venomous look, Miles threw down his napkin to add emphasis to his ire, and fled from the table.

Justin placed his eating utensils aside and stood, moved to the back of his chair and pushed it under the table. "I'm not a good influence on the family," he said quietly. "Perhaps I should take my meal in my quarters."

"You don't have to do that," said Hannah.

"I've apparently missed something this past week," interjected Michael, who had been told of Justin Laszlo but had not met him until tonight. He was astounded by the remarkable resemblance the man bore to the portrait of Webster Mayne hanging over the platform of the stairs. "I believe in giving a man a chance to prove himself. Why don't you sit . . . *Cousin* Justin, and tell us about yourself."

Liddy added, "I would like to hear about your life. My son——" She had always referred to Michael and Roby as her sons, though they were, actually, her husband's sons by his first wife, Jolie. "My son and I are very interested in what you've been doing. It is my understanding your mother knew our dear Carrie when she was in New Orleans. Do tell us what you've been told. We are so interested in anything surrounding the lives of our family."

The sweet softness of the blind woman's voice compelled Justin to retake his seat. Beneath the edge of the table Cassandra took his hand and gave it a gentle squeeze, endearing herself to him once again. He almost wished that he hated the child. If he ultimately had to avenge a "wronged" father, it would make what he had to do so much easier. The other child, though . . . Miles! Now there was one to be reckoned with. Justin had to admire the mean little rascal; he wouldn't allow the wool to be pulled over his eyes by anyone claiming to be a long-lost relative!

Some degree of normalcy returned to the people surrounding the polished mahogany table. Forks clattered against china, bowls were exchanged, the meal consumed, and all the while they talked.

"You don't say?" said Michael, dumbfounded.

"I do say," laughed Justin. "My mother, Topaz, told me that when my father was known as Junius Wade, your cousin-by-marriage, Carrie, whom he had called Flame, because of her red hair—" Hannah gasped, cutting an instant glance to her small daughter, as Justin continued, "she pushed him overboard into the Gulf of Mexico. My mother was there . . ." Justin continued the story, although Hannah didn't hear. How had Cass known about Flame?

Hannah said to her daughter, "After dinner, Cass, I would like to have a talk with you."

"Yes, mum," she replied, lowering her eyes, her good mood drifting away. She knew what was on her mother's mind—the matter of her *knowing* that Carrie had been called Flame. She silently thanked heaven for the warning so she could make up something that would make sense to her mother.

Soon, the family drifted throughout the house, Michael and Justin toward the liquor cabinet in the study, to get better acquainted, Liddy to her room on the second floor, and Dr. Redding left the house, claiming that he had to visit an elderly patient before journeying home. When Cassandra attempted to sneak off toward the stairs, Hannah called her to the kitchen, where she was preparing a plate to take up to the hotheaded Miles.

"Now, young lady, I want you to tell me how you knew Webster called your grandmother Flame." Hannah's eyes narrowed at the silent child. Sitting at the small table in the kitchen, she patted the table, calling Cassandra to her. And, before she could utter a single word, Cassandra tucked her hand beneath her mother's tapping fingers and began to wail in the most godawful way. Instantly, Hannah drew the distraught child to her. "What on earth is this for?" she asked softly.

In between her sobs, she managed to say, "Miles said . . . when you use . . . that tone of voice . . . you're going to . . . wallop me good!"

Hannah drew her daughter slightly back and shook her gently. "Now, when have I ever walloped you, Cassandra Elizabeth Gilbert? Tell your mother . . . when!"

Cassandra shrugged slightly, "N-n-never, mum. B-b-but, Miles says there must always . . . be a first time."

Hannah touched her thumbs to Cassandra's cheeks, to wipe away the tears. "I just wanted to know how you knew that Grandmother Carrie was called Flame by Webster Mayne."

"Grandma told me?"

"I don't think so." Hannah shook her head slowly, then smiled to alleviate her daughter's small sobs. "Did Webster tell you?" Cassandra shrugged, her mouth pinching into a frown as her eyes found a spot on the floor to hold her attention. Immediately, Hannah's fingers went beneath her chin to force her to make eye contact. "Did he?"

Cassandra rolled her eyes heavenward, her voice assuming a tiny note of sarcasm. "Mum, Webster is *dead!* How could he tell me *anything?*"

Hannah insisted, "Did he?"

And Cassandra, tears once again filling her warm green eyes, mumbled, "Yes, mum, he did." Then she stood against her mother's knee, waiting for the lecture to come.

But Hannah hugged her daughter and said, "I believe you, Cass. If you say the ghosts talk to you, then I have no reason to doubt it."

Cassandra was immediately suspicious, though her arms did ease around her mother's waist to accept the hug. Of course, she wasn't so distraught that she didn't wonder what her mother was up to.

Nine

It was the most horrible scene Mariette had ever come across. The long, narrow cove was littered with the grisly remains of approximately thirty Indians, the months since their slaughter having left little but bones and the rotting remnants of their clothing and personal effects. The remaining evidence identified them as Seneca, and the weapons still piercing their remains were Mohawk. No doubt, these Seneca were renegades because, like the Mohawk, they were of the five nations of the Iroquois. The Iroquois usually kept peace among themselves, but considered renegades, even those of their brethren, as open game and contradictory to the welfare of the nation.

"Why did we have to take this route?" groaned Mariette, turning away to collect her bearing. She felt nauseous and weak, and could scarcely move her feet one in front of the other as she ascended the hill.

Adam growled, "Because *you* said it was a shortcut to that village where Roby might have taken the girl. I don't know these damned woods, and I certainly wouldn't have gone off the trail."

His vicious tone smarted and Mariette was unsure why he was suddenly so angry. She gave him a hateful look as she said, "Well, I'm so *damned* sorry. How was I to know there had been a massacre?"

Adam remounted his horse and edged up the hill, halting beside her. He was immediately sorry for his testy tone, but he didn't like these strange woods that might be hiding treachery behind every tree and in the depths of every shadow. He could not protect Mariette if he didn't know what to expect of their surroundings. "Remount and let's get out of here. This place gives me the spooks."

"Shouldn't we report this to someone?"

"Who?" came his sensible response.

She shrugged. "Well—oh, I don't know. They should be buried."

"We don't have time to do it *ourselves."* He had deliberately emphasized the words that would tell her forthright that he *could not* undertake the monumental task alone, though on the other hand, he wouldn't feel right about her helping him with it. So, he dragged in a moment of calm and continued, "The trapper we met yesterday who saw Roby and the girl told us they were only a few hours ahead. It was your idea to take the shortcut and intercept them before they reached the village." As an afterthought, she snapped, "We would have had help from my cousins if you hadn't said we could find him ourselves. I think you just want to be alone with me!"

His condescending lectures always infuriated her, and fury always brought tears, which Mariette now stifled with great effort. Remounting her horse, she lagged behind him as they moved on to the west. A fog had risen and they were riding under the cover of broken clouds. Occasionally, the sun would break through, but as noon approached, thunder was immediately overhead and the horizon flashed threateningly. By the time they reached the shelter of the fortified Pitkins community deep in the

Allegheny hills, the rain was falling in angry sheets, washing down the tendrils of fog that had seemed to cling to the hooves of their horses as they'd ridden along.

The people of Pitkins community had spent decades building a small city in the hills and fortifying it for attack against the Iroquois. They might have been considered a reasonably intelligent people, simply because they had managed to survive the constant threat of attack. However, in those same decades the family had regenerated by inbreeding, uncle marrying niece, cousin marrying cousin, until the current generation hadn't hardly the makings of a full brain between them. So, the old ones of the family still ruled the community, and the young ones, afflicted in various and sundry ways, both mentally and physically, took their orders and instructions by instinct.

At the center of the community stood a long house constructed of elmwood poles and seasoned elmbark, where several families lived under one roof. On the outer perimeters of the settlement, but still within the palisades, small cabins had been erected to house the occasional passerby. That is where the young man named Harley Pitkins now took Mariette Donovan.

While Adam stabled their horses in a sturdy lean-to behind the cabin and graciously accepted hay from one of the elders to feed them, Mariette used a small blanket to wring the water out of her hair, then changed into her only other suit of clothing. By the time a soaking Adam Cassidy entered the cabin, she had a warm fire going to alleviate the chill caused by this sudden midsummer downpour. She gave him little more than a perfunctory glance as he began to shed his clothing.

After a moment, he said, "Harley Pitkins invited us to have lunch with his family in the long house. Do you want to go?"

She looked to him now, his muscled back exposed, and the rain from his hair dripping to his shoulders. "I just want to be alone," she said, lifting her gaze to his quiet one. "I just need some time away from you for a little while." She wasn't sure why she felt the need to be hateful, because all she really wanted was to be in his arms, feeling those rigid muscles beneath her caressing fingers.

He seemed to take no offense. "You're not hungry then, I assume?"

"I'm not."

"Good." He turned about, pulling on his shirt as he did so. "I need time away from you, too. You're the most exasperating woman I've ever known, and I do wish you'd go on back to the city and let me carry on by myself." Climbing to his feet, he fastened his shirt buttons, then tucked the tails into the waist of his trousers. Finally, he was using the same small blanket she had used to half dry his hair. "The horses are bedded down, probably for the afternoon and night. It doesn't appear as though the storm will let up any time soon."

She eased onto a small, hard pillow, then tucked her booted feet beneath the edge of the blanket. Her arms crossed against her waistline, she gave him a rather smug look. "I won't be going back to the city, and I am quite willing to wait out the storm. If we cannot travel, then neither can Roby and Lara. He is probably holed up somewhere himself, perhaps in one of the caves dotting the mountains. He knows them all by heart—"

"Good for him!" Adam pivoted toward her, gave her a half grin, then turned toward the door. "I'll bring something back for you if you'd like."

"I can get my own food!"

Without another word, he exited, slamming the door soundly behind him. Mariette listened to his retreating bootsteps on the hard-packed earth outside, breaking into a run as he sought shelter from the downpour. *Why are we always quarreling?* Mariette wondered, wishing he were back in the cabin so that she might make amends for her haughty ways. After all, she had started the quarrel, as usual.

And she wasn't sure why she always felt the need . . . perhaps to keep him on his toes, always wondering what she will do next?

Mariette hadn't realized how sleepy she was. Making a feeble attempt to fluff the pillow, which had the same effect as trying to make small, hard pebbles more comfortable, she soon closed her eyes and enjoyed the warmth of the small cabin. The activity outside had droned away with the deepening of the storm, and now she heard very little but the crackle of the logs in the hearth, the thunder ricocheting through the roof, and an occasional laughter of those seeking the amenities of the long house at the center of the community.

Dreams began to float all around her . . . dreams of a laughing, mischievous Cassandra, even Miles, his normally sullen features breaking into a warm, childlike smile. In her dream she could almost catch the whiff of Hannah's early morning baking, hear the sniggers of the horses in their stalls at the carriage house and the creakings of the old house that was still, after two centuries, trying to settle upon its foundation. In her dream, voices of the past came drumming back . . . she vaguely remembered her great-grandfather's voice, thick with its Scottish brogue, and his gentle chiding. He had been dead for fourteen years now, and it hardly seemed possible that so much time had passed since she'd drawn herself up to his knee to hear him tell one of his infamous stories of past injustices and adventures shared with his beloved Diana.

She remembered that he was a gentleman, and that he was a *gentle man*. She remembered how he laughed, and how he was always first to charm over Hannah's frequent scoldings of the younger members of the house. Unfortunately, Mariette had been the *only* younger member, until the children had been born, so Mariette had often enjoyed her grandfather's soothing hugs and gentle words.

Mariette remembered that he'd often reminded her how different she was from her older sister. *Hannah is like an old lady trapped in a young body. Her thoughts are old, her ways are old, she's forgotten how to be young and, God, lass, you are only young once. Enjoy it while you can, because only too soon you will be old and all the good years will be behind you. And*—She remembered that he had winked then, continuing on a quieter note, *Nothing will keep you young as effectively as true love, like that your Great-grandmother Diana and I share. Remember it, lass, and choose wisely when the time comes.*

Cole had been Mariette's favorite kin, so sometimes she wondered why he only appeared to Cassandra now that he was the residential ghost.

But, of course, it was because Cassandra was a child, and childhood was the age of innocence. Mariette didn't really believe her niece saw the ghosts of the house, but on the off-chance that she did, she couldn't help but be envious.

Suddenly, Mariette realized she was no longer alone. Behind her closed eyes a shadow moved across the room, and she wondered why Adam Cassidy had felt the need to sneak back into the cabin. Did he think she was asleep and was up to some mischief? Well, she could play his game as well as he could—

A hand closed over her mouth. Mariette's eyes flew open and she attempted to see through the vague shadows of the small room. The hand muffled her scream, and when her fingers lifted, then slid across the wrist of the offender, she realized it was not the hand of Adam Cassidy. She tried to lift her gaze, but could see nothing but dark features and shoulder-length hair.

"Don't scream, Mariette!" he warned.

She wasn't sure whether Roby's voice brought relief or deeper fear, but she nodded, though his firm grip made the small move almost impossible. Slowly, his hand slid away and she spun onto her knees to stare him down with all the fury she could muster. "What are you doing, Roby? For God's sake, where is Lara?"

"She is safe." One of his knees pressed into the pillow where her head had been resting, and now both of his hands dropped to his thighs. "I want you and the stranger to go back home."

So, he knew she was traveling with Adam Cassidy, though he didn't know his name. "Not without Lara," she responded. "Bring Lara here by day's end and you can go wherever you choose." Her eyes adjusted to the failing light; immediately, she was shocked by his appearance. He was bare from the waist up, and his sharp, bronze features were painted, much like an Iroquois warrior taking to the warpath. His brows were pinched and mean, and his dark eyes were like deadly snakes about to strike. Mariette had known this man all her life, but now she didn't know him at all. In a somewhat shaky voice she reiterated, "Bring Lara here, Roby, and go where you please. That is all I ask."

His knee slid off the bed. "You ask too much. I told you she is safe and I will let her go when it pleases me."

"Don't hurt her, Roby."

"Hurt her?" Sarcasm laced the two words. "Why would I do that?"

"Who knows why you do anything?"

"Who, indeed—" Then, for a moment, the rebellion was gone, the hatred that was so much a part of his character flown off with the wind. In a quiet voice that echoed his education, he asked, "How is Michael?"

"He was recovering when I left Philadelphia. Dr. Redding says he will make a full recovery."

Roby sighed deeply, his relief as readible as a children's book. "I didn't want to hurt him, Mariette. You must believe that."

"I know you didn't. I imagine that Michael instigated the altercation." When Roby neither admitted nor denied that observation, Mariette continued with haste, "He cared deeply for Lara. You must have known that, Roby."

His excuse was, "She isn't good enough for Michael." He took a step back toward the window that had, apparently, been his access to the cabin just moments before. "But she's good enough for me. You can have her back when I'm tired of her."

He had just swung his left leg over the window ledge when the cabin door burst open, bringing in, not only the storm, but Adam Cassidy. Immediately, the plate he had been carrying clattered to the floor, and Adam drew his weapon to face down the man he thought was climbing *in* the window.

Mariette screamed, "Don't shoot him! Adam, put down your gun!"

Adam hunkered down and held the gun straight out, aimed for Roby Donovan's heart. The man, however, at whom it was aimed showed no alarm whatsoever, so calm and passive were his features as he stared down the long barrel.

Neither man said a word for what seemed like a thousand hours. Then Roby asked, "Who the hell is he anyway?"

"He's traveling with me, Roby. Please . . . end this now. Say you'll bring the girl here before nightfall."

"No!" When Roby made a move toward Mariette, Adam lifted his sidearm. Roby gave him a somewhat smirking look and, his gaze holding Adam's threatening one, his fingers eased across the space and found a perch on one of Mariette's slim wrists. Turning her hand so that she could touch him with gentle affection, Mariette offered the tiniest smile.

Suddenly Adam fired the gun firmly gripped in his right hand. Roby's hand was wrenched from Mariette's, and with a small cry of pain, his body fell through the cabin window to the outside.

Heavy footfalls echoed from all corners of the compound. With a hysterical cry, Mariette buried her fingers into her loose, damp hair as Adam, reholstering his sidearm, moved toward the window.

Momentarily, his hand came up, covered with blood. He attempted to see through the blinding veil of the storm, but beyond the window no human movement could be discerned. Roby Donovan had not been so badly wounded that he couldn't make a getaway.

Adam had just turned when a screaming Mariette thrashed his chest with her balled fists. "Why did you shoot him? Damn you . . . why—?"

He caught her wrists, holding them to him. "I thought he was going to hurt you." The door burst open; Harley Pitkins entered, followed by two older men. Releasing Mariette's wrists, Adam turned toward the three men. "It was the man, Roby Donovan. He got into the compound."

"An' you shot 'em?" asked Harley Pitkins.

"I nicked him enough to bleed."

Mariette stared in horror at the blood Adam's grip had deposited to her hand. Roby's blood . . . the blood of a man who was her family . . . the blood of a man she loved—

She only half-heard the men leave, the door close with a dull thud, then their bootsteps carrying them away from the cabin. They would search the premises for Roby Donovan, but Mariette knew they would not find him. He was too stubborn to be taken down by a bullet, but Mariette knew in her heart he was badly hurt. As tears filled her eyes, she prayed to the Almighty that Roby could make it back to Lara, and that she didn't hate him too much to take care of him.

Lara didn't dare leave the cave. Roby had said there were bears in the immediate vicinity, and she didn't care to be breakfast for any ferocious creature of this untamed wilderness. Roby had been thorough; not only had he frightened her with tales of maneating predators, but he had ridden away on their only means of transportation. She was effectively held prisoner, both by her fear and her unfamiliarity with the terrain.

She wondered where Roby had gone, and why he hadn't taken her with him. As much as she didn't want him to be away from her, she hoped he might return with food. She was starving, and the storm—as well as those ferocious bears waiting outside to gobble her up—prevented her from going in search of berries. She had become quite good at hunting out the best ones, and telling the difference between blackberries and dewberries.

A horse whinnied nearby. Pressing her back to a large

rock, she watched a shadow ease along the dry hardness of the cave wall. Then she saw Roby, dripping wet, his shirt half-dragged up his arms and one hand holding a stained handkerchief against his waistline. Dropping to his knees before her, he offered the handkerchief. "Berries, again. Sorry it couldn't be something better."

With a small smile she took them from him, immediately popping one into her mouth. "It doesn't matter. I'm so famished I could eat your horse." She gazed into his eyes, noticing at once that his brows were furrowed, his mouth pressed into a thin line, the muscles of his jaws clenching and unclenching. "What is the matter?" she asked in her crisp English accent, her fingers rising to trace a path along his taut jaw. "What has happened?" Gripping the soaked lapels of his shirt, her fingers eased along the edge of the fabric. Then, touching the warm stickiness of blood beneath, they withdrew, a look of ashen horror in her pretty features. She looked at the blood coating her fingers in disbelief.

"What can I say?" he grinned painfully. "Mariette's fella didn't like me very much." Then he quietly collapsed against her shoulder, scattering the berries he had picked for her lunch.

She might have been only seventeen years old and sheltered English royalty, but she knew a gunshot wound when she saw one. Still, when she pulled back the fabric of his shirt and saw such a tiny hole, she could scarcely believe it could be so serious. Gently laying him on his back, she rushed to the horse, retrieved the blanket tied to the back of the saddle and soon was tucking it beneath his head. She wasn't sure what to do beyond that, except use the remaining fabric of her petticoat to attempt to staunch the bleeding. She felt totally helpless. *Blast it all!* she thought, finding very little fabric remaining of the once full petticoat. Why had she felt the need to leave a trail to be followed?

The bullet had entered his right side, at the level of his waistline, and an exit hole at his back relieved her mind that she would not have to dig for the bullet. Still, how to stop the bleeding? Should she plug the hole with a bit of the fabric, or would that only make matters worse?

Lara didn't know what to do. She rocked back and forth on her knees beside him, her eyes closed and tears falling across the smooth curves of her cheeks. She tried to think, but her thoughts were muddled and indistinguishable. What if he died? What if the horse ran away? As that fear flashed through her mind, she climbed to her feet, took the reins of the horse and led it a dozen or so feet deeper into the cave. There, she used a large rock to weigh down the reins, assured herself the horse would stay there, and returned to Roby. He had not moved. Dropping to her knees once again, she drew her ear down to his face, instantly feeling the lightness of his breathing against her hairline.

"Lara? Lara?" She startled, drawing back. Roby's hand was now groping for her and she took it, pulling it down to her lap.

"What should I do?" she whispered emotionally. "I don't know what to do, Roby."

"Pour . . . whiskey. Wrap the wound. Let . . . me sleep."

"That's all?" Annoyance edged her voice; why couldn't he give more in-depth instructions. "And what do I do if you die?"

"At that point . . . I don't give . . . a damn—"

As he passed into unconsciousness once again, Lara balled her fist, wanting to strike him but daring not. How could he place her in this predicament? Trapped in a cave in the middle of a fierce storm, with a man who had been gut-shot and . . . without food! Suppose the glen should flood and the cave fill with water? Suppose the two of them, and their only horse, should drown? Frowning, curling her hands into hard balls against her thighs, Lara thought Roby's thought . . . *At that point, who gives a damn?*

So, Lara drew a deep, weary sigh and began following the instructions he had given her. She cringed as she poured the raw whiskey into the bleeding wounds, to which he did not respond, cursed as his heaviness made it difficult for her to wrap the torn lengths of her petticoat around his middle, and cursed him, also, because he appeared to be sleeping soundly and she was so hungry her stomach hurt. For a few minutes she moved gingerly around the darkening cave, gathering the berries he had brought to her, and ate them in silence. Soon, she filled the one small cup they had shared between them with rain water and sat against the cave wall, sipping the water and watching him through treacherously narrowed eyes.

She was so angry with him, and yet fearful that he might die. She hated him . . . but she knew that she loved him, also. She didn't know where he had been taking her before somebody decided to shoot him, but she had wanted all along to go with him, she wasn't sure why she'd left a trail to be followed, perhaps for the adventure of the pursuit, but she didn't want to be found and taken back to the boring, stuffy city of Philadelphia and the dreary old house where her grandparents had sent her to get her away from the stable boy!

She was lost in a paradox of emotions, sure of only one thing. Roby would live . . . and she would stay with him forever, if he would have her.

Philadelphia . . . Rourke House . . . England . . . and Lord and Lady Seymour be damned!

* * *

An hour after the shooting Mariette was still trembling.
Her eyes were red both from rage and from tears, and all
of Adam Cassidy's explanations had been for naught. He
had been fearful for her, thinking that Roby would harm
her—he had fired by instinct and he was sorry now.

One thing was certain; the storm would leave no trail
to follow. If Roby Donovan had left the English girl
bound and gagged somewhere, and he died returning to
her, then she might certainly die, as well. The hills were
dotted with caves, and by the time they found her—if,
indeed, that is where Roby had taken her—she could well
have been dead for weeks.

Adam cursed his own impulsiveness. He should have
realized the man wouldn't have harmed Mariette. But
what was the purpose of his visit with her? And, blast it,
she had yet to tell him! He knew she was angry with him,
but that was no reason to shut him out now! He needed
to know what the man had told her, and he needed to
know now! The woman's life might depend on it.

He was just about to ask Mariette once again when her
gaze lifted to him and she spitefully said, "I won't tell you
anything! You'll be wasting your breath by asking!"

Mariette watched him approach, circle the bed, then sit
on the edge beside her. His fingers drew toward the folds
of her gown, then withdrew, and his eyes watched her
own intently. He understood her frustrated anger, because he *shouldn't* have shot Roby Donovan. But, dammit,
she had to understand that not only had he agreed to go
after the man, but part of his job was to protect Mariette
as well. Couldn't she see that? Did she have to be so
narrow-minded that she couldn't see this was as frustrat-
ing for him as it was for her?

Mariette was feeling a little self-conscious. Adam Cassidy watched her intently, and she couldn't seem to find her voice to say anything to him, whether it be friendly or rude. Certainly, he deserved the latter, but her heart simply wasn't in it.

She didn't like the way his eyes were flickering indifferently across her features, as though he were watching for some small emotion she was deliberately holding at bay. But for the moment, she felt nothing inside, and she wanted only for him to go away and leave her alone, and don't come back until she'd decided the sight of him wouldn't make her sick.

Who was she trying to fool? The sight of him did everything to her . . . except make her sick.

She didn't like his closeness, and she didn't like the musky, manly scent of him so close to her. She didn't like the way his hand rested so close to her skirts and his fingers flexed and unflexed. She didn't like the way his eyes bore holes through her, and she . . . oh, she just didn't like him at all. Couldn't he see that?

So, she forced her mouth into a grim smile and remarked lazily, "If you've gotten your fill of looking at me, why don't you scat."

"Scat? I don't think I've ever done that. Why don't you show me how it's done?"

The smile slid away. She hated it when his sarcasm bested her own. For a moment, she studied his rugged good looks, the way his silver-blond hair gleamed in the gentle flames of the hearth. He was gritting his teeth; the muscles of his jaw grew taught. She liked the way his eyes briefly widened each time the thunder clashed, and she liked the way his full, masculine mouth parted, though she wasn't particularly fond of the sneer that instantly twisted it.

Before she could quite prepare for the move, his hand had circled her neck and his fingers dragged painfully into the tangled masses of her hair. She drew a short gasp, her eyes curiously wide. When his mouth drew close to her own, and she protested with a demure struggle, he asked, "What's wrong, Mariette, frightened of a man's kiss?"

She searched his features carefully, finding it, strangely, free of sarcasm. That, alone, left her speechless. To save face, so that he would not think she was indeed waiting for his kiss, she arched a pale, copper-colored eyebrow and met his gaze, transfixed, in a bold stand-off. She got just the response she expected . . . his fingers slid from their hiding place in the depths of her hair and he rose, turning his back on her. She watched his slow, deliberate retreat, and when he reached the door, she asked, "If you find him, let me know right away."

Without facing her, he asked, "What makes you think I'm going out searching for him?"

"I heard the men talking. They think if he's not badly wounded that they won't find him. And I think that's what you're counting on."

He turned to her now, frowning. "I do hope we don't find him," he admitted. "Because if we do, he's—"

When he hesitated, she finished his statement. "Dead. Yes . . . I know. But, you won't find him. He got back to where he left Lara. I know it."

"You don't know any such thing," he argued, his hands drawing up to find a perch against his hips. He wasn't really sure why he felt the need to contradict her. "You are merely hoping," he ended on a paler note.

"He's my kin, Adam Cassidy, and I care for him. I may not like him very much, and I might not approve of the hot-blooded things he does, but I care deeply for him. If you find him dead, I'll hate you forever."

"I can live with it." He jerked the door open, but then paused, drawing a deep breath as he contradicted himself, "No, I couldn't live with it, Mariette." He turned to face her now, and a world of pain was easily distinguishable in his gaze as he looked to her. "Somehow you've wormed your way right into my heart . . . and I don't want you to hate me. I couldn't bear it."

She sat forward, startled by his declaration. But as she fought to recover her lost voice, the door closed and he was gone, nothing left of him but the quiet echo of his boots as he merged into the falling rain.

Ten

Cassandra read the passage with great interest. *Sir Cole Cynric Donovan died two days past. He has been buried on the grounds of Donovan House beside his dear wife, beneath the oak where he buried his sword a few weeks ago. How long will it be visible, the gold gilt that his loving hands once caressed? My dear father once said that he would rather bury his sword in a young tree than bury it in the heart of a man, and it pains me so to think that at the time my own heart was the young sapling in my father's eyes. Even so, he should have died more nobly than to have wasted away in bed—*"

Cassandra was both intrigued and confused by the final passage written by a woman named Emilia Rourke in her father's diary. Cole Cynric Donovan had been her grandfather Andrew's father, and Andrew had been an only child, so who had Emilia been?

"I can explain that one," Cole Cynric Donovan said as he stepped out of the shadow in the corner of Cassandra's room. He moved toward her, then sat on a wide chest and placed his hand on her shoulder. "This is a different man . . . *my* namesake, and he lived a hundred years before I was born."

"But Great-grandpapa, why was he so unhappy? Why

was he angry with his daughter, that she should believe he did not love her, and that he would as soon have buried the sword in her heart as in the young sapling? I don't understand."

"It is a story of a man whose wife, Emilia, had died in childbirth. After he buried his wife, he mended his sorrows in his love for his daughter, named Emilia, after her mother. When she was nineteen, she met a man named Moss Rourke, whom her father did not think was good enough for her. Emilia met Moss in secrecy, because her father had forbidden them to see each other, and she eventually married the young man, without the blessings of her father. Thereafter, her father's health began to fail, and though Emilia made daily trips to the house, then called Donovan House, he refused to see her. As the story went, one evening after she had made one of her trips, Cole Donovan plunged his gold-gilted sword into a small oak sapling beside the grave of his dead wife. From that moment on, he brooded and drank and cursed the darkness, until mere exhaustion took conscious thought away. Emilia was summoned to the house when her father was dying, and when she sat at his bedside, he cursed her and every child conceived of her union with Moss Rourke. Then he died, and after his burial Emilia and Ross moved into the house, immediately renaming it Rourke House."

In the moment of silence to follow, Cassandra looked to her great-grandfather, soon asking, "And the sword is still in the little tree?"

Cole laughed, rising, walking a few feet across the carpet, then turning back. "The tree is now a giant. You've seen it many times, Cassandra, centrally located in the family cemetery. The next time you go there, you look very closely at about this level—" Cole held his hand at his waist, "—and I guarantee, lass, that you'll see a neat, round hole that grew around and over the sword. Aye, it is still there, and human eyes will n'ere behold it again."

"Did Emilia and Moss have any children?" asked Cassandra, now closing the diary among the folds of her gown.

"Aye, they did . . . Standish, a son, who was my beloved Diana's father, and Jocelyn, who was the mother of Webster Mayne. You are of Diana's lineage, Cassandra, and the man, Justin Laszlo, is of Webster's lineage."

"Mum thinks Cousin Justin is not to be trusted. Do you think so too, Great-grandpapa?"

"I din't know," Cole responded reluctantly, moving back to Cassandra and retaking his seat. "You must be very careful of him. I know you like him, and I suspect he likes you—" He grinned now, patting her hand in gentle comfort. "Who wouldn't like such a sweet lass? But I din't know him, and I want him to go away from Rourke House, before he causes any trouble for you."

"What kind of trouble could he cause?" Smiling, she asked, "Can he cause nearly as much trouble for me as the ghosts of this house, including you, Great-grandpapa?"

Cole Cynric Donovan did so love this child . . . her big green eyes fringed by honey-colored lashes, her cute nose and dainty, dimpled fingers, her sweetly puckered lips. She had styled her hair in thick braids, and a few wispy curls gently framed her pale features. He was just about to order in a stern, but loving voice that she must "be careful," when an almost timid knock sounded at the door.

As Cassandra called sweetly, "Come in," Cole stepped back into the dark corner.

Hannah Gilbert momentarily stepped into her daughter's room. "Who were you talking to, Cass?" When

Cassandra dropped her eyes, she continued, "One of your ghosts, daughter?"

Cassandra shrugged, pressing her mouth into a pout, and refusing to meet Hannah's stare. She didn't want a motherly lecture before she tucked herself into bed. Then, redirecting her attentions to the diary, she raised it to Hannah's view, brightening immediately. "No, mum, I was reading this old diary. That's all, I wasn't talking to ghosts. Really, mum, I wasn't."

Hannah had decided on a new course of action a few days ago. Lecturing Cassandra would only give the ghosts more exposure, and Cassandra might turn more frequently to them for friendship. Now, she dropped to the small, wooden chest, then bent across and looked at the diary. "Oh, yes, that's a very interesting diary. He was your Great-great-great-grandpapa. And his name was—"

"Cole Cynric Donovan, same as Great-grandpapa Cole." She sneaked a glance toward the corner where he was standing, then immediately looked back. "I'm learning all about the family, mum. I'm very interested."

Hannah drew her daughter's hand into the folds of her gown. "Yes, I know you are. And I want you to know that it is *all right* to be friends with the ghosts."

Cassandra gave her mother a skeptical look. "Really, mum? And which ghosts in particular should I be friends with?"

"Any of them," her mother replied indulgently, "except Webster. He's not nice, that one."

Cassandra opened her mouth, though her defense of Webster immediately halted. So, she nodded, then managed a somewhat timorous smile for her mother. "Very well. If you say so, mum."

Hannah moved gracefully upwards, then let her daughter's small hand fall from her own. "You need to be getting into your nightclothes, Cass. Have you finished the reading assignment Miss Lee gave you?"

Cassandra nodded. "Mum?"

Hannah was now at the door, straightening a few items of clothing clinging precariously to a hook. "Yes?"

"Is there a hole in the oak tree at the cemetery?"

Hannah offered a motherly smile. "Where the sword was driven, you mean?"

"You know about that?"

"Of course. I was a girl once myself, and I enjoyed reading the old diary. Yes. There is a hole."

"May I go see it?"

"Perhaps in the morning after it stops raining. Now— good night, Cass."

Hannah opened the door, as Cassandra smiled and answered, "Good night, mum."

She listened to the retreat of her mother's footsteps, scarcely giving Cole much notice when he stepped out of the shadows. But when he said, "Listen to your mother, Cassandra. *Don't* go out into the night," her livid green eyes turned straightaway to his gray ones.

"Ghosts!" she smarted. "You're always giving orders . . . just like mothers!"

Folding her arms across her chest, her little mouth pressed into a firm, angry line as she turned away from him. Soon, he withdrew into the shadows, and Cassandra jumped to her feet. She looked for him for a moment, thinking that he might simply be hiding, then, assured that he had gone on his merry way to wherever it was ghosts usually went, she moved toward the chifforobe and found her favorite wrap, a large, crocheted shawl that her grandmother Carrie had given her. Soon, her small, slippered feet were easing toward the servant's stairs at the end of the corridor.

Within a matter of minutes, her feet were easing onto the hard-packed earth outside the kitchen entrance, and as she left the shelter of a narrow lean-to, she saw that the lamps were lit in Cousin Justin's apartment. It occurred to her that with the rain pouring down, and an occasional crack of thunder, he would not have heard her moving across the lawn. Yet she still exercised caution. By the time she reached the cemetery gate, she stopped worrying that she'd be heard and did not ease the gate open to avoid its ever-present creak. The rain pelted her; she could scarcely see the dark, hanging branches of the oak beneath the black sky, and drew back, a little frightened, when it stood within her reach. Here, beneath the thick masses of leaves, the rain scarcely touched her, and she spent a few moments studying the trunk of the oak, "about this high," as her great-grandpapa had indicated. Within minutes, her small finger eased into a dent and, catching her breath in wonderment, worked it deeply into the hole. There was something smooth and metallic deep inside the hole and she strained to circle her finger around it. Yes, it must be the end of the sword's handle; she felt a raise in the metal that might be a decoration of sorts.

Cassandra was so excited that she released a delighted squeal. "It's here, just like the diary says." Then Cassandra squealed again, as she suddenly felt herself being snatched up into a man's arms. Her frightened gaze penetrating the veil of darkness, she easily discerned Cousin's Justin's thin, angular features. "Will you tell mother?" she immediately wailed, hugging his neck so firmly that he chuckled.

"You shouldn't be out, Cassandra. You'll catch your death!"

She gasped, a little surprised by his declaration. "Oh,

no, Cousin Justin. I would *never* try to catch death. I'm much too clever for that!"

Turning toward the house with her snuggled against him, Justin smiled. He could not know that the naughty adventure enjoyed by the child this night would have severe repercussions.

Adam Cassidy hunkered down into the small cot, trying to drown out the gentle sound of Mariette's breathing across the short spanse of space, mildly grateful that the compound was filled, requiring that they share the cabin, and everyone believed that Adam was a gentleman and thus a perfect escort for Mariette in the danger-filled wilderness. He tried to listen to the frequent claps of thunder outside the cabin but it did not reach his ear as effectively as did the sound of the enchanting creature who was his traveling companion. He was still a little perplexed by the light nervousness she had displayed in the late evening. He knew she was worried about Roby but he didn't think he was in her thoughts this time.

Mariette was aware of Adam Cassidy's even breathing. She lay quietly on her side, watching him, seeing only the wide expanse of his back covered by the coarse blanket. She had been upset when Harley Pitkins had informed her they would share the cabin as long as they were here, but now Mariette was glad of his company. Adam filled her thoughts. Certainly, she was angry that Adam had shot Roby and felt it was hot-headed and needless, but she understood that it had been a tense moment. And her little talk with Bree Pitkins, the wife of Harley, early in the afternoon, had disturbed her very much. Bree had told her that Adam had asked Harley to take his place in the quest for Roby Donovan and the girl he had kidnapped.

Mariette didn't want another companion, and she certainly did not want the odorous, cigar-smoking Harley Pitkins taking the place of the charming, and often moody, Adam Cassidy. She had to keep Adam with her, and she would do so at any cost. All afternoon and well into the night, Mariette thought about her course of action and she had known what she had to do.

She was a woman, and it would take womanly wiles.

When Adam suddenly turned on the small cot, Mariette snapped her eyes shut. She imagined that he wouldn't have been able to distinguish her features, or the fact that she was watching him, but she wouldn't take the chance. He might take her spying upon him in the cover of dark as an admiration of him, and she simply couldn't allow that. Could she?

Now, she cracked her eyes a bit, able to see only the dark outline of him through the fringes of her lashes. Then a glitter caught where one of his eyes might be, and she knew then that he was watching her as well. *Weren't they a pair?* she thought, drawing in a deep sigh. It seemed neither one of them could sleep.

Moving her head up on the pillow, she whispered across the dark, "Are you asleep, Adam?"

He immediately replied, "Yes . . . sound asleep."

"Oh—" Her mouth twisted into a wry smile, "then I won't bother you." In the lack of a response to follow, she threw off the blanket and swung her feet to the bare planked floor. For a moment she sat there, bent over, her elbows pressed into her thighs and her fingers tunneling through the rich, thick masses of her hair.

Adam watched her intently, admiring the way a single lamp beyond the window and the veil of rain surrounded her flaming head with an almost angelic aura. He could easily see that something was on her mind, something important enough to her that she could not sleep. And he knew she had to be tired. They had traveled sixteen hours the day before, had gotten only a half dozen hours of sleep that night, then had weathered the mountain trails made slick and treacherous by the storm that had rolled across them.

He watched her arise, make a feeble attempt to tuck her blouse into the waist of her trousers, then, leaving her boots beneath her cot, moved across the floor and soon stepped out to the small, narrow porch. She did not close the door, but stood there, facing the rain and the thunderous night.

Mariette felt the ache of tension through her shoulders. She knew she would not be able to sleep as long as Adam was determined to turn her over to Harley Pitkins, and yet she was so tired she had to grip the rough-hewn porch rail for support. She was worried about Roby, and about Lara, and afraid that Roby had died out in the forest, leaving Lara bound and defenseless somewhere where she would not be found. But would he have done that? She imagined that he would have left her sheltered from the storm; her unfamiliarity with the mountains, and possibly her fear of wild animals, would be all the confinement he needed to keep her from leaving without him. Mariette knew they had only the one horse; John had seen them ride away, Lara thrown recklessly across the pommel of Roby's saddle. He should have had the good sense to take another horse, though that would make traveling easier, and put more distance between them.

Mariette raised her eyes to the flashing night, to the wild, ominous tumble of black clouds across the gray-black sky. A mid-summer storm like this one could hang on for days; she'd seen it many times before. She could be effectively stuck at Pitkins community. She knew if Roby

wasn't too badly hurt, he would travel beneath the treacherous storm and put even more distance between them.
While Adam was concerned with keeping her safe, and
since he was a man of some medical knowledge, he would
know that being wet day in and day out was not good for
a soul. She imagined that he would protect her from the
elements, just as he might protect a child. It should annoy
her that he might treat her like a child, but for some
strange, inexplicable reason it did not. She liked the idea
of his protection.

But, he was planning to part from her! She wanted to
think he felt enough loyalty to see the mission through to
its end, but if Bree was correct, then Adam would abandon her. She wasn't sure what was bothering him, but if
he was upset about shooting Roby, then—

Then what? she thought, dragging in a deep breath of
the wet evening air. He should stay with her to trip's
end because he wanted the stallion. He should stay
with her because he wanted to protect her. He should stay
with her because that was what she wanted!

Suddenly, and she couldn't recall that he had moved,
his strong, slim fingers were closing over her upper arms.
She started, then relaxed, a smile touching her mouth that
was so brief as to be nonexistent. Without really thinking
how he might read it, she let herself fall against him, and
felt the heat of his body penetrate the barriers of fabric
and warm her skin.

"What is bothering you, Mariette?" he asked in a gentle, husky voice.

She wanted to tell him that he was the reason she
couldn't sleep, but not for the reason he might suspect.
From the first moment her eyes had met his own, she had
been denying that she was drawn to him, that the very
thought of him wrapped her in a blanket of molten fire.

She wanted to tell him that she was repulsed by him because he would even consider leaving her. But her body was not responding to his nearness as though she were repulsed by him. Should she simply tell him that she knew he was planning to turn her over to Harley Pitkins, and entreat him to stay with her? Wouldn't that be the forth-right thing to do? But she didn't want him to know how much she cared about him. She wanted to tell him that she hated him for shooting Roby, but she knew how badly he felt about that. She wanted to turn and sling insults and degradations at him . . . but her heart simply wasn't in it.

She turned in his arms and pressed her cheek gently to the broad expanse of his chest. "I confess, Adam. I'm brave—" She had deliberately forced humor into her voice as she spoke those last words, but now quietly con-tinued, "But I'm not nearly as brave as I would have everyone believe."

"I disagree," he murmured, his hands folding across her slender shoulders. "You're about the bravest woman I've ever come across." Then he wondered, quite off the subject, what a woman like Mariette might wear beneath a man's trousers, and a bit of crimson flowed into his cheeks.

"Adam?"

"Hmmm?" *Bloomers would be too full. Something of her own design, perhaps?*

"You didn't really think I would shoot the cardinal the other day, did you?"

Or, better yet. Nothing at all! "Ah, so that is why you can't sleep! Because you're worried that I might think you're a cold-hearted woman!" Pride eased into his tone. "I saw the way you smiled when you saw the beautiful creature," he half-chuckled. "And I knew you wouldn't have shot it." He laughed now, holding her more firmly to him. "And if you had, I *would* have made you eat it!"

Joining in his laughter, she said, "You're a gentle man, Adam Cassidy. Why do you have to be so angry all the time? What has so deeply hurt you that you're always on the defensive," she hesitated to add, "against, I would imagine, all women." When he failed to respond, she forced herself to ask, "Who is Emily?"

His breathing instantly stopped. She was sure she had felt a shudder as he put a small bit of space between them. When she lifted her gaze to his own darkly narrowed one, he asked, "Where did you hear her name?"

She shrugged lightly, attempting to return her cheek to its comfortable spot against his chest. He would not allow it. His rueful gaze forced her eyes to slide upward once again. "That night in Michael's room," she replied. "When I opened the window, I heard you murmur her name in your sleep."

His fingers closed firmly over her shoulders, and when he saw her wince, the grip loosened. "I don't ever want you to speak her name again. If you do, you will never see me again."

Her gaze gripped his angry one. "You would leave me here alone?"

"I would," he said, his teeth gritting so hard his jaw was a sharp line. His body softened as he drew her back to him, and his arms circled her shoulders. "I love holding you, Mariette. You're soft and warm and, blast, so—"

When he hesitated, she prompted, "So what?" She was surprised that his warning had instantly transcended his anger and his tone was now soft and loving. Though she didn't plan it, she lifted her eyes to him, her lips parted, and she watched his full, masculine mouth through narrow, thoughtful eyes. There was very little expression in his features, and what did fill his eyes, she did not fully understand. She imagined that if a man had a lusty gaze, then this was it, his eyes narrow, gleaming, one dark eyebrow slightly raised, as if in contemplation. When his head moved slightly, and his breathing now whispered hotly upon her cheek, she lifted her mouth, expecting his kiss.

She was not disappointed. As his full, moist mouth covered her own, gently, commandingly caressing it as it had never before been caressed, she savored the wondrous moments, pressing her body close to his own. She was trembling, but she didn't know why. She wasn't afraid, she wasn't cold,—her body was trembling in anticipation. She had never before felt so much desire, nor had she been with a man who made a river of hot fire encompass her flesh from head to toe. She could feel his sinewy fingers threading through her hair, to keep her from breaking away from his kiss. But couldn't he see that she wanted to be in his arms, enjoying the full command of his mouth, and feeling the wanton surrender of her body to his own, so completely that she was too irrational to feel even a moment of apprehension and fear.

Suddenly, Mariette was embroiled in a quandary. She wanted to make love to Adam Cassidy, not to ensure that he would stay with her, but because she wanted to. She wanted to be in Adam's arms, feeling his magical touch awaken and sear her wondrously through, but she had to know that Roby was all right. *Oh . . . what to do?* she asked herself, her hands closing over his shoulders so firmly that he winced from their brutal pinch.

"Mariette—" He put the smallest breath of space between them, but immediately pulled her back into his arms. "I think you bruised me." Then he saw her eyes, wide . . . fearful, or so he thought . . . her mouth trembling as though she might suddenly burst into tears. "I'm sorry. Shouldn't I have kissed you like that?" In his heart, he knew he shouldn't have, especially since he was planning to leave her in the morning.

"You should have," she breathlessly answered, "but it is so wrong. There is Roby, lying out there and possibly dying from a bullet wound, and there is Lara, whose grandparents will visit at Christmas and expect to take her back home with them. And I want only to be in your arms, Adam—" she hesitated. "And that is wrong . . . so very wrong! I should be worrying about my family and what this horrible mess is doing to them. I should be back at Rourke House, helping Hannah . . . oh, she does have so much to do, what with the children being so exasperating at times, and Michael being bedridden, and our parents in San Francisco, and Uncle Noble being gone to Charleston with his brother, and—"

A gentle index finger touched her mouth. Then without warning, Adam swooped her into his arms. When he turned toward the door, he paused, smiling. "Blast, girl . . . I can't get over you wearing these britches. I've never seen anything like it before in my life."

"They're practical," she explained, her fingers linking behind his neck. "Don't you think so?"

I think I've simply got to know what you wear under them!
"They're very practical," he agreed, "but I do like ladies in skirts—"

She grinned mischievously. "Because a man can get beneath them a little easier, I suppose?"

"Mariette!" He feigned the reproof, refusing to smile, though he smiled inside. Moving into the cabin he soon deposited her to the narrow cot she had moments before left. Now, he knelt beside her, then took her hand in his own. "I believe you need to get a good night's sleep. If the storm lets up, we'll need to get an early start."

She was a little surprised when he moved upward and her hand went immediately to the back of his neck. "Adam?"

His eyes narrowed beneath dark, hooded brows. "Yes, Mariette."

Her mouth trembled, her gaze skittering across his sharp, good looks. "Make love to me."

The smile playing at the corners of his mouth instantly slid away, his eyes narrowing to mere slits. He wanted to make love to her, dammit, he wanted that more than anything, but if he did he would feel obligated to stay with her. "Go to sleep," he ordered gruffly, peeling her hands away from him. "Tomorrow will be a long day."

Her misty emerald eyes followed his movements as he arose and put distance between them. She watched him stand beside his cot, his back turned to her, his right hand rising to sweep back a lock of his rich blond-silver hair. She wondered what he was thinking, why he hesitated to climb beneath the blanket and seek much-needed sleep of his own. Making a pillow of her arm, Mariette's gaze remained upon him, as first he turned toward the door, and then turned back to the cot. Twice, it appeared that he would leave—a humiliation she felt and attempted to hide—and as she realized that he was as confused as she was, she smiled. She had only to wait, because he was thinking about her and the small request she had made. If he accepted her, and made love to her, then he would not leave her come morning.

Adam's teeth gritted so firmly that pain shot through his neck. The alluring creature lay just a few feet away, and he could feel her eyes boring through him. Good senses warned him to walk away from her, but the painful reaction of his body to her request made it impossible to put distance between them.

He turned to face her now, his dark, lusty gaze full upon her, though he could see only the vague outline of her features through the veil of darkness. Then he returned, dropped to one knee and groped among the covers for her hand. Holding it against his mouth, he asked, "Now, this love you want to make with me . . . is that holding and cuddling and a little kiss now and then . . . or do you mean *love,* and will it obligate me?"

"I think the proper word is fornication . . . and yes, it will obligate you."

"I don't like that word. It's vulgar."

"Obligate or fornication?"

"Mariette . . ."

"Then call it what you will. Or don't call it at all, and let's just do it."

"For a well-born Philadelphia lady, you're being very coarse, Mariette."

His low, husky tone, scarcely a reprimand, managed to bring a smile to her lips. "Am I really coarse and vulgar, Adam Cassidy?"

He quickly responded, "No," lest she change her mind. Rising, throwing off his shirt, he moved toward a large braided rug before the hearth, where only a few glowing embers hinted at life. Dropping to his knees, his hand went out, coaxing her to him. Damn what making love to her would do to him! Let it obligate him! Let it do what it would because he could not deny himself.

Mariette slid from the cot and sauntered toward him. He watched the gentle sway of her hips, the way she circled him, then dropped to her knees before him on the rug. Soon, she was bending forward, her fingers plying a gentle coarse up both of his thighs. Then she touched her mouth to his own, her fingers evading the hardness of his loins and moving across the sinewy muscles of his chest to close over his shoulders.

Her kiss played sweetly across his cheek, much as a child kissing a favored doll to soothe away an imaginary hurt. She did not protest as his fingers deftly began to unfasten the buttons of her blouse, but when his hands eased beneath the fabric and it began to flow down her arms, she caught her breath and held it, her gaze skittering across his dark, lusty features.

Now, the fear and apprehension flooded her. Now, when his hands were roaming over her warm, exposed flesh, did she wonder what she was doing. But as his fingers slid into the tight waistband of her trousers, she knew there was no turning back.

Not now.

Not that she wanted to.

Eleven

Adam's fingers eased beneath her pert chin and lifted her mouth to his own, caressing it with a gentleness that he thought would make her feel safe, secure, and happy. Yet, he wanted her to want all there was of him; though this moment had been of her own making, he feared she might suddenly change her mind. The tender kiss deepened into a touch of fiery passion as his hands firmly, though gently, traveled a path from her shoulders, along the smooth skin he had moments before exposed, then on a deliberate course down her spine. His mouth followed a hot, moist path across her cheeks, her temples, her violet eyelids, then plummeted into the tiny throbbing pulse in her neck. He wanted the treasure of supple flesh beckoning to him, peaking against his chest like hot pokers, and as he captured one, then the other, he felt the breath rush from her body in one swell swoop.

His movements instantly ceased, his passion-filled gaze connecting to her now frightened one. "Do you want me to stop, Mariette?"

Her body eased backward on the carpet, her arms lying limply on either side of her. Alien emotions struggled within her, driving her into a vortex as confusing as anything she had ever experienced. What a time to question her own motives! Of course, she wanted him to stay with her as they kept to Roby's and Lara's trail, but was that reason enough to make love to the man? And was it, indeed, the reason, or only the excuse?

It was certainly a quandary, and she wasn't sure at the moment what she should do. When the weight of his slim body dropped to her soft one, she felt his iron-hard chest fuse to her tender breasts and suddenly all her tugging emotions flew off with the wind. She wanted only to be with him, like this, to love and be loved by him. She knew that she should be afraid, and in a very small way she was. She knew she should have scooted out from beneath him, intent on preserving her virginity, but it was the last thing on earth she wanted to do. She wanted him, to enjoy the awakening she had been longing for since she was a girl of seventeen. She wanted to see fireworks, like on the Fourth of July, and she could almost see them now, within the darkened cabin.

She had thought of nothing but this intimacy since meeting Adam Cassidy. She had dreamed of him at night, and had struggled with her opposing emotions by day.

Her hands moved to claim his shoulders, hard and tense, as he perched above her, his mouth tasting the delicious warmth of her own. She was aflame . . . her slender body craved the attentions of his commanding one, and as his mouth moved lovingly over the curves of her overly warm cheeks, she closed her eyes so that she might completely, uninhibitingly enjoy the musky, manly scent of him against her, filling her lungs so that she might explode for want of him.

"If you want me to stop," he almost grumbled against her damp hairline, "then this is the time to tell me." He wasn't sure why she wanted this, and he quietly cursed her timing. Just this morning he had asked one of the Pitkins men if one among them would take his place as her escort, and now . . . here this remarkably beautiful angel lay gently on her back, her eyes like beacons of love, her full, sensual mouth having quietly uttered, "Make love to me," just moments ago . . . words that still echoed in his head. If he didn't know better he would have sworn that she knew of his plan, and that this was her way to make him stay. She knew that he wouldn't be able to leave a woman he had lain with in intimate passion.

But he had asked Harley Pitkins to say nothing to her, and he had no reason to believe he hadn't honored that request. And now, the velvety softness of feminine flesh lay beneath his caressing fingers, and he raised one hand, gently touched her chin, then traced the line of her profile. He only now realized that she had crossed her hands upon her breasts, and with an admiring smile he took one of her hands and kissed each finger in turn.

"Don't hide yourself, Mariette. You are so perfect. Don't you realize that?" Her thick, flaming masses had fanned out on the rug, and her eyes were moisture-sheened, gazing at him with something akin to fear. Ceasing his movements for a moment, he touched a kiss to her pert nose. "You look as though I will hurt you, Mariette. Are you afraid of me?"

She shook her head, then slowly nodded, attempting to extract her hand so that she might again cover herself. But he would not allow it.

The feelings swelling inside of Mariette confused and disoriented her. Her heart beat almost painfully, and though she wanted to feel his hard muscles against her softness, she was also fearful of that same touch. Suppose he hurt her, though she didn't think he would do so deliberately. She was almost glad of the tight trousers that would scarcely allow for the explorations of his hand, were he to make the move, but in the same moment, she wanted to be free of the restrictive bindings. Oh, what was the matter with her, and why couldn't she decide exactly what it was she wanted?

She knew only that she was much too conscious of her nudity above her waist, of the lustful admiration of his eyes and the masterful explorations of his hands along the throbbing pulses of her lithe body. She had felt something strangely wonderful happen to her breasts when he had touched them, and now they hurt for want of his attentions once again. She was glad of the cover of darkness, and she hoped he could not see the tears gathering in her eyes, or her mouth trembling so violently. She sucked her lower lip between her teeth, biting it hard enough to hurt, and hoping that the trembling might stop. Her entire body, from head to toe, was a dead giveaway that she had never been with a man.

Suddenly, she realized that his hand was at the waist of her trousers, his fingers gently popping the buttons. She fought the urge to slap away the offensive intruder, but in the same moment, she felt an aching heat crawl through her abdomen. When he began to slide the trousers down her hips and her slim thighs, she slightly lifted her buttocks, to allow for the undressing. She saw a smile touch his mouth through the foggy darkness.

Adam smiled as he witnessed the undergarment beneath her trousers that had kept him wondering for the past half an hour. The garment was small, silky, open at the sides with a narrow band hugging her waist and one small button at the left side. He'd never seen anything like it, and imagined that she'd made them especially to wear on those special occasions when trousers were necessary.

He liked the way they looked on her, hiding very little of her, and yet keeping from his view the beauty of her most intimate place. Now his gaze traveled upward and settled on her pale features.

"I like this little silky thing," he half-chuckled, easing his fingers into the waist. "It's quite flattering—"

"I had my seamstress make them," she said softly, "and I'm afraid she was quite appalled by the request. I believe she remarked that they should be red and worn by a woman of the evening."

"White—" His body moved to cover her, and his hands balled into her open palms above her head. "Virginal white, Miss Mariette Donovan. And how much longer will you be entitled to wear them?"

"I would imagine . . . not much longer." His loins were hard against her, and she wished that he'd taken the trousers down the full length of her legs. She felt a little awkward, and her feet were bound by the fabric. But, perhaps that was good. It kept her knees together for a little while and allowed very little room to accommodate his male body. She smiled, remembering her Grandmother Diana telling her when she'd had her first gentleman caller at the age of seventeen, *Be sure to keep your hand on your little bit of fluff . . . and if you forget, remember the date to tell the doctor.*

Adam buried his right hand into the rich, silken tresses while his other stroked a hot trail along her most intimate curves. Then he kissed each peaked breast in turn, traced a line from the valley between to her navel with his tongue, then rose to his knees so quickly that it startled her. Gently, he pulled her trousers down, exposing the slim columns of her legs and when his finger eased into the waist of the underpants, her hand curled around his wrist, halting him.

"Don't—"

He halted at once, fearing that if he rushed her, she might suddenly scoot upward and dash away from him. His fingers eased from the band of the silky garment, then began to unfasten his trousers. Mariette gasped in awe and surprise when the maleness of him was free of the trousers and she immediately snapped her eyes shut. When again she opened them, to his dark, hooded features this time, he was completely nude, his clothing lying in the pile with her own at the edge of the rug.

Now, the only things standing between them were fear and "her little silky thing". And now, she felt his attentions returning to that; he made no move to take it off her, but his fingers had wrapped around the thin band at the left side, where the little button was located.

The breath again rushed from her body as his other hand moved gently down her outer thigh, then to her overly warm inner thigh. Momentarily, she felt the penetration of his fingers beneath her "little silky thing", and instinctively, her thighs fell apart to allow for the intimate caress. She dared not open her eyes, because she was sure she would see the explosion of fireworks within the small room, so bright that he would be able to see every detail of her features. He would see her own lust and desire, and then he might laugh at her.

Adam's loins ached so badly that he wanted only to rip that blasted thing from her and bury himself deeply. But he suspected that she *was* a virgin, though he couldn't imagine how she could remain so at her age, and he wanted her to enjoy every moment. He forced calm into his hard body crawling with brutal passion and, with one unpredictable movement, popped the button and tore the garment down her slender thighs. A small groan escaped her, and though she tried to grab the garment before it was flung away, he was much too quick for her.

Now the flashes of lightning betrayed the treasure of her body to him, slim and ivory, without so much as a small mole to mar its beauty. She was magnificent there, as his hands eased across her now drawn up knees, and he touched a kiss to the triangle of tight copper curls. She gasped, attempting to scoot out from beneath him, but he dropped quickly between her knees and his kisses traveled a deliberate path from her naval, up to circle each of her full, firm breasts, then along the slim column of her neck to capture her mouth in sweet, tormenting, teasing caresses.

"Don't be afraid, Mariette . . . I will not hurt you. I won't," he murmured, pressing his maleness against the apex of her thighs, but making no move to enter her.

Something painfully hot and exciting grabbed at Mariette's insides. She was a novice at lovemaking, and yet she knew what she wanted. She wanted to feel the fullness of him inside her, the heat of his torso pressed to her own . . . she wanted to snatch the kisses he offered her and drink in the lust of his eyes . . . yes, she wanted all this . . . The fear flew away.

His hands masterfully traced a path over every passion-sensitive inch of her body. When his finger dipped into the honeyed sweetness of her most intimate place, she rose to meet his caress. His mouth dipped to claim hers again and again she nipped him with the playfulness of a wild cat. And when she felt his movements and the positioning of the smooth, velvety hardness of him against her, her knees pressed invitingly against his hips.

Adam's fear of hurting her in any way was very close to causing his complete withdrawal. She had only to look at him with fear and he would leave her alone . . . she had only to draw in one gasp of horror, and she would still be a virgin in the morning.

But her long, tapered fingernails were digging into his flesh, closing over his shoulders in an effort to draw him close, and her hips were rising to accept him.

And when she whispered deliriously, "Now . . . please, now, Adam," her body arching against the throbbing length of him, he eased into her hot, moist depths and dragged his fingers through her flaming hair in the same moment.

Mariette felt the fullness of him, pleasant, erotic, naughty. She had thought there would be pain, but there was only delicious torment. She had thought tears would sting her eyes, but they were clouded by pure, unadulterated lust for him. She waited for him to move within her, but for the moment, he seemed content to simply fill her, and she knew there had to be much, much more than this.

She was confused by his deeply growled, "Now, Mariette . . . are you ready for me now?" She gently nodded. At that moment, he drove himself into her with such force that she cried out as the reeling pain burst within her. The surprise made her try to crawl out from beneath him, but his hands had held her hips, his mouth bruisingly claiming her trembling one.

He quickly kissed away the unrestrained tears traveling down her temples and into her hairline, with a promise, "Relax a moment, sweet Mariette."

The pain subsided at once, and she instinctively moved to accept his trembling mouth against her own. The fullness of him was wonderfully exciting, and she began to match his rhythm and pace, her mouth claiming his kisses again and again.

She had never realized that the powerful strength of a man could be so naughty, so enjoyable, and she wanted their union never to end. She wasn't sure if the rumble was of the thunder outside, or of the now frenzied gyrations of their own bodies seeking fulfillment. She wasn't sure if lightning flashed, or if it was the lusty gleam of his eyes. She felt a gripping strangeness fill her abdomen, and her hands closed over his shoulders just as his seed exploded within her. Then, with a deep, pleasant groan, he pulled her into a tight embrace and collapsed against her.

Mariette realized only then that the pulsation ricocheting through her abdomen was not only his, but her own, as she shared in the mutual, rapturous culmination of their lovemaking, fully, and completely.

When his breathing slowed its erratic pace, Adam whispered huskily, "There is a god after all." He snuggled against her cool, damp shoulder, enjoying the touch of her fingers as they swept back his unkempt silvery-blond hair. Then, with a low groan, he withdrew from her, falling to her side to pull her close. "It'll be better for you next time, Mariette, I promise. And it won't be so quick." With that he lay quietly, closing his eyes and enjoying her womanly softness in the aftermath of their love.

She did not dwell on the fact that it was wonderful for her, and she could not imagine it being better. "Adam?"

His mouth touched a tiny kiss to her cheek. "Ummmm?"

"Will you respect me in the morning?"

His head snapped up, his dark, hooded brows easing immediately into his forehead. "What the hell?"

"Will you respect me in the morning?" she repeated. "It's a reasonable question—"

"No, Mariette." Humored sarcasm touched his voice as he looked at her. "I'll see you as a wanton hussy who spread her legs to a man she's known for two weeks."

Then he laughed, drawing her into a tight embrace. "Of course, I will respect you! What kind of question is that?"

Sharing his smile, she said, "I sort of enjoy having you around, Adam Cassidy. You're—" she hesitated, then added, "fun." She simply had to find a way to interrogate him on his plans for tomorrow, and whether he had changed his mind about giving her over to one of the Pitkins men for the rest of the journey. But could she bring it up without him being suspicious, without him knowing that she'd gotten wind of his plans? And, thus, would question her motives for making love to him? Well, she had to take that chance. "Adam?"

"Hmmmm?"

Diplomacy ruled the moment. "Thank you for taking this journey with me. I don't know what I'd have done if you hadn't agreed. And . . . I forgive you for shooting Roby. I know you thought you were protecting me."

"It was hot-headed," he responded regretfully, "and I wish it hadn't happened." Closing his arm protectively across her shoulders, he lightly ordered, "Now . . . let's get some sleep."

Mariette closed her eyes, enjoying the warmth of him, the way his arm clasped her shoulder as though he were making a claim to her, and she fought back the tears stinging behind her eyelids.

Why was she having her doubts now as to her motives? It wasn't only so that he would stay with her, but because she had wanted to be loved by him. She didn't know what she would do if he found out that Bree had told her of his plans.

It took a long time to fall asleep, though she heard him lightly snoring a few minutes later. Well past midnight, she listened to the thunder and rain, and watched the treacherous flashes of lightning across the jagged form of the palisades, and just before sleep finally overcame her, she knew it was almost time to arise and face the new day.

She awakened first, dressing hastily as Adam slept, then crept from the cabin just as the sun was topping the woodline. The rain had stopped, but the compound was a carpet of thick red mud and she did not want to step down into it. She stood on the porch for a moment, tucking in her blouse and dragging a comb through her thick, tangled masses, then retrieved a length of ribbon from the pocket of her trousers, hastily braiding her hair and tying the end with the ribbon. As she finished, she saw Bree exit the long house, throw out a bucket of murky water, then wave to her as she reentered the interior.

For a moment, Mariette's eyes scouted the dryest trail to the long house. Choosing a trail, she moved onto it and soon knocked at the door Bree had just entered. The older woman called, "Come in," and Mariette stepped into the long house.

"Good morning," she greeted, catching a whiff of frying bacon and eggs cooking on a grill.

Bree flashed a wide smile, asking, "Well, did you convince him to stay with you?"

Mariette shrugged, then dropped into a chair at a long, narrow table. Harley Pitkins entered from another door, and Mariette said, "Good morning." When he had moved down the length of the long house and out of hearing range, she responded to Bree, "I think he will stay, though he hasn't said so. I thank you for telling me of his plans."

Bree's finger went immediately to her lips, hushing Mariette. "Harley'll be fit to be tied if he knows I told you." She grinned, resuming her work at the frying pan. "Tell me, what did you say to convince him?"

Mariette liked the woman. She was easy to talk to, and she felt comfortable confiding in her. "It wasn't so much what I said," she replied, guilt lacing the few quiet words, ". . . but what I did."

"And what did you do?" Mariette spun in the chair, her eyes wide with shock as she stared into the features of Adam Cassidy. "Well, Miss Donovan . . . what *did* you do to convince me to stay with you?"

Her mouth trembled; tears moistened her eyes. "I . . . I don't know what you mean," she continued with more inflection. "Bree and I were just making conversation."

"Oh, I see."

The murderous look in his eyes frightened her. "When will we leave this morning?" She watched him observe their surroundings, then, spotting Harley, move in that direction without answering her.

She knew he thought she had tricked him into staying with her, but that was so far from the truth that she wanted to drag him around to face her and sling her denials. At first, she had wanted to make love to him because it would ensure his loyalty to the rescue, but that had only been the excuse. Oh, couldn't he see how much she cared about him, and how much she had wanted to make love to him? Could she have pretended to enjoy being with him so much, if she had merely been tricking him?

Tears touched her lower lids, but she quickly wiped them away. Then she looked to the silent Bree and said, "I believe he's very upset with me."

"As well he should be," she responded at once. "A man doesn't like to be tricked."

What had happened between Adam and her was their business, and not open to discussion with anyone else.

The people of the compound were beginning to stir, fully awake. Within moments, several men had entered the long house, nodded politely, then filled plates with biscuits, eggs, and bacon.

Mariette watched Adam exit the south end of the long house with Harley Pitkins. He believed that she had made love to him for selfish reasons, and she didn't know how to convince him otherwise.

She wasn't sure how long she sat there, exchanging mindless small talk with the inhabitants of the compound, but she did notice the sunlight becoming brighter at the windows. Soon, she stood from the table, exchanged polite amenities and moved into the warm, rain-sogged morning. Immediately, she saw their horses saddled at the cabin, ready for travel, and she breathed a sigh of relief. Adam would stay with her, and somehow, someway, she would convince him of her deepest feelings for him. It wasn't just his company she wanted. She wanted the man. She wanted to be with him always.

Stepping to the muddy ground, she moved precariously in the tracks of larger boots. Then she stepped up to the porch, made a half-hearted attempt to scrape the mud from her boots on the planked boards, then entered the cabin to gather her things. She had thought Adam would be there, but he was not.

"Are you ready, Miss Donovan?"

Surprised by the voice of Harley Pitkins outside, Mariette spun about. He was standing in the doorway, one large hand against the facing. "What . . . yes, of course, I'm ready to go. Is Mr. Cassidy waiting for me?"

"I'll be with you until we locate your people," he said

huskily. "Mr. Cassidy says he'll return the stallion to Rourke House."

Feeling sick and faint, Mariette dropped heavily to the edge of the cot. When a concerned Harley Pitkins approached her, she waved her hand away. "It is nothing personal, Mr. Pitkins, but I started the trip with Mr. Cassidy, and I will resume the trip with Mr. Cassidy. You tell him that, and then you tell him I'm waiting here to talk to him."

"He said you're a treacherous vixen, Miss Donovan, an' he don't want nothin' more to do with you—" Her eyes caught his humored features, and when they filled with tears, his grin slid away. "I'm sorry. I reckon he was jus' funnin'—"

"Tell him to come talk to me. Please, Mr. Pitkins."

He had scarcely cleared the door before she collapsed into a sobbing bundle on the cot. Dragging her balled hand against her forehead, she muffled her sobs in the hard pillow, drawing her legs up to the coarse fabric of the blanket. No . . . no, she couldn't allow him to catch her crying. He would think it another trick; he wouldn't believe she was genuinely distraught.

Lord, what had she done? She was the most vicious kind of woman, and he deserved better than her. But didn't he know how her heart was breaking, and couldn't he find it in his own heart to forgive her? Swinging herself erect, Mariette dried her tears on the sleeve of her blouse, then grabbed up a comb and began dragging it through the tips of her hair. It snagged her loose braid at once and pulled it free, so that when she heard his footfalls on the narrow porch, she was an untidy mess, and probably presented herself to him as a mad woman.

She pivoted smartly, seeing only a narrow line of him through the curtain of her hair. But she saw enough of him to notice that he was livid. She managed the smallest of smiles as she parted the hair from her face.

"You came. . . . Good—"

"Of course," he responded with heavy sarcasm. "Wasn't I summoned?"

She had thought she would throw herself at his feet and beg for mercy, beg him to stay with her. But as she looked into his lethally narrowed eyes, she knew he would not succumb to that. He was so angry she was sure all of her entreaties would fall on deaf ears. So in that single moment, she devised a new scheme, one that she prayed would work.

Assuming her most professional tone, Mariette said, "Mr. Pitkins said you would return the stallion to Rourke House. I would request that you allow me sufficient time to write a letter to my sister. I will travel on alone to find Roby and Lara, and should anything happen to me—"

"You'll do no such a damned thing! Harley will go with you."

"He will not. And if he tries, I'll shoot him dead before he has time to say his prayers. Now—" She turned to the small valise she'd brought with her from Philadelphia. "I'll write the letter and I'll bring it to you in a few minutes."

"You're not going on alone."

"I am." She sat at a small, handmade table, her back turned to him, and her hand preparing the pen, ink, and paper she'd taken from the valise. "I can take care of myself—" She listened to his approaching bootsteps, preparing for almost anything . . . but she had not prepared herself for being dragged up by his powerful hands and jerked around to face him. Now, she was the livid one. "How dare you!"

His eyes raked her, his mouth sneering so viciously that

she wasn't sure what he would say—or do—next. She felt her feet being lifted off the floor, only her toes maintaining contact. His grip on her upper arms was so hard that she fought to keep the pain from marring her features. Then, when she thought he might toss her away like so much rubbish, he dragged her against him, and his mouth roughly, bruisingly claimed her own . . . so quickly and so painfully that she instinctively bit him.

Now she was tossed off, and as she righted herself against the cot, he raised his fingers to his bleeding mouth. "You bitch—"

"A bitch who can take care of herself, Adam Cassidy," she hissed. "Now, get out!"

So sure was he that she might suddenly spring and kill, that he turned, shouting at her across his shoulder, "I'll wait ten minutes for that damned letter . . . and then I'm leaving here!"

Twelve

Roby had been shot before, and he knew from experience that the wound inflicted on him by the stranger was not too serious. Still, he wanted only to sleep in those three days since he'd been to the Pitkins compound, and Lara was so fearful of him dying that every time he'd fallen asleep, she jabbed him in the ribs to awaken him.

In his lucid moments, he'd decided that she was quite a good little nurse, even though her bedside manners left something to be desired. Still, he would rather see her pert, pretty features when he opened his eyes than to see nothing but the darkness of the cave. She had gone to hunt berries and graze their horse in the misty aftermath of still another mountain storm, and had managed to talk an old Indian out of a small venison roast. Now she sat, cooking it over a fire she had made herself. He watched her from beneath the rim of his hat; as the meat cooked, she would cut off a piece and eat it. But the nibbles were coming less frequent now, and Roby imagined that she was getting full, perhaps even leaving some to fill the emptiness of his own stomach.

Her gaze cut across the dark interior and connected to

his own. He smiled. "You were afraid I'd die, weren't you, pretty lady?"

"You're a halfbreed Indian pig." She grumbled the insult. "And I couldn't care less if you died." Lara knew that wasn't true, but she couldn't let her guard down, or give him reason to think he was winning her affections. He should be punished for what he'd done: taking her from the comfort and security of Rourke House, dragging her off to the mountains and ravishing her. She imagined that some judicious form of punishment would be awaiting him when he was taken back in chains.

"What are you thinking?" he continued in his same light tone.

"I was thinking that I'll laugh when they tie the rope around your hideous neck and leave nothing beneath your boots but air. Yes, I think I'll laugh my bloody head off!"

Roby managed to sit up, groaning in pain as he did so. Then he scooted across the hard ground toward her, momentarily tearing off a small piece of the cooking meat. As he popped it into his mouth, he watched her long and hard, waiting for the small, certain flinch of self-consciousness his stares always produced. He did not have long to wait.

"What are you looking at, you bastard!" Jerking her shoulder around, she managed to show him a good part of her back. "I don't want you looking at me," she ended on a quieter note.

"Why . . . I thought you liked the way I looked at you. Didn't you want me to look at you when you took off your clothes at the river? Didn't you want to see my reaction to your very charming state of undress then? So, why can't I look at you now that you are my woman?"

"I am not your woman. You . . . you raped me!" she brutally reminded him.

"Ah—" His fingers moved to the fringe of her neckline. "And you *fought so hard,* didn't you, my sweet? I certainly didn't have to push those pretty knees apart. So, it can hardly be rape if you were willing enough to scratch the hell out of my back as you pulled me down to you."

She turned to face him now, her eyes spitting fury. "Shut up! I don't want to hear your version of what happened! The authorities will believe *my* version. And as far as I am concerned, you raped me. For that you will die by the white man's law—"

"And I've been fairly well out of it for three days. You could have taken the horse and high-tailed it for Philadelphia."

She might have continued the argument if a flapping of wings hadn't sounded very nearby. As they turned, a large black bird pitched on a rock, then sat there and stared at them.

"Get rid of it!" Lara harshly whispered.

Roby laughed. "It's just an ugly old crow."

Then the bird, turning his small, dark eyes full upon them, said, "Quote the raven nevermore."

Roby laughed, his hand going out to invite the bird to it. "Why you little skunk," he continued to laugh as the bird perched on his wrist. "What are you doing here?"

"Get rid of that beast!" Lara ordered, her eyes wide with horror. "Crows are evil—"

Roby tore off a small bit of meat and handed it to the bird called Poe by its master. "He's a raven."

"Same difference."

"And he belongs to a friend of mine. An Iroquois—" When he turned his eyes and saw the sheer terror in her features because of the bird's presence, he waved it off and it again settled on the rock near the entrance to the cave. "Damn, girl, what is wrong with you?" She was trembling so violently she could hardly move. Roby drew her into his arms. "What the hell is this? It's just a bird, for God's sake . . . and he's gentle as a kitten—"

Beads of sweat popped out on her forehead, and Roby noticed her watching every movement the bird made. It felt her fear, for its small eyes intimidatingly held her wide-eyed stare.

Roby thought it the oddest thing he'd ever seen in his life, the bird and the woman staring each other down, the woman so afraid that she could only tremble in his arms. It was time to end the standoff, before the rest of the venison burned, and as Roby picked up a small rock to frighten off the raven, a dark human form appeared at the entrance to the cave.

The Iroquois hunter, known as Erie through the region, immediately brought up his long rifle, for a man who would attack a tame bird would attack him as well. Then, recognizing Roby the instant the darkness parted from his eyes, he smiled engagingly. "So, the bird has found a friend who chunks rocks at him," Erie said, moving into the cave, then settling onto his knees beside the fire. "And the friend has found a woman, eh?" Then he looked to Lara, his head cocking to the side for a moment, and said, "But one whose sky is filled with pigeons!"

Roby took his friend's proferred hand and held it tightly. "It is good to see you, Erie." The hand offered to Erie in friendship now returned to Lara's slim shoulder. "No, the woman is all right. I believe the raven frightened her."

With that, Erie flicked his hand at the bird and it flew off into the forest. "There, the bird is gone. Now . . . how about some of that meat?" He did not await permission, but withdrew his knife and cut off a thick slice.

Absently, Lara's gaze drifted to the harsh bronze features of the Iroquois hunter. She thought him most primitive looking: his leggings and loin cloth filthy, his bare chest gleaming with sweat, and his dark hair adorned by a multitude of feathers. But he smiled easily, which took away some of the panic she felt. After a moment, Lara apologized, "I'm not particularly fond of ravens since being attacked by one when I was a girl. My grandfather had brought it home to Holker Hall, as a novelty, he'd said. The nasty creature immediately flew at me and pecked my face."

"You are still but a girl," Erie laughed. "But Poe will not attack you. He will speak to you in the poet's tongue, and he will teach you to count to four—if you cannot already do so—but he will not be unkind."

"Why is it that you speak so well?" asked Lara, recovering her prior mood. "And with an English accent?"

"Cambridge. My white father sent me to be educated in England." Then a thread of sunlight caught upon his face, and piercing blue eyes surrounded by bronze skin smiled at Lara. He continued, "I am unpopular in the ranks of my mother's people, so I keep to myself and to the mountains. My friends are the animals . . . and a few good people like your man there."

"He's not my man!" Softening her voice, though sarcasm lightly laced it, she continued, "I suppose you apologize to the animals you kill to eat?"

"Listening to those stories told by your English fathers about the Indians, and how they respect all life except that of the white man, eh?" Erie finished off the piece of meat. "I do not kill animals to eat," he continued. "I eat meat only if I come across it already dead—like this. I am an eater of fish—" He shrugged, dropping to support his weight on one bent elbow on the hard-packed earth, "and occasionally I will eat a chicken, if I can get it out of the coop before my backside is filled with buckshot." Only now noticing the bandage surrounding Roby's middle, he asked, "Came across a white man, did you?"

Roby settled against the cave wall, then eased Lara against him. "I ran into a particularly mean westerner at the Pitkins place. They're fortifying again. Are your brothers on the warpath?"

"I claim no Iroquois as my brother," said Erie with a strong note of boasting. "I claim only the mountains as my kin and my spirit." To Roby's inquiry, he continued, "I hear rumors, and the rumors are that they will avenge the death of one of their own at the hands of Jasper Pitkins. You know that his daughter-in-law, Bree, is Iroquois stock. The man she had first been betrothed to came to take her back and the old man killed him. Nay, it'll not be safe in the mountains—" Using a small stick to stoke up the fire, Erie asked, "And who is this young English girl you have with you?"

"I'd imagine you already know."

"I'll admit, news travels through the mountains like a strong wind. The Donovan woman is after you." Laughter hid behind the Indian's voice. "And a stranger from the West, as well. Ah, that must be the Westerner who put a bullet in you. I heard that your brother has offered a five-hundred-dollar reward for return of the woman."

Roby's grip instinctively tightened over Lara's shoulders. "Michael is a fool!" Then, with narrow suspicion, "And do you intend to collect that reward?"

"What need have I for five hundred dollars? My father would give me a hundred times that much, if I would don the white man's clothes and walk down the white man's streets with a white man's cane clipping upon the bricks, on my way to a white man's job in a white man's building. Being Indian is better—life is free and entertainingly treacherous, more challenging to a man's heart. No, Michael can keep his money. But the Westerner may want to collect that reward—"

"He'll die trying," boasted Roby, shoving Lara from him in his moment of anger, but immediately drawing her back. "The woman does not want him. The woman wants me!"

Lara turned now, her eyes treacherously narrowed. *"The woman* wants neither of you!" Easing onto her knees, she pulled a piece of venison from the skewer. *"The woman* wants only to eat. Men be damned!"

Mariette Donovan had the same thought. She had pretended illness three mornings ago, when Adam Cassidy had recklessly turned her over to Harley Pitkins. She had enjoyed the small cabin these past few days that the storms had hung over the Alleghenies. Adam was still at the compound, though he'd taken to sleeping elsewhere, and she hoped that he was hanging around because she was still here. She hoped that she had been right about him . . . that he would not leave her after they had made love . . . but thus far he had found a multitude of excuses for hanging around, and none of them had been because of her. In fact, she had only caught a glimpse of him these past few days, and they had exchanged no more than a few words in passing.

Mariette had made easy friends with Bree, the Iroquois wife of Harley Pitkins. She was a little rough but she had a good heart, and she was quick to offer advice to Mariette, even when it was not solicited. Bree was perceptive;

she knew how deeply Mariette cared for Adam Cassidy, and she knew that she was much too stubborn to admit it.

Mariette settled onto the edge of the cot and began to pull on her boots. Quickly dragging a comb through her hair, then tying it back in a length of blue ribbon, she exited into the Allegheny morning, the first in three days that had not been drenched in rain. But the ground was a river of muck and mire, and, blast it, she had just cleaned her boots!

So, she stood on the porch, contemplating which path to take.

"Over your feminine ills, Mariette?"

She turned, narrowly watching Adam Cassidy approach from the side of the cabin. "Were you spying on me?" When he failed to respond, offering, instead, one of his devilish grins, she continued with haste, "I wasn't suffering from feminine ills. I never said I was."

"Just assumed—"

"Don't assume. Just go on your merry way, Adam Cassidy!" She paused, then added, "And leave me be!" When he ended the glaring look, then continued on his way to the long house, Mariette, called out, "And just why are you still here, Adam? Are you staying around just to see what I am going to do?"

He turned, sarcastically tipped his hat and said, "I don't give a damn what you do, Mariette Donovan. Now, quit finding excuses to retain me. I really am hungry for that ham and eggs cooking on Bree's fire."

"Go to hell, Adam Cassidy," she hissed at his retreating back.

Lifting a hand, though not turning back, he drawled, "Yes, ma'am . . . I'm on my way, ma'am. Do you want to go with me, ma'am?"

She watched him until he had disappeared into the

warm, dim interior of the long house before allowing a slight smile to curl her lips. She was fairly certain the man was kin to a demon of some kind.

Justin Laszlo had not effectively played the role of the demon that Dr. Bertrand Redding had assigned to him. Though he had become somewhat of a puzzle to the inhabitants of Rourke House, he had never once done anything even remotely demonic. Hannah had grown very fond of Justin, and was especially grateful to him for the time he had spent with Cassandra. Bertrand, however, had other ideas which he related to Hannah in the warmth of her kitchen that morning.

"I do believe you misinterpreted something he said that day, Bertrand," Hannah argued with little feeling. "He had been shot. Perhaps he'd said something that you just read the wrong way—"

"I'm telling you, Hannah Gilbert, that you need to be wary of that fellow. He's up to something, and whatever it is won't be to the benefit of this household."

With a small sigh, Hannah turned to the table with a skillet, momentarily spooning scrambled eggs and bacon onto the plate she had earlier set for Bertrand. Placing the pan on a trivet, she took a chair across from the doctor and watched him put healthy portions of butter onto two of her freshly baked biscuits. "He's been very cordial, Bertrand," she continued the argument in Justin's behalf. "He has spent time with Cassandra, and has taught her a few Creole words. He and Michael get along beautifully, and Liddy thinks he's the top of the morning. And I have no complaints, Bertrand." With a sigh she added, "Actually, it's been quite pleasant having him here—"

"And Miles? What does the boy think of his distant cousin?"

Hannah shrugged now, taking one of the biscuits and pinching it off in small pieces to put in her mouth. "You delivered Miles, Bertrand. In the years since have you once seen him smile? I'll wager he hasn't smiled half a dozen times in his life. Why? Because he dislikes all people. I would hardly think he'd like Justin . . . even if he *liked* him. Now, I don't want to hear any more negative thoughts about Justin. If, and when, he does something that doesn't settle well with me, then I will ask him to leave. I do believe you know I have good judgment, and that I would not put my children in danger."

"You're too good a woman, Hannah." Bertrand laid his fork aside for a moment. "Just watch him. Don't let him out of your sight."

Hannah wasn't sure where her hostility came from. A small part of her heart did *not* trust Justin Laszlo. Hadn't she forbade Cassandra to visit his apartment, or to be alone with him? Perhaps it was just that she didn't like anyone who was not family, even Bertrand Redding who was *like* family, telling her what to do.

Besides, there was something about Justin that she found very appealing. Though he appeared to be awkward and a bit clumsy, he was, rather, an extremely graceful man. The one time he had touched her, he had done so with gentleness. Instinctively, her fingers curled around her right wrist, and she could almost feel the warmth of his touch, even after these two days. She couldn't recall what had occurred that he should have touched her, but she did remember that it had made her heart flutter with something she hadn't felt in years.

With that thought, Hannah saw Bertrand Redding silently watching the movement of her fingers, and a bit of crimson crawled into her cheeks. She patted them, explaining, "The kitchen is getting too hot. Perhaps I should mellow the fire in the stove."

He grunted a wordless response, then resumed his meal. Presently, he pushed himself from the table, patted his stomach and said, "I should look at Cassandra's arm now, to make sure the ringworm is well healed. Then, I should be on my way to check on Mrs. Trevor, who's due any day now."

"Yes, I know," Hannah absently replied as she busied herself cleaning up the kitchen. She needed to check on the children, to see if they were attending their studies with Miss Lee. They did so hate the hours of summer spent in the school room, and Hannah frequently had to keep after them to pay attention. Usually, a motherly stare from the crack of the door halted any naughtiness they displayed in the school room.

Soon, polite amenities accomplished, she saw Bertrand Redding away in his carriage. Hearing a clatter in the summer room, she moved in that direction, and came across Michael, cleaning his weapons. Before she could question him, he explained, "I'm going after Mariette."

"No, Michael, you're going after Lara. For mercy's sake, let Mariette and Mr. Cassidy bring her back. You needn't go. You and Roby will simply get into it again."

Michael looked down the bore of his rifle. "We'll get into nothing, Hannah, as long as he releases Lara. I think I'll ask Justin to go with me—"

"No!"

That single word caused Michael to halt his labors. Slowly, he lowered the rifle, then stared at the tall woman he considered his cousin. He hadn't realized how thin she had gotten, or how much gray had eased in among the dark strands of her hair. He had never before noticed the tiny lines stretching from the corners of her eyes, eyes that now moistened with tears. "Hannah?" He rose now, laying the rifle aside to approach and close her shoulders within his slim hands. "Do you not want Justin to go with me, because in your heart you do not trust him—" He hesitated to continue, "Or do you wish that he remain here, in the house, with you?" When she lowered her gaze, he continued in a tone of disbelief, "By damn, Hannah Gilbert, you've allowed another man to walk into your heart."

She shook her head in denial, though not with much feeling. "That's not true, Michael. You know that I said I would never love again after Tom was killed."

"You might have said it—" His fingers gently tucked beneath her chin and lifted her gaze to his own. Smiling for her, he continued, "But you didn't mean it. And if my opinion means anything, Hannah, I say, hurrah for you!"

To end the intimidating moment, Hannah hugged him tightly. She had once wished that Michael would notice her in the same way he noticed Lara. They were, after all, not of the same blood. But these past two weeks that Justin had been in the house, she had begun to think more of him each day, and to dream of him at night. She didn't know what it was about him that attracted her so, but she knew that, if he gave her even one iota of encouragement or hinted that he might feel the same about her, she could—and would—fall deeply in love.

So, she drew back from her cousin, then smiled prettily for him. "Men! You're always thinking about falling in love. Well, I think it's all a silly emotion, and you men may have it." Turning away from him now, she moved toward the doorway. "Do reconsider going after Roby, Michael. Mariette can handle herself, and Mr. Cassidy seemed a competent sort. I'm sure Lara will be brought back unharmed and, I pray, before Christmas when her grandparents arrive."

Roby moved to the divan, picked up the rifle and prepared to commence his work. "Then I will join Mr. Cassidy, so that Mariette can return home. Tracking a scoundrel like my brother is no job for a lady like Mariette. She needs to be at home, making herself pretty and appealing for a man. She's past the age of marrying—"

"Pooh! Mariette can take care of herself. And I don't think she does much worrying about men."

Mariette had done enough worrying about one particular man—and his unreasonable moods—in the past three days to last a lifetime. This Westerner . . . this Adam Cassidy . . . she was sick of worrying about him! She wasn't sure what he was hoping to accomplish by hanging around the Pitkins compound, but she imagined he was waiting to see if she would dare carry on alone. Well, she decided with a huff, she'd wasted enough time waiting for him to change his mind about staying with her, and it was time to go on with life . . . and finding Lara before her grandparents got wind of her little adventure. Penley and Anne Seymour had expected the Donovans of Philadelphia to take care of Lara (though Mariette now suspected that they knew that was a considerable job to hoist on innocent people) and by George, she would bring the girl back, even if she had to do it alone! She had a fair idea where Roby would head—if Adam Cassidy's bullet hadn't killed him!

Moving off the porch into the well-tracked mud, she eased toward the lean-to at the back of the cabin. There, she saddled her horse, then brought her around to the front of the cabin. Collecting up her few things from the cabin's interior, she tied the bundle on the back of the saddle, all the while, her eyes watching the movements of the long house. She wasn't really sure whether she wanted Adam Cassidy to appear and try to stop her, then give in and go with her, but she was disappointed when she finally mounted her horse and he hadn't made an appearance. As she eased the mare toward the gate, Bree called to her, then slipped across the mud in her approach of Mariette.

"I packed a knapsack for you, meat and biscuits . . . a canteen of sweetened tea."

Mariette gratefully accepted the woman's thoughtfulness. "Please, don't tell Cassidy that I'm leaving."

Bree placed her finger at her mouth. "Not a word, I promise."

Then they said goodbye and parted. At the palisades, one of the compound residents on the wall opened the gate for her and she moved into the narrow clearing, paused at the edge of the woods and watched the gate being closed again.

Adam Cassidy couldn't care less what happened to her. He would probably be terribly inconvenienced if he rode into the woods later in the day, found her murdered and scalped, and had to take the time to bury her. Well, so much for getting to a man's heart through his loins. She should have listened to Hannah years ago, who had told her to always go through his stomach if she really wanted to make an impression. Adam Cassidy be damned!

The storm would, of course, have erased any trail that Roby might have left. Mariette had only her instincts to guide her through the mountains. With that same instinct, she closed her fingers over the sidearm hanging at her hip, then urged the mare into a trot deeper into the woods.

The morning was overcast, damp and hot, and her mood wasn't much better.

Soon, Mariette managed to forget her troubles. The ground seemed to rise up to meet the hooves of her mare, and when horse and rider dipped into a deep valley between the mountains, she felt a sense of peaceful isolation, as though nothing of this earth could do her harm. The sun was low in the east; the hour was still early, and Mariette felt the heat of the morning as nonchalantly as she might feel a breeze. Still, she kept alert for any sound out of the ordinary.

The miles and the hours rolled by until she knew the time of day only because her stomach growled in protest. She pulled up beneath the thick overhang of a spruce and dismounted. While the mare grazed in the sparse grass of the dale, Mariette ate a meal of biscuits and beef, as warm as if it had come off the fire a few minutes ago.

A bird called across the mountains. Relaxing against the trunk of the spruce, Mariette watched a hawk float gracefully on the wind, its circle becoming wider and wider, until finally the horizon swallowed it up. Then a movement caught her attentions in the thick underbrush, and momentarily, a rabbit darted out, saw her and froze, then dashed for the cover of the forest once again.

Here in this lush, summer retreat, Mariette could almost forget that a world existed beyond the line of the mountains. Though she closed her eyes, she could still see the green freshness of the land; though the air was still damp and heavy, she caught the delicate fragrance of honeysuckle; though her ears caught hardly a sound disturbing the peace, the mountains screamed their strength and bounty. She could become one with this land and be happy, because she'd never been happier than when she was here. But, that wasn't quite true—she'd been blissfully happy in Adam's arms, no matter the motive that had initially driven her there.

Mariette became acutely aware of a sound nearby. Cracking open one eyelid, she watched a blur of dark feathers scurry past her features. Darting forward, she saw a great black bird pitch on a branch overhead. As she feared having her eyes plucked out, it suddenly called, "Quote the raven nevermore."

Mariette grinned. Poe was a notorious resident of the Alleghenies, and he was usually not far from his master, the Iroquois hunter, Erie. "Where is he?" Mariette asked, looking around and expecting to see the tall, statuesque, bronze-skinned Erie. "I'll bet he's right over that mountain there," she continued with teasing laughter. "I'll bet he would help me find Roby and that English tart."

"I'll bet he wouldn't," came a masculine response. Startled, Mariette turned on her knees, her fingers moving quickly toward her gun. Just at that moment, Erie moved from the cover of the spruce against which she had been resting. Dropping to his knees, he placed his bow against the tree. "I think I frightened the color of the evening sky right out of your hair," he laughed. Looking about, a critical gaze soon returned to her. "You're not out here alone, are you?"

Mariette relaxed a little. "I lost my traveling companion," she informed him, regret only too noticeable in her voice. She quickly brightened, "But you know me, Erie, I can take care of myself." She studied the man she had not seen in over a year. If she did not know that he was thirty years old, it would have been hard to guess his age. The agility of youth moved in his tall, slim body, but the lines of age—or he might call it "wisdom"—etched deeply into his features, tanned by the sun to a much darker hue. "I'm looking for Roby," she said. "Have you seen him?" When he hesitated, she asked, "Have you?"

He responded then, "Yes, I have seen him—"

"When?"

"This morning. I shared meat with Roby and the English woman he is traveling with."

"You must tell me where he is."

"I cannot. I will tell you only that his wound is not serious. I know that your man shot him."

"Adam Cassidy is not *my* man." She paused, gaining a moment as she tried to calm the anger she felt at Erie's withheld information. "Why won't you tell me where he is?"

"Because I promised that I wouldn't."

"He took the woman by force."

"She did not appear unhappy to be with him."

"She is young and foolish."

"That is her business."

Mariette realized only then that Erie was watching her strangely, his eyes darting past her, then returning to her quiet gaze. She looked around, immediately catching sight of the timber rattlesnake slithering across the log just behind her. She stiffened, afraid to look back to Erie, afraid to move lest the poisonous beast spring and sink its fangs into her.

Then, without warning, Erie sprang for her, and together they rolled down the hill, until both lay in a crumpled heap in the soggy bottom of the dale.

Erie turned to his back and whispered harshly, "Damn, that was close."

Mariette, struggling to free her leg from the weight of one of his own, was glad of his agility and his quick thinking.

Neither of them saw Mariette's horse take off over the hill.

Nor did either of them see Adam Cassidy perched atop the stallion, rifle aimed for Erie's heart.

Thirteen

Mariette's horse, fleeing across the mountain, was the least of Adam Cassidy's worries at the moment. He knew only that he'd topped the hill just as she was being attacked by an Indian. Sliding the stallion down the treacherously slick hill on its haunches, he soon sprang from the saddle and was rolling with the savage attacker. He might die now, but at least Mariette was safe . . . if only she would have the good sense to drag herself into Charlie's saddle and hightail it over the mountain.

Staving off the Indian's attack, Adam screamed at Mariette, "Go . . . get out of here—For God's sake—"

Instead she rose from the mud, parted her boots by a foot and stood looking down at the two of them with her hands drawn to her slim hips. "Adam Cassidy, what the hell do you think you're doing!" Her hand moved to her sidearm, hesitated, then drew it from its holster.

Adam halted at once, his legs spraddling Erie in the mud, his hands holding the man's wrists down so firmly that they were lost in the muck and mire. His disbelieving gaze moved first to a seething Mariette, holding her sidearm with unwavering calm, then returned to the Indian beneath him. Instantly, Erie smiled. "I believe you better move, Westerner, or the lady will shoot you."

"She's aiming at you!" Adam argued, the rage darkening his features again.

"I'd take another look if I were you," Erie half-chuckled.

Adam glanced up, seeing that her weapon was, indeed, pointed at his own head. "Do you know this man?" he growled, still holding Erie to the ground.

"Of course, I know him!" she said, now reholstering her sidearm.

"But I saw—he was—I thought he was attacking you!"

"He saved my life." Slim hands now flailed the air, to add emphasis to her ire. "We were dodging out of the way of a poisonous snake and lost our footing in the mucky ground. For Heaven's sake, Adam Cassidy, must you shoot everyone you think is going to cause me harm?"

With a low, aggravated grump, he moved from Erie, but kept his eyes full upon the man as he rose from the ground, his body sucking up out of the mud with a somewhat disgusting sound. "So," Erie said, sliding the mud from his arms with a thumb and index finger, "this is the man who shot Roby."

"You told him that?" Adam hissed, "Without telling him the circumstances? Damn, Mariette, why must you constantly make me look like a black-hearted rogue!"

"She told me nothing, Westerner," Erie interrupted. "Roby told me that you had shot him."

"My horse is gone," huffed Mariette, turning, his hands moving slightly upward to pinch the air in her frustration. "What are we going to do about my horse?"

"I'll fetch her," offered Adam, cutting a warning gaze at the Indian.

Adam mounted the stallion and rode off in the direction that the mare had bolted. When he was out of hearing range, Erie asked, "How did you get involved with that hotheaded bastard, Mariette?"

"He's not a bastard. He's—" She fought for the proper words, without betraying that she was sticking up for him, "He's just earning the bounty I offered him to find Lara, and keeping me safe as well."

"Have you shared his lodgings?"

Her eyes widened in surprise as they returned to Erie's features. "What do you mean? Have we slept beneath the same stars? Well, of course, we have—"

"No . . . have you *shared* with him."

"That is none of your business!"

"Ah, so you have." Though he was one to be delicate in his manner of interrogation, Erie was not one to be bashful when he wanted information. If he wanted to assess a situation, he had to know all the details. He had heard Roby's version of the incident that had brought Mariette into the mountains, and not only did he wish to know her version, but he wanted to know why she was traveling with the Westerner. He had promised Roby that he would pick up as much information as he could. He supposed that, considering the dark anger in Mariette's pretty features, he should not have brought up such an intimate subject as a shared bed. So, after the long pause, he said, "Walk with me to that stream down there, while I clean some of this mud off. We can talk—"

"There is nothing to talk about!" Though her response was sharp, she fell in beside him, then stepped gingerly down the muddy slope. She needed a bath as well, because she was as muddy as Erie. "You're notorious, Erie," she shouted, now making the subject more personal. "For sticking your nose into other people's business. And equally as notorious for taking sides, and usually not the sensible one. I don't care what Roby told you, he was wrong to do what he did. And the girl is only sixteen!"

"She said she was seventeen."

"Well she is just barely!"

Halting in the shallows of the babbling brook, she crouched to clean herself up somewhat while Erie moved into the water until he was waist-deep. The raven perched on a limb half a dozen feet above them, fussing and flapping its wings at its bathing master. As Erie began to clean himself off, he got back to the subject she had brought up. "I have not taken sides, Mariette. As for what Roby told me, he said he took the girl from the house in the dark of night, against her will, and dragged her off to the mountains." Erie chose not to inform her that Roby, speaking with deep regret, had confessed to ravishing the pale young Englishwoman. "He feels very badly about what he did, but he said he cannot return her. Not now—"

"Why not now?"

"He claims to care for her." Without warning, Erie went beneath the water, where he stayed for several seconds, then emerged much cleaner than before. Dragging back his dark hair as he moved toward Mariette, he continued, "Why don't you and the Westerner go on back to Philadelphia? Let Roby bring the girl back when he gets damned good and ready. If you insist on going after him, especially in the company of a man who is quick to draw his weapon, someone is going to get hurt." He hesitated to add, "Again." When he stood beside Mariette, one slim hand fell affectionately to her shoulder. "And I don't want that someone to be you, Mariette. You've been a good friend over the years."

When his hand traveled a path along her arm, Mariette climbed up, a little embarrassed by his soft caress. "You were supposed to spend time with us in Philadelphia this past Christmas. Why didn't you come?" She twisted the water from her hair, then flung it at her back.

Turning her in his arms, Erie coaxed her toward a fallen log, where they both sat. "My father and I haven't been getting along very well. When he asked me to come to Virginia at Christmas, I thought that, perhaps, he and I could mend the tension that has existed between us. But the visit did not go well and I left shortly afterward. I wanted to come by Rourke House, but the visit with my father had left me in an especially foul mood." He smiled now. "You forgive me, don't you?"

"Of course I do," she responded, giving him an affectionate punch on his shoulder. "We just missed seeing you, that's all, and we were afraid something might have happened. How is your mother, by the way?"

"She died in March."

Mariette gasped, instantly surprised that she hadn't received news from Hester at the trading post, who kept up with the goings-on of everyone in the region. "I'm so sorry. I didn't know."

"It was kept quiet," Erie said with a note of regret. "Her father was hoping that I would not find out until after her burial. I'm a constant reminder of my father's blood and he keeps his distance from me." Erie laughed, relieving the melancholy he was beginning to feel. "But his stubbornness is his loss, isn't it, Mariette? Why, who wouldn't want a blue-eyed halfbreed hanging around, eh?"

Mariette was well aware of the rejection he had suffered at the hands of his mother's people and his sadness saddened her as well. Hoping to lighten the moment, she smiled, "No one that I know, Erie." She looked up the hill, wondering what was taking Adam so long, then wondering in the same moment if he had simply left her there because Erie was with her. Adam Cassidy was exasperating.

But, could he be jealous? And could he be watching them even now? Mariette slid her arm around Erie's strong one in a friendly embrace then dropped her head against his shoulder.

Erie caught the direction of her gaze, and gave her a reassuring pat. He also knew exactly what she was doing by her uncustomary show of affection toward him, though he took no offense. "Don't worry. He will return. The mare probably made it halfway back to Philadelphia."

"I don't care if he never returns!" Her heated response had elicited a smile from him, though he said nothing to fuel the moment of humor. To change the subject, she entreated him, "Will you please take a message to Roby for me? Please, before Adam comes back?"

"I cannot leave you here alone," he argued unhesitatingly. "It would be unsafe."

Mariette patted the sidearm. "Don't worry . . . I'm not alone. And I really need to dunk myself in that stream the way you did. I am filthy!"

His eyes narrowed as he absently watched the raven follow an insect along the bough of the tree. "And if I agreed to take this message to Roby, what is it that you wish me to tell him?"

"Tell Roby that if he will allow you to bring Lara to me that we will return to the city and that no charges will come against him, nor will her grandparents find out what happened. Tell him that if he will release her, then he will be able to return to the city, if he so wishes, but that he is not to come to the house while Lara is there. Tell him that all we want is for Lara to be returned, because her grandparents trusted us to take care of her." Mariette cut her gaze to the quiet Erie. "Will you take that message to him?"

"And suppose he should choose to keep the English girl with him?"

Mariette huffed up a little. "Well, he took her in a moment of anger, and I would imagine that he regrets it now and would like to be rid of her. I'm sure that if he would think with his brain, rather than his . . . his loins . . . he would realize we are doing him a favor—"

"He'll realize no such thing. I believe he cares for the woman."

"And why would you think that?"

"A man can tell," Erie said, nodding thoughtfully. "Believe me when I tell you that a man recognizes love, even if women believe men have no eye for romance."

"Roby is too sensible to fall for Lara Seymour. She's a little tart and a troublemaker. No, Roby might be hotheaded, but he is wise in many ways, and much too wise to be fooled by a wisp of a girl like Lara Seymour." When Adam Cassidy suddenly appeared atop the hill, she quickly continued. "Good. He has caught up to my horse."

Erie drew upright. "I will take your message now, Mariette, but do not tell the Westerner. If I am followed, I will not return to Roby. I will be back, and I will have his message for you. Wait for me here."

"If I am not here precisely, I will be nearby. You will find me, won't you?"

He nodded, taking up his bow. "I will simply follow Poe to you, if you are not here."

"Then be on your way," she rushed the order. "Before that rascal approaching us can ask any questions."

With a shrill whistle, Erie called the raven to his shoulder, and the two of them disappeared into the overhanging darkness of the deep forest.

Adam approached. "Where is he going?"

"I don't know," she mumbled the small fib, shrugging lightly. "I guess men have needs to attend without an audience." Then with acute sarcasm, "Why don't you follow him?"

Ignoring her attempt to prickle him, he dismounted, then handed her the reins of her exhausted horse. "Next time, tie her off before you go wallowing down the hill with strange men."

"He's not a strange man. I've known him forever." *Why am I explaining to Adam Cassidy?* she wondered. It was none of his business. "Besides, I wasn't wallowing!"

"Yes, you were!" Slinging out his hand with such force that the stallion drew back, Adam gave her a glaring look. "You were wallowing down the hill with that man, and I demand to know just what the hell was going on! And don't give me some damned story about dashing out of the path of a snake and losing your footing."

"Well, that is exactly what happened, Adam Cassidy! Do you think I could make up a story like that on such short notice? Or, am I too stupid to think that quickly? Did you expect to hear me babbling like a fool as I try to come up with something logical?"

He almost winced at her renewed bout of sarcasm. When she whirled away from him, he caught her shoulder and forced her back. "Don't you walk away from me, Mariette! I'm talking to you—"

"I need a bath in that stream," she shouted as she ran into the water.

"Mariette!" Tying the horses to a sturdy oak sapling, Adam threw his boots and sidearm beside her own and soon joined her at the stream, though he allowed several feet to separate them.

When she noticed Adam, she very quickly emerged from the brook, wringing the water from her hair and dragging on her boots.

Then Adam followed her, and his hand grabbed her shoulder. "Don't walk away from me."

Her mouth fell open, so dumbfounded was she by his patronizing tone and the lethal glare of his eyes. She returned the glare, then focused it on his hand at her shoulder and the pressed anger upon his mouth. "Don't ever forget, Adam Cassidy . . . I bite as the treacherous she-cat you called me. Remove your hand from my shoulder."

Adam suddenly saw something in her features that repulsed him; he snatched his hand back and dragged it down the front of his shirt as though to wash away the ugly memory that had attacked him inside. Then he looked again at Mariette's ivory features, finding that the little expression that had brought back another face, one condemned to his brutal memories, had slid away, leaving behind Mariette's endearing little quirks. What was it that he had seen in her face . . . the viciousness of a screaming woman scrounging through the pockets of dirty clothing, looking for a few overlooked coins so that she could stumble her way to one of China Town's notorious opium dens?

He visibly shuddered, and when Mariette saw the pallor in his features, her anger went the way of spent words. She started to touch him, though she really didn't know what to do then, but he drew back with that same repulsion he had exhibited just moments ago.

"What is wrong with you, Adam?" she asked quietly. "One minute we are having a good row, as usual, and the next minute you look as though you have seen a ghost." In an attempt to lighten the moment, she said, "As you know, only our little Cassandra is allowed to see ghosts."

His gaze turned to her, though she suspected he really did not see her. Then he blinked several times, and a small expression came back into his features, replacing the blankness that had taken her off her guard. "Sorry," he said.

In a soft, accusing tone, she said, "You were thinking about her, weren't you? . . . Emily—"

His eyes narrowed once again. Turning, pulling into his saddle, he spurred the stallion toward the hill and the east. When he drew up briefly, he reminded her, "I said if you ever mentioned her name again I would leave you." He coaxed the stallion a few feet ahead at a slow pace and called to her, "I trust the Indian, your friend, will return momentarily. I'm sure he'll take care of you."

Panic hit Mariette until she believed that he was bluffing. "Oh, of course, go on your merry way. Erie will be back in a minute or two. Who knows, we might decide to do a little more of that wallowing." Flicking her wrist, she ordered light-heartedly, "Well, go on. I'll be all right."

He turned his head from her and sat for a moment, appearing to be deep in thought. Then he dragged his hat low on his forehead and spurred the stallion ahead.

Mariette watched him with fear squeezing her insides. He wouldn't leave her; he wouldn't dare. And as she anticipated his return, she practiced her most sarcastic and knowing smile so that when he eased the horse around and returned to her it would be the first thing he saw. But he was now topping the hill, and he had not looked back. The smile slid from her mouth and her heart began to beat rapidly. She wanted to call after him, but she wouldn't give him the satisfaction. Should she pretend that she didn't care? Yes, that's exactly what she would do. *He will be back any minute now,* she thought. Even when his descent of the hill had carried him from sight, she watched for his return, mentally rehearsing the tone of sarcasm she would use to make him look small and foolish.

But the minutes passed; she sat against the fallen tree, dragged her boot up and continued to watch in the direction he had gone. She could not hear his horse, nor did her instincts tell her that he was very near by. Surely . . . surely, he would not ride off and leave her all alone.

As she waited, Mariette watched the movements within the mountains, the circling hawks, the underbrush being parted by a scurrying creature, a small fish breaking the surface of the stream. Then she stood up, her gaze cutting into the brushes to the right. There was something very familiar about this part of the mountain, though she knew she had never been here before. She knew of the vicinity, but who had told her about it? An old memory fought to surface. Yes . . . there was something familiar, endearing and yet, oh, so lonely about this stretch of the mountain, and she was suddenly very anxious to remember what it was.

Rising, taking the reins of her mare, she moved up the hill, and when she stood at the rise, it was not Adam Cassidy she was looking for but several small, long-abandoned cabins, and a trading post that hadn't been worked in years. She looked for a clearing that had probably grown over and now bore very little resemblance to the lively community it had once been. Her long scrutiny produced nothing of the ghosts she was looking for, and she thought that, perhaps, she had dreamed about another trading post in another region of the mountains.

So, she returned her attentions to her solitude.

Adam Cassidy, the rascal, had, indeed, left her alone, to fend for herself in the hostile world of the Allegheny range.

Adam had found one of the small cabins that probably had not been occupied in half a century. It was only a quarter of a mile through the woods from where he had left Mariette, and he expected that she would show up any moment now to give him a good piece of her mind. He had fully intended to leave her, but when he had put enough distance between them that he could not see her, he had known that he couldn't let her fend for herself in these mountains, even if she did have the security of a sidearm she could handle as well as any man. She might have lied about Erie returning in a few minutes—it wouldn't be the first time she'd told a lie—and he would never be able to forgive himself if something happened to her.

Checking a very old bentwood chair for dependability, Adam carefully sat down on the remains of a narrow porch and looked around. The place might once have been a small trading post, though only a few boards remained of the roof of the building that might have been used for bartering, and very little remained of the small cabins. Most of the boards at the north wall, facing dense underbrush, had rotted away years ago. Off in a narrow glen, he could see piles of rocks, possibly marking graves in no particular form or fashion. The well that might once have been centralized in the clearing, probably had dried up as many years ago as Adam had been alive.

The area portrayed a certain charm, though, with white birches and conifers clinging precariously to the steep side of a small cliff, trailing vines sitting like fingers over what remained of roofs and porches, farm tools covered with rust and surrounded by weeds lay scattered about. He could hear water babbling in a small brook that he could not see, and smell the decaying ground of a deep valley that had not been touched by sunlight in years.

He liked this place; it whispered its history through the shroud of trees cutting off the noonday sun. He leaned back, drew in a deep, weary breath—and one, certainly, that still maintained a bit of anger—and tried to think pleasant thoughts. But try as he might to keep those thoughts on mundane things, they persisted in returning to the tall, slim figure of Mariette Donovan encased within the tight trousers, to eyes the color of emeralds in sunlight, to wild masses of hair that looked as though it might burst into flames any moment. He thought of her mouth, full, sensual, slightly parted, betraying a thin line of her straight, perfect teeth, of the crimson flooding her cheeks so that he wanted to kiss away the hotness lingering there. How beautiful, naughty, and erotic she had been beneath his exploring hands, how sweet the taste of her. . . .

"So . . . here you are!"

With surprise, the chair hit the dry-rotted boards of the porch with a dull thud. But Adam immediately leaned it back against the wall and did not give Mariette the satisfaction of one of his long, smug looks. "What do you want, woman?" His tone was meant to anger her, and he was a little surprised that one of her boots did not kick out to whip the chair from under him.

"I knew you wouldn't leave, Adam Cassidy," Mariette said with a smug smile.

"I am merely resting before resuming my journey. Tie that blasted horse off if you're going to stay. I don't want to have to go after her again."

His eyes cracked open, and he saw that she was not looking at him, and did not appear to be listening to him either. Her gaze moved fluidly over the antiquated ruins of what had surely been a trading post, and she had turned away, the tips of her fingers tucked into the front pockets of her trousers.

"I know this place," she remarked absently. "I'm sure that I know this place." Mariette moved around the chair in which Adam sat and entered the small cabin, ignoring the warning to "be careful" that he called out to her. Any furnishings in the interior had fallen apart years ago, and there were still the remnants of rotting bedding and curtains lying here and about. A glazed white ewer and bowl sat, unbroken, in a corner that had rotted away, settling both upon the hard-packed earth. Beyond the frame of the back wall, where the boards had fallen in decay to the outside, she watched a flock of martins skimming across the sky, high above the timberline. But her attentions did not linger there, because thoughts were flooding through her so quickly that she felt dizzy. She had read about this place somewhere . . . she knew it was the place, because when she had ridden in she had seen the remains of four cabins, a T-shaped building that had surely been a trading post, and the brick well that might once have held a place of distinction at the center of the compound. Drawing a warm palm to her temple, she tried to grab from the array of memories flooding her that one certain memory eluding clear thought. Then, as though something had clicked in her brain, she began to quietly recite, "It is a quiet, peaceful place deep in the Alleghenies that captured my heart before I met dear Rufina. I'm sure it is long abandoned now, because most of our race are fearful of the Iroquois, but if anyone cares to know who I am, there is where the answer will be found—"

"What on earth are you talking about, Mariette?"

She turned quickly, a little embarrassed to have had her private moment interrupted. "This place is part of my family's past," she quietly responded. "My grandmother, Diana, was taken away from Rourke House when her mother left her father. She brought her to a trading post—the one we visited a few days ago, which is run by Hester and her family—and when she died suddenly, my grandmother was raised by her mother's aunt, Rufina Chambers. Rufina's husband had died several years before, and she had a gentleman friend who lived at the trading post with her, and the only name anyone ever knew him by was Hambone. Even several years after my grandmother returned to Rourke House, and Rufina married Hambone, she had to continue to be known by her first husband's name—Chambers—because Hambone refused to betray his true identity. Rufina and Hambone lived together for over thirty years, and when he died, I believe just before my sister, Hannah, was born, the only name put on the wooden cross above his grave was Hambone."

Adam had listened intently, more interested in her story than he was willing to admit. He found everything surrounding Mariette exciting, even her reminiscences of the past. "But what has all that to do with this place?" he replied after a moment.

"This is where Hambone lived before he met Rufina and moved to Wills Creek to be with her. This is where his identity lies concealed—"

"Then leave it concealed—"

"No—" She threw up her hands now. "Don't you see, Adam? Right here, within my touch, is one of the most intriguing mysteries of my family's past. The subject of Hambone's identity has been brought up so frequently in the past that I feel that I knew the old man, even though he died many years before I was born. If I could solve the mystery and take back to Rourke House Hambone's true identity, well, I—" When he gave her a narrow, patronizing look, she continued with haste, "He was a very educated man who kept journals of his life, and yet he looked like a grizzled old mountain man and anyone who knew him automatically assumed he hadn't been educated. But you should have read his journals, Adam, and you would be as intrigued as I am. You would want to learn his identity every bit as much as I do. And that identity lies here, buried somewhere in all this rubble." Her eyes brightened as she smiled. "Will you help me find it? Perhaps he buried earlier journals somewhere, and I know Hambone as well as anyone by his later journals, and he would have left clues as to their whereabouts. I simply *must* know Hambone's true identity. Wouldn't it make something exciting to print in the *Gazette?*" She looked to him now, instantly surprised at the expression marring his remarkable good looks. There was something she hadn't seen in a few days . . . a smile . . . and it was neither offensive nor sarcastic. Quietly she asked, "Why are you looking at me like that?"

"I was thinking what an incredible woman you are, Mariette Donovan. One minute you are at my throat, and the next moment you are telling me family histories with the glee of a child and eliciting my help in solving an old mystery. I do believe you're the most charming creature I've ever met."

Without hesitation, Mariette tucked herself into his arms and held him tightly. When his hands moved to circle her shoulders, she said, "Let's not quarrel any longer, Adam. Let's forget the problems of Roby and Lara and just enjoy being with each other for a little while—"

She lifted her smiling face to him and continued brightly, "And let's put together this puzzle. Wouldn't it be wonderful if Hambone's name could finally be put on his tombstone? My grandmother would be so pleased. What do you say: kill two birds with one pebble?"

"I believe that's 'stone.' " He grinned. "And suppose your Hambone is found to be an escaped murderer?"

"But suppose he is an exiled prince?"

"Or a bloody pirate?"

"Or a hero from one of our great wars?"

"Point taken," said Adam, touching a tender kiss to her forehead. "All right, let's do a little exploring and see what we can come up with." She chose that moment to tell him of the message Erie was taking to Roby. "Do you think he will let the woman go?" he asked following her recitation.

"If he's thinking sensibly, perhaps. Erie will return with his answer before nightfall. He'll find us here . . . searching for a long-lost identity."

"Does sound intriguing," he admitted. When she attempted to pull away from him, to begin their search he stubbornly refused to release her. Lifting her gaze to his devilishly glazed one, she smiled a little wickedly. At which time, he said hoarsely, "I can think of more exciting things to do right now than search for old journals."

"Tell you what, Adam Cassidy," she murmured, touching a kiss to his mouth. "Mystery solved . . . rewards exchanged. Deal?"

"Deal," he echoed the single word, then held her long, lovingly and gently, as he breathed the delicate fragrance of her.

There was only one reward he wanted.

Fourteen

He stood near the secret opening, just to the right of the large chifforobe where Cassandra's pretty dresses and accessories were neatly hung and packed. He thought her pretty and pale, lying against the sunny blue sheets her mother had put on the bed just the day before. He had watched her gather them from the line, where they had briefly spoken.

But she was a Donovan.

Though he admired Cassandra and thought her a kind, good-hearted little girl, he wanted to cross the room, press a pillow to her face, and snuff the life out of her.

He might have acted on his impulse if the child had not suddenly awakened and turned her green gaze toward him. He saw them widen in her moment of surprise, and when he drew quickly back into the darkness, he was not sure if she had recognized him.

He could say she had been dreaming, he reasoned, as he made his way through the interior walls of the house. Within moments, he had settled into his familiar surroundings, waiting for the woman, Hannah, to come to him with tales her daughter had told him. He had already composed a reply in his mind and was prepared for her.

* * *

Hannah was surprised to find Cassandra tucked warmly into her bed this late August afternoon. When Miss Lee had revealed that Cassandra had asked to be excused from her lessons due to illness, Hannah thought the child was simply up to more of her charming mischief and had an adventure to undertake. She blamed Justin, in a way, since he encouraged Cassandra to "follow her heart." Hannah would have let the matter go, but Miles had created such a scene at having to do lessons alone, that Hannah had decided she would have to send Cassandra back to the schoolroom. Now she sat on the bed, touching her lips to the child's forehead. She was fevered and trembling ever so slightly.

Coaxed by her mother's soothing voice as she spoke her name, Cassandra opened her eyes. "I saw a man in the corner of my room, mum."

"One of your ghosts?" queried Hannah.

"No, I believe it was John. He disappeared just before you came in."

With a quick glance, she assured her, "You were just dreaming, Cass." She had now dropped her hand to her daughter's forehead. "You have a little fever. Perhaps I should send for Dr. Redding." Cassandra had taken the time to pull on her white bedgown with the tiny pink flowers, her favorite. That alone alarmed Hannah, since Cassandra had always protested wearing her bedclothes any time of the daylight hours. Now, Cassandra dropped her full lashes and pressed her overly pink cheek to the pillow. Hannah stood, touched another small kiss to her forehead and moved quietly from the room.

Exiting into the corridor brought her face to face with Miss Lee, and approaching from the stairs was Justin

Laszlo. Presently, he halted beside Miss Lee and asked, "How is the child? I hear she isn't feeling well."

"I was coming to check on her, also," said Miss Lee.

"She's a little fevered. I'm sending John into town for Bertrand."

"Shall I sit with her until he arrives?" offered Miss Lee.

"No—" Justin smiled his apology for being abrupt. "If you don't mind, Hannah, Miss Lee, I'll sit with Cassandra. I had promised her a story about New Orleans."

"Thank you," Hannah replied, then returning her attentions to Miss Lee, "Please, do assure Miles that his sister *really is* ill, and that he is not to pout. If he is too much trouble for you, you may cut the lessons short for the day."

Miss Lee retreated, and Hannah turned to the door of Cassandra's room. Justin had already pulled up a chair and was speaking in a soft, loving voice to the child. She stood there for a moment, noticing at once that Cassandra smiled warmly for Justin.

Though sending for Bertrand was first and foremost in her mind, some invisible force compelled her into the room. She approached quietly, dropping her hand to Justin's shoulder. She said nothing when he lifted his dark gaze to her own, and when he gracefully arose, then pulled her into a warm embrace, she did not protest, but accepted the intimacy as though it had been a part of her daily life forever. Then she drew back, their fingers touching for the longest of moments as she began to withdraw, and soon she turned to the corridor.

Within minutes, John was hurrying into town to fetch Bertrand Redding, and Hannah was seeing Miss Lee off in her own small surrey. As she turned to reenter the house, she saw Miles moving down the lines of stalls, talking to the horses. She imagined that he was choosing one to ride that afternoon, and she took a moment to be thankful Mr. Cassidy had chosen the stallion for his venture. Miles usually rode the beast, simply because he knew that his mother would be worried sick until he returned.

Hannah realized that she hadn't been as attentive to Miles as she had been to Cassandra, but that was because Miles had never seemed to need her affections. Instead of returning to Cassandra, she paused on the walkway, watched Miles for a moment, then turned in his direction.

Miles had hoped she would go on to the house. He didn't need his mother doting on him; he was a man now. So, to ward off any motherly concerns, he quipped as soon as she was within hearing range, "You *told* Mr. Cassidy to take the stallion, didn't you?"

Hannah halted abruptly, though she was not surprised by Miles's unfounded accusation. "No, I did not, Miles. He chose that one because it appealed to him. I never even knew that your aunt had told him to choose one of our horses." She attempted to drop an affectionate hand to his shoulder.

But he immediately scooted out from beneath her hand and moved toward the bay mare closest to him at the moment. "How is Cassandra?" asked Miles. "Miss Lee said she was feverish. Shouldn't you be with her?"

"I should, son."

"You shouldn't leave her alone if she's ill."

"Justin is sitting with her."

Miles cut dark, narrowed eyes to her with such venom that Hannah withdrew. "That despicable man shouldn't be here! I don't believe he's kin! You shouldn't be so easily duped, mother!"

Hannah dragged in a breath of surprise. "Don't you take that tone with me, Miles Gilbert! You're not too old for me to take a strap to."

Hannah wasn't sure why she ever tried to be pleasant to her son. Their encounters always ended in anger and harsh words, with him pleased that he had riled his mother. So, rather than continue the confrontation and thus, add another victory to his youthful belt, Hannah turned and moved slowly down the length of the carriage house, crossed the lawn and did not respond to the tears streaming down her cheeks. Try as she might, she could not understand where she had gone wrong in raising Miles.

Why couldn't he be more like Cassandra?

"You know, you remind me a lot of young Cassandra right now."

Mariette turned from the hole in the floor that she'd been inspecting, then looked warily into Adam Cassidy's smiling features. "And just why is that, Adam?"

"You're like a child hunting for Easter eggs. A charming little girl who is so sure she'll find the treasure that the very thought of it not happening draws a pretty pout to her mouth."

Rising, her boots stepping across the precarious floor boards, she soon dropped into Adam's lap, circling her fingers at his back. "Well, look at you, sitting here in this rickity old chair while I do all the work. I'll wager, Mr. Cassidy, that somewhere nearby is that Easter egg I'm looking for." Laughing, she continued, "I remember the last time Cassandra and I dyed eggs, it took seven weeks for the colors to fade from our hands. Imagine that!"

Adam's smile grew out of faint reminiscence; he could remember dying eggs one Saturday with a little girl in San Francisco, because her mother had been "much too sick to worry with the mess." But as he felt the heat of moisture sheening his eyes, he roughly circled Mariette's waist and pulled her firmly against him. "What do you say we cease and desist this ridiculous hunt and do something much more enjoyable—"

Breaking from his embrace, she stood before him, her hands drawing to her hips in feigned annoyance. "Adam Cassidy, you have only one thing on your mind. And why should I play man–woman games with you when you said that you were leaving me?"

Drawing to his full height, a move which toppled her from his lap, Adam pulled her into his arms. "Well, I'm *not* leaving you."

He was just about to back her against the wall, to keep her from escaping from him, when the stallion appeared at the door. "Get out of here," Adam ordered roughly. The stallion rolled his head at Adam, then pawed the ground three times. "That's only three . . . one more," ordered Adam, and the stallion obeyed his command.

Mariette stared at horse and man in disbelief. "How did you teach him to do that so quickly?"

"I taught him that three years ago," Adam murmured, stealing a kiss from her, then drawing back, "before some sorry bastard stole him from me—"

"My father purchased him from a horse trader in St. Louis. He's *your* horse?" asked Mariette in surprise. "Why haven't you said anything before?"

"No need—" he said shortly, his mouth capturing hers in brief, teasing kisses. "Dammit, I don't want to talk about horses!"

When his hand moved to the waist of her trousers, she caught it up short, murmuring brokenly, "No . . . Erie . . . might catch us . . . we can't—"

"Blast the man! He won't be back for hours. Besides—

we'll hear that blasted bird first, before the man shows up—"

Again, his hand moved and again she stopped it. "No—no, Adam—we shouldn't—" But even as she spoke, her hands moved along the buttons of his shirt, popping them one at a time. She was suddenly, erotically lost in the moment, as she frantically dragged her trousers down her slim hips and threw off one leg and one boot. As her thigh rose against his hip, she sought the warmth of his mouth with her own, her hands now moving to the buttons of his trousers.

With a husky growl, he dragged his trousers down, and without prelude, without the teasing caresses of his hands awakening her, she was against the wall, offering the sweetness of herself to him. Dragging aside the loose satin garment she wore beneath her trousers, he buried his maleness within her, drowning out her gasp with a roughly taken kiss, his hands cupped over her buttocks to bring her firmly against him.

Mariette had never felt so much enjoyment—or naughtiness—or even imagined that a man and woman could make love in such a position. She loved the way he took her without hesitation, and when she began to whisper sweet sentiments against his ear, she loved the way he responded with raw passion and yet so much tenderness that she wanted their union never to end. His mouth was upon her breast, caressing it to hardness, and she braced herself against the wall, giving herself willingly to his brutal pounding.

Then, she heard the familiar cawing of the raven not very far off in the woods and she whispered, "He's coming, Adam . . . Erie is coming—"

"To hell with him," he whispered with husky need. His glazed, lusty look let her know that his passion would peak only too soon, and as her wide-eyed gaze caught sight of Erie two hundred yards through the woods, Adam buried his seed within her.

Though she knew that Erie could not see them in the overhanging darkness of the rotting timbers, she half-pushed Adam from her and hastily dragged on her trousers and the one boot she had kicked off. Tucking in her shirt to return some semblance of order to her clothing, she combed her fingers through her wild, tangled masses, then drew them across her shoulders. As Erie exited into the clearing, she turned in the doorway, smiling timidly.

Adam, the pace of his breathing still quick, joined her a few minutes later.

"So, you saw Roby?" she brightened when Erie faced her.

The Indian gave her a narrow scrutiny, then cut his gaze to the man standing slightly behind her. A smile curled his mouth, as he realized what he almost interrupted. "Roby says he will not return the woman. He said that if you will go back to Rourke House and give him time to decide whether he wants to keep her—"

"What does he think she is?" Mariette angrily cut him off. "Chattel? Bank notes? A horse to be traded off? No, that simply won't do." Then she entreated, "You simply must tell me where he is hiding, or at least take me to him. I believe I could make him see reason. And, I really do need to see for myself that the English tar—umm, woman is all right."

Erie shrugged with deep regret. "I cannot do that, Mariette. I made a promise, and my father might think I am a prideful bastard who cares only about himself, and I certainly might be. But I do have some virtues, and one of them is that I never break a promise. I will not betray him."

She knew it was useless to argue with a man who had such pride in his given word.

"Is the English girl faring well?" Adam asked.

"She fusses a bit . . . all women do, I suppose, when modern conveniences are denied them . . . but she seems to want to stay with Roby," Erie replied. Sharing a look between the two people, Erie issued a warning, "I would suggest, Mr. Cassidy, that you take Mariette back to Philadelphia. There will be trouble between the Iroquois and the people of the Pitkins community. I have been to visit the Pitkins elders, but they will not heed my warning and leave the area."

"What kind of trouble?"

"Much death," somberly replied Erie, "Much death on both sides. If you will take her to the city, I will bring news as soon as I am able."

"But what about Lara?" worried Mariette. "If we are not safe, then neither is she."

"Roby will keep her safe. The Iroquois respect him . . ." Erie continued with haste, "If he has not returned the woman to Philadelphia by the time the trouble has ended, then you can journey back to the mountains in search of him. But for now, you are safer back in Philadelphia."

When she hastened to issue a protest, Adam whispered, "Remember the grisly scene we came upon a few miles back, Mariette—"

"Yes—" Erie had heard his softly spoken words. "That is what the Iroquois do to each other, so imagine what they will do to those of the Pitkins community. They are too foolish to clear out. I hope you will not also be so affected, Mariette."

"We'll depart in the morning," said Adam.

"And stay away from the Pitkins place," Erie suggested. When Adam slowly nodded, Erie lifted a crooked finger to his forehead in departure, and as swift as the wind, man and raven had made themselves a part of the darkening forest.

"I'm frightened for Lara," said Mariette, tears stinging her eyes. "I don't know what we will do if something happens to her. Her grandparents trusted us to take care of her."

"What has happened is not your fault." His hands affectionately closed over her shoulders. "We'll return to Philadelphia and get the ache of the saddle out of our bones. When this crisis is over, if Roby hasn't returned, we'll come back."

"Do you promise?"

"I do."

Forcing her mood to brighten, she shrugged as she said, "Then we still have the rest of the afternoon and the night to find Hambone's journals."

"There's nothing here," he said discouragingly, "and I wish there was . . . for you—"

She turned, refusing to be discouraged. "No, they're here. I know they're here, just as surely—" flashing a wide smile across her shoulder, "as I know my own heart."

Instantly his hands circled her small waist and dragged her against him. "And what is your heart, Mariette Donovan? And is there a place in it for me?"

As she pulled away from him, she felt her stomach churn, though she didn't know why. His question was sensible enough . . . they had, after all, made wicked, passionate love, and he probably knew she wasn't the kind of woman to give herself easily and willingly if there wasn't a commitment somewhere in the future. Still, the fact that he was eliciting his position of prominence in her heart frightened her somewhat, because he was a man she hadn't known until a few weeks ago, and a man with a